Catch Me if You Can

Racing Series, Book 3

Sequel to
Déjà vu Bride
Racing Series, Book 2

The Bride Wore Coveralls
Racing Series, Book 1
(Barbour Publishing)

By
Debra Ullrick

Catch Me If You Can
Copyright © 2014 by Debra Ullrick

Scripture taken from the New King James Version®
Copyright © 1982 by Thomas Nelson, Inc.
Used by permission. All rights reserved.

Published by: Sweet Impressions Publishing
ISBN-10: 0692309314
ISBN-13: 978-0692309315

Cover Design by Lynnette Bonner
Cover images © BigStock- 41331460, 33807104

Printed in the United States of America

Dedication

To my brothers Slim and Oskie
for passing your love and passion for racing onto me.
I love you both so very dearly.

"Though one may be overpowered by another,
two can withstand him.
And a threefold cord is not quickly broken."
Ecclesiastes 4:12 (NKJV)

Chapter One

Playing chicken with other vehicles sure didn't top Audra Darron's list of things to do before she went on to meet her maker.

Charity, West Virginia's hot July sun bore down on her back. Her clothes clung to her body, not from humidity and heat but from a bad case of the nerves. Inside the dirt racetrack at Cole Speedway, she glanced around at the various different shapes, sizes, makes, and models of the demolition derby cars. Obviously, quite a few other women were crazy enough to do this demolition derby competition thing too.

She cut a glance to her right and shook her head at her best friend Olivia Cole. "How did I ever let you talk me into this, Liv?"

"Ah, c'mon. It'll be fun." Olivia winked and tossed her caramel-colored braid over her shoulder.

"What happened to the gal who once feared adventure? Huh?" Audra asked, tilting her head and hiking an eyebrow at Olivia. There was a time before Olivia met her husband that adventure was something she had grown to greatly fear.

Olivia looked over toward the bleachers. There on the very top row stood her husband Erik, leaning against the rail with his heel hooked over the bottom rung. Livvy waved at him, and he blew her a kiss. "Need I say more?" Olivia smiled, her face glowed like a ray of sunshine.

"Drivers, get ready." The announcer's voice boomed over the loud speaker.

Do I have to? Audra's stomach dropped with the question only her mind heard.

"You can't chicken out now."

Oh yeah, just watch me, she wanted to say. But instead, against her better judgment, she forced one foot in front of the other and bent her knees, ready to sprint to the souped-up, silver '57 Chevy with the ginormous 777 painted in black on both doors.

If only her legs would cooperate and stop shaking, but that wasn't likely to happen any time soon.

"On the count of three, dash to your cars," the announcer continued, "put your safety gear on, and buckle up. When you've finished, raise your flag, and do not, I repeat, do not start your engines until the flagger gives you the green flag."

So, this was it.

There was no backing out now.

Sweat beads dotted the top of her nose, something that usually happened when she got nervous or scared. Right now, she was both. "C'mon now," she whispered to herself. "*You can do all things through Christ who strengthens you. There is no fear in love, but perfect love casts out fear.* So, this is just one more fear for ya to overcome. So buck up, girl."

"You talking to yourself again?" Livvy shoulder bumped her.

"If you must know, I'm quoting scripture to myself. I need all the courage I can get before I do this crazy thing." She wanted to shoulder bump Olivia back, but her feet wouldn't budge and felt cemented into the dirt.

"Ready," the announcer drew out the word.

Uh, no, not really. So feel free to take your time, Mister Announcer person. Please.

"One..."

"Lord, how'd I let Olivia talk me into this? Is it really necessary that I face this particular fear? I mean really, it's not like I need it to live or anything," she mumbled. Okay, grumbled but only she and the Lord heard it.

"Two..."

Of all the things she'd confronted before, this one had to be the craziest of them all.

Well, that is, if she didn't count the time she had climbed the side of a steep cliff that left her dangling in the air hundreds of feet above the rocky ground.

Or the time she jumped from an airplane with only a parachute between her and the earth's floor.

Or the time she'd ridden a bucking bull. Okay, a small steer, but it was still of the male cow species, and muscle-bound bulls were something she was deathly afraid of.

Right now, even all of those things sounded better to her than crashing into someone else's car on purpose and having them do the same to you. Just thinking about it, her focus darted toward the exit. Maybe, just maybe, she could make a mad dash for the gate before the competition started. Surely, this one time of not facing a fear head-on would be okay.

Head-on?

Yikes!

Why did she have to use that particular term at this precise moment? *I can't do this, Lord. I'll try it another time, okay? Okay? Are ya listening?*

"Three!"

Guess not.

Audra's take off was one even an Olympic sprinter would be proud of.

Adrenaline pumped through her body as she pushed her short legs to run as fast as they could toward the driver's side door of her car.

It only took her a few seconds to reach her Chevy. She splayed her right hand across the top of the glassless window frame. "Ouch." She yanked her hand off the scorching metal. "That puppy's hotter than hades." She tugged her leather gloves out of the back pocket of her slim-fit jeans and slid her hands into them.

Once again, she held onto the top of the window frame and straddled her leg over the bottom part. Hot metal seared through her jeans. She resisted the urge to yelp out loud. Climbing inside the vehicle proved to be more difficult than she had anticipated, especially since the door was welded shut and the only way inside was through the open window.

She glanced at the other cars to see if she was the only one struggling to get inside. Two other women must have had the same trouble she was having because they were still outside their vehicles as well. There was no way she wanted to be the last one inside, so she braced herself against the onslaught of pain and quickly dropped herself behind the steering wheel.

She slipped the mouthpiece into her mouth, strapped her safety helmet with the protective eye gear on, and latched the safety harness just as Olivia and Erik had shown her.

Now for the flag. With more bravery than she possessed, she lowered the red stick with the fluorescent orange flag. It said she was ready, her trembling body said otherwise.

Riveting her eyes on the flagger, her pounding heartbeat echoed inside her helmet as she waited for the go ahead from him.

The flagger waved the green flag.

Time to race.

With trembling hands, Audra turned the ignition key and the Chevy roared to life, crackling and purring, and sending goose bumps pebbling across her arms. She swiped the moisture away from the tip of her nose.

She stomped the clutch to the floorboard, jammed the stick shift into first gear, and let out the clutch at the same time she pressed the gas pedal. Dirt clouds shot out behind her as she raced to the other side of the oval racetrack out of harm's way from all the other competitors. Okay, so she was being a chicken. *So, sue me*, she thought, mashing the fear down and letting survival take over.

Crunch!

Bang!

Her gaze darted wildly at the other cars ramming and banging each other. "This is insane!"

A bright yellow station wagon with sinister eyes painted on the front of the hood turned and headed straight toward her.

Audra's eyes widened. She stared at the oncoming, hypnotic eyes, unable to tear her gaze away.

A loud crash to her right and she blinked and shook her head. If she didn't get out of the way, within seconds that thing would hit her head on. There was that word again.

Audra threw the car in reverse and spun a loop, barely missing the head-on attack. "Whoa, that gal means business. Well, Miss Sassypants, two can play this game. You're going be sorry you ever messed with me," she yelled even though she knew the station wagon driver couldn't hear her over the loud noise of the muffler-less cars.

Audra rubbed her gloved hands together. "Now for a counter attack." Seeing her opportunity, she spun back around, and the back of her Chevy rammed the front fender of that big ole yellow car nice and hard. "Hah, hah, take that!" Audra laughed, feeling rather smug and elated about her victory slam. Somehow, the fear had gotten lost in the exhilaration of the conquest. With that, she took off after her next victim. "This is so-o-o fun."

Cars battled around her. An orange Camaro charged after her, but Audra gunned her car out of the Camaro's way. "Catch me if ya can, Hotrod!" Audra drove like a mad woman, dodging every attempt that aggressive woman with the lead foot and several others made.

Off to her side, Audra spotted Olivia's purple '66 Chevy Malibu with the white number 1 on the hood and doors.

Audra's lips curled into a smirking grin as the temptation to ram into her friend for talking her into this guzzled over her. Before she could follow through with her wicked scheme, a black Studebaker crashed into Audra from behind. "Whoa. That could've really hurt." Audra jammed the gas and popped the clutch to get out of the woman's way.

Minutes later, after ramming and being rammed by several more vehicles, only Audra, Olivia, and the old Studebaker remained. The other twelve cars had their flags raised, indicating they were out.

Once again, Audra avoided the black car's attempt to attack her.

Olivia hit it.

"Way to go, Liv." Audra fisted the air.

Metal mashed against metal, crunching and denting both the cars until they looked like wreckage in an auto salvage yard.

Olivia backed up, obviously positioning herself to hit the stalled Studebaker in front of both Audra and Olivia again.

Dirt spun as Olivia shot toward the side of the black car straight ahead of Audra. Audra decided to join her in sandwiching the car between them. Bracing herself for the impact of the collision, she squinted, bunching her face.

All of a sudden, the old Studebaker lurched forward.

Audra slammed on her brakes, but it was too late.

She and Olivia hit head on, and her engine quit.

Steam rolled out from under the hood of both her and Olivia's derbies.

Audra tried starting the Chevy. "C'mon now. Start. Please," Audra pleaded with it as if it could understand her. Gas-fumes wafted through the car's interior, but Audra refused to let that stop her.

She glanced at Olivia's car. It hadn't moved yet either.

Movement at her side caught Audra's eye. She turned in time to see that big ole black Studebaker charging straight for them.

Audra cranked the starter over and over, glancing at the Studebaker every other second or so. She put the car in neutral, took it out of neutral, held the gas petal to the floor, and still nothing.

Only yards away, the oncoming beast raced toward her at full throttle.

The scene before her reminded Audra of a movie she'd seen a long time ago. In the movie, the guy's car stalled on a railroad track. Only feet away from the man was a fast-moving train headed straight toward him.

The film shifted into slow motion.

Right before the locomotive was about to hit him, the guy's arms flew up to cover his face.

Audra held her breath.

Bam!

Crunch!

Just like the train in the movie, that old Studebaker rammed into Audra's door. Her body barely shifted from the impact, but her insides rattled like the tail of a rattlesnake ready to strike.

It backed up, no doubt to ram Audra again.

For the twentieth time, Audra cranked the starter of her Chevy, and still nothing. The thing was deader than a mummy.

Not about to get bashed into again, Audra thrust her flag up.

The Studebaker switched directions and headed straight toward Olivia.

Audra cringed as the car slammed into Olivia's passenger's side door.

Olivia's flag went up, and just like that the demolition derby was over.

That ole black Studebaker, with very few dents in it, had won.

Well, Audra would get her next time. Wait! What was she thinking? There would be no next time. Or would there?

Audra unbuckled her harness and climbed out of the window. After she removed her gloves, helmet and mouth guard and tossed them onto the seat, she shook out her long hair, enjoying the coolness the movement created.

She turned around and saw Olivia sprinting toward her with a huge smile on her face and her hand poised in the air.

They high-fived each other.

"So, what did you think? Did you like it? Were you scared? It's a rush, isn't it?" Olivia's turquoise eyes and smudged face gleamed.

Audra raised her hand. "Whoa! Whoa. Slow down there, Hotrod. Questions overload."

"Get over it, Audie, and just answer them."

"Boy, are you bossy." She rolled her eyes all dramatic like. "Okay, okay. You were right. It was fun." She hooped her arm through Olivia's and the two of them strolled over to Erik who was making his way down the bleachers. "When can I do it again?"

"I knew it!" Olivia jerked free from Audra's grasp and faced her. "I knew you would like it. Admit it, I was right."

"I just did." She wrinkled her nose at Olivia. "So, when can I do it again?"

"We have one every week during the summer. Is next week too soon? I'll make sure Erik has another car ready for you."

"No it's not too soon, but what's wrong with the one I just used?"

Olivia glanced toward the '57 Chevy, then back at Audra. One eyebrow curled into a horizontal question mark. "I think that car has seen better days."

Audra looked over at it. One rim was bent, steam trickled from the engine, and it had so many dents it looked like a bad case of cellulite explosion. "I think you're right."

They both laughed.

With a spring in their step, they all but skipped toward Erik.

"One more fear conquered. Yes!" Audra yanked her fist toward her body.

"Why you find it necessary to confront everything you're afraid of is beyond me. We all have fears."

"Yup, we sure do. But, I've seen too many people whose fears have kept them from enjoying the life God has for them. I don't want fear to control me. Besides, I love anything that challenges me spiritually, physically and emotionally. There are still a few more challenges and fears I wanna overcome." One in particular, however,… Um, not so much.

"I shudder to think what they are." Olivia's eyes darted to the sky. "Still, you're right. Where would I be if I hadn't overcome my fear of loving people?"

Audra shuddered too thinking about where Olivia would be today if she hadn't overcome her fear of love.

Olivia had lost her parents and grandma at a young age and had been forced to live with a wicked, evil aunt she didn't even know existed. One who had gone behind Olivia's back and had sold her parent's home and every single memento Olivia had of her parents and grandmother. Then her fiancé died in a plane crash. All of those things had not only left Olivia paralyzed with fear of loving but with an ocean load of guilt. Thank God, the power of love had defeated all of that.

"Oh, by the way, I like that you've gone all natch-ur-elle again," Olivia said, winking at her friend.

"Huh?" Audra blinked and looked at Olivia. "What do ya mean?"

"You're hair. Black looked good on you. The pink, purple, green and yellow, well, enough said. Your natural auburn color looks the best. Same with your eyes. Why you wear all those different colored contacts when you have such beautiful hazel-gray eyes is beyond me. I mean, it's not like you need them or anything. You have perfect 20/20 vision."

"I know, but I wear them 'cause I can." She raised her chin in a teasing, haughty gesture. "And I like being different."

"Oh, you're different all right."

"Hey." Audra gave Olivia a playful elbow-nudge.

"So how was it, Audra?" Erik asked as he stepped up to them.

"Oh my goodness." Audra gave a little hop. "It was so-o-o much fun."

"She wants to do it again," Olivia chimed in.

"That can be arranged." Erik slipped his arm around Olivia and kissed her.

Audra was used to their public displays of affection. It warmed her heart seeing her friend so happy. Erik was a prince amongst princes.

If only there was a prince out there for her. But her abilities to find a nice guy and to hear clearly from the Lord on that subject were sorely lacking. So much so, that she no longer trusted her judgment where men were concerned. Especially after her last relationship with her ex-boyfriend Neil Jetts—liar extraordinaire. Just thinking about him and what he'd done set her blood to boiling. She needed to cool off. A walk to the concession stand across the way would do her good. She turned to her friends. "I need something to drink. I'll catch y'all later." Without waiting for their response, she whirled and stormed over to the food stand.

~♥*~*

Barrett Camden followed the driver of the '57 Chevy with the numbers 777 on the door to the concession stand. He stood behind her in line and waited for her to order. As soon as she did, he stepped alongside her. "I'm paying for the lady's food."

She turned and looked up at him in surprise.

His breath hitched. Frown and all, she was even more beautiful up close than she was at a distance. A man could easily get lost in those hazel gray eyes of hers.

"Thanks just the same, but I can pay for my own meal." She handed the man behind the counter a twenty, pocketed her change, and without saying another word to him or even giving him a second look, she headed toward the stands.

Not one to be brushed off, while he ordered a corndog with chili and a Coke, he kept his eyes on her as best as he could so he would know exactly where she went. Her long hair swished back and forth against her swaying hips.

She stopped and talked to a woman and a crying boy. A blob of pastry lay on the ground at the boy's feet. She said something to the little boy and then handed him her funnel cake.

Barrett couldn't believe it. Not only was the petite woman pretty as a princess, she was compassionate too.

Determined even more than before to get to know her, he quickly ordered another funnel cake, and as soon he got his order, he strode to where he last saw her.

He scanned the bleachers until he spotted her seated on the second row from the top.

Barrett climbed the bleacher steps two at a time. When he reached her, he looked down at her and asked, "Is this seat taken?"

She slurped the food off the side of her finger. "No, but there are plenty of other empty seats, I'm sure you can find one."

Feisty. He liked that in a woman. Showed she had spunk. And he loved that Southern accent of hers too. Not one bit deterred, he grinned, and then sat down behind her on the top row.

She twisted sideways in her seat and looked up at him, frowning.

"Name's Barrett." He lowered himself next to her.

"Didn't ask." She scooted away from him, but that didn't discourage him one little bit.

Nope. Barrett loved a challenge. It was game on. He scooted closer to her.

Her eyes narrowed, and her lips puckered. "Excuse me."

The urge to kiss those lips drove through him. It took every ounce of willpower he possessed not to. "So, you going to tell me your name or not?"

"Not." She took a bite of her slaw dog, which left a piece of cabbage clinging to her lower lip.

He took his napkin and brushed it across her full lips. Lips that were soft even under the napkin.

"Uh, excuse me, what do ya think you're doing?" Her southern drawl snapped with all the attitude of a diva, but this woman who had just raced like a hotshot was definitely no diva.

Or at least he didn't think she was. The divas he knew didn't race derby cars. "You had slaw on your mouth, so I did you a favor and wiped it off."

"I can wipe my own mouth just fine, thank you very much." Using her own napkin, she did so with a vengeance. "Why don't ya go bother somebody else?"

"Am I bothering you?"

"Yup."

"Why?"

"'Cause. I know your type. That's why."

"Oh yeah, and just what type am I?" He couldn't wait to hear her answer.

"The type that thinks he's God's gift to women." She sipped her drink through a straw, her hazel gray eyes gazing up at him, daring him to deny what she'd just said about him.

Well, deny it he would. Plus, he'd show her. "I've met your type before too."

She lowered her drink. "Oh yeah, and just what type do you think I am?"

"Beautiful. Stuck on herself. Thinks she's too good for anyone else."

"Well." She slammed her drink on the seat. "Of all the nerve. You don't even know me. I am *not* stuck up!"

"Prove it. Go out with me."

Her big eyes widened. A smirk slowly curled her lips. "You're on, Hotrod."

He sat back, pleased with himself. "Good." He took a bite of his corndog to put a stamp on it.

Her eyebrows curled with skepticism. "That's it, just 'good'."

Barrett shrugged and lifted the corndog to his lips again. "What else did you want me to say?"

She rolled her eyes and put a half-frown on her face. "Audra."

"You want me to say Audra?"

"No. That's my name."

Audra. He liked the sound of that.

"Audra what?"

"Audra Darron."

Barrett held out his hand. "Barrett Camden."

She glanced at his hand then shook it. He was amazed how strong her grip was for such a tiny little thing.

Now that he'd accomplished what he'd set out to do, before she changed her mind, he stood, gathered his food and glanced down at her. "Seven o'clock. Here."

Turning back to the track, she shrugged. "Whatever. See ya then."

He set the funnel cake on her lap, nodded and strode down the bleachers. He couldn't wait until seven o'clock.

Chapter Two

Audra still couldn't believe she'd told a total stranger that she'd go out with him. Not just any old stranger either, but the type of guy she usually avoided and with good reason. But the instant the gorgeous man with sandy blond hair and hazel eyes challenged her, she had to say yes. If nothing else, to prove to him that she wasn't stuck on herself or that she thought she was too good for anyone.

She thought back to how angry she'd gotten when he had prejudged her. When really, isn't that what she herself had done? Prejudged him? All she could do now was hope and pray that he proved her wrong.

A quick glance at the clock, and she groaned. "Ech. Late again."

Pocketing her money and driver's license, she headed out the door, straddled her Harley, slid on her helmet, and fired up her chromed-out motorcycle.

Down the street and up the highway she drove, heading straight to Cole's Speedway to meet Barrett Camden.

She showed the man at the gate her pit pass, the one Olivia gave her so that she could come straight to the contestant's pit any time she wanted to because more than likely that's where Olivia would be.

Slowly and cautiously, she wove her Harley past the monster trucks and made her way to where the rest of the motorcycles parked. She shut her Harley down, climbed off, and removed her neon lime, yellow, and pink flamed helmet.

"You drive a Harley?"

"Ahhh!" She whirled around, her helmet dangling precariously from her fingers.

There stood Barrett, looking all gorgeous and smoking hot in black jeans, squared toed boots, and a black tee shirt that showed off his broad chest and buff arms. He really was handsome. Too handsome. That alone made him dangerous in her book. She wasn't in the market for a man, and this date-thing wasn't about going out with him, it was about making a point, and that was all.

"Do you always sneak up on people?" She turned her back to him, her heart slammed against her ribs. Without being obvious, she drew in a couple of small breaths and let them out slowly, hoping to calm her racing heart. Something about the man made her heart rev up like a racecar on speed.

"Didn't sneak up on you," he said. "You were so busy, you didn't hear me."

"What are ya doing here?" She strapped her helmet onto her cycle.

"We have a date. Remember?"

"Of course I 'member." She faced him. "Why do ya think I'm here?"

"You're late." He tapped his watch.

Audra grasped his hand and turned his wrist until she could read the time on his Rolex. "Only fifteen minutes."

He arched a brow at her. "Only?"

Her eyes snapped up to his. "You didn't answer my question. What are ya doing here?"

"If you must know, I was heading to my car to come look for you."

She planted a hand on her hip. "And just *where* were ya planning on looking to find me? I didn't give you my address." She rested her backside on the seat of her cycle, crossed her arms and ankles, and sent Mr. Sure-of-himself a smug look.

"523 Hummingbird Lane." He recited her address, then her phone number, her date of birth, and even what she did for a living.

Audra shot off her cycle. "How—how did you find out all that information? What are ya, some sort of psychopath or something?" Now that was a dumb question if she'd ever heard one. What was he supposed to say? Why yes, I am. How did you guess? She mentally rolled her eyes at her own stupidity, simultaneously asking herself if going out with him was even a good idea.

His smirk dug into her patience. "Well, if I were, I surely wouldn't tell you, now would I?"

He had her there.

"Barry."

"Barry?" She tilted her head and stared up at him, wondering what in the world he was talking about.

"Barry Brown. He's the detective I hired to do a background check on you."

Was this man for real? "You've got to be kidding me? You ran a background check on me?" Who did background checks on someone they'd just met? More people than she cared to admit, but still it annoyed her that he'd run one on her.

"Yes."

"I can't believe this," she mumbled. "This date is so over, boy-o." She reached for her helmet just as his large hand clasped her wrist.

"Come on. Don't go having a tizzy-fit. I wanted to learn as much about you as I could. You should be flattered."

Flattered? *Oh brother,* she rolled her eyes again and yanked her helmet from off its perch. "You really are in love with yourself, aren't you?"

He smiled down at her "Nope. Just confident."

"Well, I hate to be the one to shatter your confidence, Hotrod, but…" Before he could stop her, she hopped on her cycle and within seconds she spotted him in her rear view mirror, standing there, arms crossed over his broad chest, smiling. Well, he could just wipe that smug smile off his face because she had no intention of ever getting anywhere near Barrett Camden ever again.

Barrett stood there, staring at the tail light on her motorcycle. Every so often the brake light lit up as she wove her way past the monster trucks and out of the contestants' pit.

If she thought he was going to give up that easily, she had another think coming. He strode to his roadster, hopped in behind the wheel, and fired it up.

He typed Audra's address into his phone's GPS and drove that direction. Feisty. He liked feisty.

When he turned down her street, the houses and neighborhood immediately reminded him of those in the movie *Meet Me In St. Louis.*

Large brick houses.

Huge lawns trimmed nice and neat.

Porches with swings.

Children playing in the front yards.

White picket fences. The whole enchilada.

Several people waved at him as he drove by, reminding him of The Andy Griffin Show this time. The folks of Mayberry live and they live right here.

He waved back.

In the middle of the street, he stopped and checked the address on his GPS against the one on the large Victorian house. **523.** The Harley Audra rode was parked in the driveway. No doubt about it, this was definitely the right place.

Barrett pulled his roadster alongside her motorcycle and shut the engine off. He strode to the front door and knocked. A yapping dog peered out from the front window curtain, barking like crazy.

"Louey, hush." Barrett heard Audra's stern voice on the other side of the door. The dog stopped barking.

Seconds passed before the door opened.

Suddenly, Audra stood there behind the screen door, holding a little brown and tan longhaired Chihuahua. One look and she shook her head. "Go away." She started to close the door.

"No can do. I'll just wait here on your porch until you come out." He strode toward the porch swing. "All night if I have to."

Both doors whipped open, and Audra stormed over to him, the top of her head barely reaching his chin. "Listen here, boy-o, if you don't leave, I'm calling the police." Her dog growled, bearing its teeth at him. If the mutt wasn't trying so hard to be intimidating, Barrett might have laughed.

With half-a-shrug, Barrett reached inside his pocket and extended his cell phone toward her. "Tell Captain Marlowe I said hello."

Her eyebrows rose, then dipped. That smirk he'd seen earlier curled her full lips. "I will." She snatched his phone from him.

Barrett sat down on the swing, stretched his legs out in front of him and crossed his hands behind his head. "The number there is…" He waited until she was ready.

Holding the phone with her free hand, with her thumb poised over the touchpad, he recited the non-emergency phone number for the Charity, West Virginia Police Station.

He listened while she said there was a crazy man on her porch that wouldn't go away.

He smiled. He was crazy all right. Crazy for the cuter-than-a-basket-full-of-kittens woman standing in front of him.

"Yes, please send an officer out. And hurry. My address is—" Just then his phone rang.

Her eyes rounded and darted to his, knowing she'd been busted making her fake phone call.

"Mind if I answer that?" He chuckled and held out his hand for her to give him back his phone.

She threw it at him, and it landed on his lap.

Whirling around, she stomped toward the front door, her heavy footsteps echoed underneath the floor.

Before she got away, he snatched up his phone and answered it, hurrying over to Audra.

Her dog growled and let out a low bark now and then. Incandescent eyes glowered up at him.

Not the least bit intimidated by the dog, he used his body as a barricade to stop Audra from going inside. "I've got to go. I'll call you later." He ended the call and pocketed his phone. "Don't go away mad. Listen, I'd really like to get to know you. I'm not a psychopath or a murderer or anything like that. I'm just some guy who watched this crazy, fearless woman compete in a demolition derby."

"You calling me crazy?" She rubbed her dog behind his large ears.

Well, since she was asking. "I am."

"You're right, I am. And don't you forget it neither." Her lips twitched, then slowly curled upward into a huge smile.

And woo-wee what a smile. Never before had he met a more intriguing, fascinating woman than Audra Darron. And he'd met plenty of women in his day. Women who always threw themselves at him. Audra was the first one who hadn't. And he liked that. Right then he made up his mind he was going to catch this woman even if she didn't want to be caught, and he knew that was going to be no easy challenge.

~♥*~*

Audra didn't know how he did it, but he did. He got her to change her mind yet again. Well, no more. She'd allow it this once, then she'd send him out of her life for good.

She sat down on the swing and settled Louey onto her lap. The poor thing was so scared of Barrett that he trembled more than he normally did around strangers. "It's okay, Louey, that big, bad man isn't gonna hurt you," she cooed and ran her hand over Louey's head and back. "I won't let him." Audra looked up at Barrett.

"Big, bad man, huh?" A grin tugged at the corners of his mouth.

Her only response, a smirk of a grin. "So, ya gonna just stand there or are ya gonna sit down?"

Barrett smiled and sat down next to her. His broad shoulders filled a good portion of the swing.

A light breeze whispered across them, his pine-rain scent drifted under her nose. As discreetly as possible, she inhaled, trying to get a better whiff of the cologne that was all male.

Male.

That one word said it all.

Males had the power to hurt her.

Her past relationship had soured her on men.

Men who would stop at nothing to get their way.

Men who lied.

Men with secrets.

Men who weren't what and who they said they were.

She wondered what lies and secrets Barrett had. Well, she'd wonder no more. She was fixing to find out. "So tell me, Barrett Camden, if I were to have a background check done on you, what would I find?"

"Is that your way of fishing for information?"

"Yup. You bitin'?"

"Nope. You'll just have to spend time with me if you want to find out more about me."

What did she expect he would say? *Oh yeah, by the way I have many skeletons in my closet and those skeletons are blah blah blah.* She'd come this far, she could handle a couple of hours in his presence. But that was it. Two, three hours tops and she was done with him. "Fine. Whatever." If Barrett even remotely showed a sign of a smug grin because he'd won yet again, Audra was going to bop him over the head, or have Louey use his arm for a chew toy. Thinking of chewing... "I haven't eaten dinner yet, and I'm starving. You up for a pizza?"

"Nope. I have something better in mind. Lock up your house, grab your Harley keys and an extra helmet if you have one, and let's go." He stood and offered her his hand.

Still not wholly sure about this, she picked up Louey from off her lap and stood without Barrett's aid. "I'm not helpless, ya know." If her mother knew she had treated a gentleman like that, she'd tan her hide. But, her mother wasn't here, didn't even live nearby, and... her mother hadn't met Barrett. If she did, she would understand.

"Sorry, but I'm not going anywhere with you. When I mentioned pizza, I meant we'd order one and eat it out here." She pointed to the white wrought iron table with the glass top and the two wrought iron chairs over in the corner of her porch. "Where all my neighbors can keep an eye on you."

He looked over at the table and then back at her. "You're kidding, right?"

"Nope. I'm not gonna go to only who knows where with you. I know nothing about you, and what I do know, I'm not sure I even like."

"You agreed to go out with me, and you didn't know me then."

"That's only because we were meeting in a public place, with lots of people around, including my best friends."

Barrett sighed. "You're perfectly safe with me. Audra. I promise I'm not going to kidnap you or anything."

"Who said anything about kidnapping?" She hiked one eyebrow.

"You did."

"I did no such thing."

"Yes, you did. With your looks. Listen, if it will make you feel better..." He grabbed his phone and handed it to her. "Here. Dial the police station. For real this time." The deep rumble in his chest was so charming, and so male, and so frustrating, she scrunched her face at him. Obviously unfazed, he continued, "Ask for Captain Anderson Marlowe. You can ask him if it's safe to go with me or not."

Audra looked at the phone and back up at him. If he were some sort of killer or nut case, he definitely wouldn't offer for her to call the police captain. Still, these days one couldn't be too careful. Besides, she wanted to call his bluff. Rather than dial the number in his Contact list in case it wasn't on the up and up, looking over Louey's head, she Googled the Charity Police Station and punched the number in. "Yes, ma'am, may I please speak to Captain Marlowe?"

"May I ask whose calling?" the stern female voice on the other end inquired.

"Barrett Camden told me to call."

"Oh, okay. Just a moment, please." The stern voice turned rather perky. Did the mention of Barrett's name have anything to do with that?

It wasn't but a second before Audra heard, "This is Captain Marlowe."

"Yes, Captain. I'm sorry to bother you, but I was wondering if you know a Barrett Camden."

"Oh, great. What's he done now?" a deep voice on the other end asked.

Hmmm. That wasn't the response Audra had expected. Now she had no clue what to think or what to say. She eyed Barrett warily.

At the look, Barrett took the phone from her and pushed the speaker icon. "Marlowe, you getting me in trouble again?"

"Hey, Barrett. How you doing, buddy?"

"Good.

"Who's the woman that wants to know about you?"

"That woman is Audra Darron, and she's listening to you now. You're on speaker."

"On speaker, huh? Listen lady, I don't know what he's trying to tell you about himself, but if I were you, I'd run." Laughter followed and the call ended.

"That's it." She slammed his phone into the palm of his hand. "I'm going back inside." Audra spun on her heel.

"Oh, no, you don't." Barrett grabbed her wrist, his grip strong, yet gentle. "Grab your keys and a spare helmet if you have one."

"Uh, no, I don't think so." She wiggled her wrist from his grasp and ruffled Louey's fur. "C'mon, Louey."

"Audra, think about it. Would I have you call the captain of the police and give him your name if I were going to harm you?"

He had a point. A very good point. It was one she didn't particularly like, but it was good nonetheless.

"Okay," she finally said, "but don't always think it's gonna be this easy." As she walked to her front door, she heard him say, "Trust me, I won't. Nothing's probably ever easy with you."

"You got that right, Hotrod," she tossed over her shoulder.

His phone rang, and Barrett answered it. "Hey, buddy. You have some explaining to do. Hopefully Audra knows you were just teasing."

Audra heard Barrett say right before she stepped back into her house. She wanted to eavesdrop on the rest of the conversation, but she didn't want to look obvious. So instead, for the second time that evening, she grabbed her keys and one of the extra helmets she had available in case someone wanted to ride with her, locked her door, and headed to the driveway where Barrett was waiting for her.

"I'll drive." He held out his hand. A very large, very masculine hand. "Keys."

"Uh, no, I don't think so." She closed his hand and pushed it away from her. Her attention drifted to the black roadster and to the red, orange and yellow flames that ran on top of the hood, around the blower and along the side. "Nice ride. What year is it?"

"A '31."

"Why don't we take it?"

"Because I haven't driven a Harley in years."

"Oh yeah? Did you used to own one?"

"You going to let me drive or what?"

"You gonna answer my question first or what?"

"Nope."

Why wouldn't he answer her? What was the big deal?

"I promise I won't wreck it, and that I don't bite."

"Maybe I do."

Barrett laughed as he swung his muscular leg over the seat of her Harley and straddled it. Once again, he held out his hand and said, "Keys. Please."

What was it about him that had her giving into his requests? Whatever it was, it worked. With a sigh, she handed him the keys, put on her helmet, and climbed on behind him.

He strapped his helmet on. One second later and her cycle fired to life. "Hold on."

She did.

As they rounded the street corners and curves, she leaned the same direction as he did. Muscles of steel rippled under her hands with each movement he made as she held onto his waist.

The wind whipped through her blouse as they rode down her street and through town. An exhilarating feeling of freedom rushed over her as it did every time she rode her Harley. She leaned her head back and relished the feel of the whole experience.

When they neared the outskirts of town and headed out of the city limits, those feelings of freedom vanished. A bad case of the nervous jitters took its place.

Why had she allowed him to talk her into going with him?

Regardless of her phone call to the captain, the further Barrett drove, the more her mind conjured up all sort of scenarios of what could happen to her. With each scenario, fear clawed her stomach.

Where was he taking her?

To the back woods somewhere?

Sweat beads broke out across the end of her nose.

Lord, forgive me for being so stupid. I should've never gotten on this cycle with him. Please protect me and keep me safe.

Forty minutes later, he turned off of the main road onto a long paved lane lined with bald cypress trees.

Audra's fear of being taken somewhere in the backwoods was quickly becoming a reality.

Anger replaced her fear. If Barrett Camden thought he would take her out in the middle of nowhere and do only who knows what with her, well he'd soon find out he'd have a fight on his hands. She would use every self-defense technique she'd ever learned on the man, and after Neil, that was now more than a few.

She yanked her arms from around his middle and grabbed the bar behind her, holding on tight.

He twisted his head and shoulder back and looked at her confused.

Audra glared at him, and he cocked his head.

If you think I'm gonna explain myself, you have another think coming, boy-o.

When he stopped, he'd have a hard time catching her. Her legs might be short, but she'd won many a first place ribbon in high school field and track.

About a half mile in, she noticed a clearing up ahead. When they reached the clearing, a beautiful, large two-story brick house with rows and rows of windows came into view. A wrought iron fence with evenly spaced brick pillars surrounded the property.

Barrett reached inside his pocket and the automatic gate slowly opened.

What was this place? More intrigued than scared or angry, her eyes roamed the space as he followed the curved driveway past the front of the house and around back.

There amidst a cluster of trees and bushes stood a very large glass building shaped like a gazebo. Audra had no clue what it was. But from what she could tell, it looked like some sort of solarium.

Barrett stopped in front of the walkway and shut the cycle off. Transfixed by the spectacle before her, Audra forgot all about her plan of escape once they stopped.

They got off the cycle and removed their helmets. "Where are we? And what is that thing?" She pointed to the glass building.

"Come on, I'll show you." He clasped her hand and led her up the brick pathway. Barrett opened the door for her, and followed her inside.

Earth and a menagerie of floral scents, along with the humidity hung in the air. Blooming tropical flowers and trees and shrubbery filled the place. Butterflies of all colors and sizes danced in the air, landing on one flower then flying away to the next one.

Audra looked up at Barrett. "This is beautiful. I've never seen so many butterflies in one place before."

"It's my butterfly garden."

"Yours?" She didn't mean to sound so shocked, but the truth was, she was more than shocked. After all, Mr. Macho Man didn't seem like the type of guy who would have a butterfly garden.

"Yes. Mine. It's my hobby."

"Hmmm. I saw you more as the rugged outdoorsy, *thug* type." She emphasized the word thug and shot him another one of her smirk-laden grins.

"Well, looks can be deceiving."

"They sure can be." This macho male had a soft side.

~❤*~*

If only the woman knew just how true their statements were. Barrett counted his blessings that she didn't, especially since facial reconstructive surgery had altered his looks, and he'd had his name legally changed. The first one, the cosmetic surgery, he really didn't have much choice. The second, well, he didn't want to dwell on the reasons he'd changed his name. It was much too painful.

Besides, right now, all he wanted to focus on was the beautiful, bubbly woman before him. "Want to see the whole place before we eat?"

She placed her bright pink fingertip against her chin. "Hmmm. Let me think." She gazed up at him. "Does Barrett own a smokin' hot black roadster? Are butterflies flitting about this room? Is Barrett a psychopath?"

He chuckled. "The answer to the first two questions is yes. As for the third... Well, I'll let you decide." With that, he placed his hand on the small of her back and nudged her forward. "Watch where you step." He pointed down at the butterflies on the pathway.

He gave her the tour of his butterfly garden, pointing out each feature as she oohed and awed, asking what kind of butterflies, plants and shrubberies each one was. When they reached the fountain near the center, she stopped, leaned over, and brushed her fingers through the clear water.

Fascinated by her interest in his garden, he watched her, wanting to join her, and yet he stood back, allowing her to enjoy the feel of the water flowing through her fingers.

She looked up at him with something he could only describe as a glint in her eyes.

Next thing he knew, she shot up and flicked her wet fingers at him.

Drops of water sprinkled across his face, he blinked them back and grinned down at her. "So, that's how you want to play, is it?"

In the next second, he scooped her up. Bracing his knee against the rock ledge surrounding the fountain, Barrett held her over the pool of water and slowly lowered her toward it.

"Don't you dare!" she squealed, glancing back and forth between him and the water.

"Or what?" he challenged, lowering her even further.

"Or I'll. I'll—" She jerked her body, sending her heel into his backside, and the two of them fell unceremoniously into the water, splashing and sputtering.

Cool water penetrated the pockets of his jeans, his belt buckle, and half of his shirt. Water gushed over the edge of the fountain and onto the floor. Gasping at the sudden rush of cold, he shoved himself up. "What did you do that for?"

"Because I told you not to drop me."

"So you throw both of us in?"

She just smiled up at him all innocent like.

Water rained down from his clothes as he offered her a hand up. Audra settled her hand into his, and he pulled her to her feet.

Standing in the water, he helped her step over the rock ledge. Right when he raised his leg to step over the edge, she shoved him in the chest.

His arms did a backstroke, his hands grasped at the air as they searched for anything solid to grab ahold of to stop him from falling back into the water.

"That's what I'll do." She smiled sweetly at him, then turned and headed further into the garden, tugging at her blouse and pulling it away from her skin.

With his hands behind him, his feet flat on the bottom of the fountain, and his knees above the water, Barrett sat there, watching her stroll away, giggling. The sound was as soothing and as pleasant as the water running over the rocks.

He shoved himself up and followed the water trail she'd left on the brick walkway.

Seated on one of many marble benches throughout the garden, water pooled at her feet, as she sat staring at the butterfly perched on her finger.

Barrett stopped and watched her.

"You sure are a pretty little thing." She held the butterfly up for inspection, its wings opened and closed.

She sure was.

Ignoring her sopping wet clothing, Audra stared at the blue butterfly perched on her finger and marveled at its velvety soft wings. *God, Your creation never ceases to amaze me.*

"That's one of my favorites." Barrett came over and sat down next to her.

Audra pulled her eyes off of the amazing butterfly and gazed over at him. "Does it have a name?"

"Battus philenor. Pipevine Swallowtail." That name poured from his lips, impressing Audra even more with his knowledge of the beautiful flying insects he tended to with so much compassion and tender care.

She wasn't even going to try and repeat what he'd just said. All she could say to that was, "Oh." On a nearby leaf, she settled the butterfly. Once again, she tugged her wet clinging shirt away from her body.

"Would you like a towel?"

"No, I'm fine."

"Shall we eat then?"

"Can we come back here afterward?"

"No."

"Oh. Um, okay."

Barrett chuckled. "No because we aren't leaving. While you were getting your keys, I called ahead. Dinner's waiting for us." He stood. "If you'll allow me." He offered her his arm.

Audra stood and threaded her arm through his. "Lead the way." She expected him to lead her out the door they'd come in, but instead he led her over to the far corner of the garden, lifted the flap of a hidden keypad and punched in a code. The rock wall parted, opening up to a hidden room free of butterflies.

"Oh my." Was all she could say as she stared at the dusty rose cloth-covered table in the middle of the room. Short, medium and tall silver and gold lit candles set in the center. The table was set with two covered plates, two glasses filled with ice cubes and lemonade, and silverware.

He stepped aside. "Ladies first."

Audra stepped inside, and Barrett walked right in behind her. He punched numbers into another code box and the door shut. Her mouth hung open as she stared at the two-way mirror. In here, she could still watch the butterflies and enjoy the view without fighting them for her food. "Beautiful," she whispered. She turned around, her arm brushed against Barrett's chest when she did. Quickly she backed up, stunned by the touch. "Sorry."

"I'm not." He looked down at her, his gaze dropped to her lips, and his head lowered an inch toward hers.

She'd never let a guy kiss her on the first date, and she wasn't about to start now either. That was one of many things she refused to let Barrett talk her into doing. "I'm hungry," she blurted out and darted around him.

His chuckle echoed in the room. "Afraid?"

"Of what?" she asked as innocently as she could, turning around and looking up at him.

"That I was going to kiss you?" His hazel eyes bore into hers.

"Oh, is that what you were gonna do?"

"Yes, and you know it."

Again he had her. "Okay, so I knew you were gonna kiss me, so what?"

"What were you afraid of?"

She shrugged. "Nothing."

"Do you always bolt like a scared kitten when you're not afraid? Or were you afraid you might like it?"

That was part of the reason, but she wasn't about to tell him that. "Don't flatter yourself. I don't kiss on the first date."

"I'll wait."

"Wait for what?"

"Until the second."

"There won't be a second."

"Oh, yes there will. You can count on it."

Ech, this man was so infuriating.

Only because she knew he was right.

Chapter Three

"Lands O' Goshen! Are you crazy?" Olivia blurted.

"Probably." Honestly, how else did Olivia expect her to answer that?

Sitting on the patio at Olivia's house, Audra watched the cardinals swoop down to pick up the scraps she and Olivia tossed out to them. There was a time when Olivia wouldn't go anywhere near birds. It was such a blessing to see her friend not only feeding them but actually enjoying them.

"You don't even know this guy. What were you thinking going out with him? To his house no less."

Audra placed her hand on top of Olivia's. "Thanks for worrying about me, Mama."

Olivia frowned. "I'm not your mama, but I am a friend who loves you and cares about you and is concerned that you might get hurt."

"I'm just teasing ya, Liv. I know you care, and I appreciate that."

Erik leaned his elbows on the glass table and clasped his hands. "What do you really know about this guy?"

"Nothing really. Except he's friends with the police captain."

"Interesting." Erik rubbed his chin. "If you don't mind, I'd like to run a background check on him."

What was with guys and running background checks?

"Oh, that's a great idea, hon."

Not Olivia too.

Okay, okay, in fairness to her friends, she knew they were worried about her. In order to put their minds at ease, she decided to let Erik run one. And if she were being honest with herself, she'd have to admit that she, too, was relieved. After what she went through with her ex-boyfriend Neil, she wouldn't mind a background check done on Barrett especially if she continued to see him. At the present, she had no plans to do that, but Barrett could be very persuasive. She had already learned that much about him. Therefore, all the more reason for a background check. "I agree with Liv. That's a great idea. After all, if he can do it, so can I."

"What do you mean if he could do it? Did he run one on you?" Erik exchanged a confused look with Olivia.

"Yup. He knew my address, what I did for a living, and a whole bunch of other stuff too."

"That's weird. Why would he do that?" Olivia asked.

Audra shrugged. "Same reason we are, I suppose."

"Touché," Erik agreed.

"Honestly, judging by the looks of his place, he's got money. Maybe he's just protecting his interests."

"That may be true, but promise me you won't see him again until Erik finds out more about him." Concern filled Olivia's voice.

Audra thought back to how much fun she'd had the night before and how her stomach had fluttered about like the butterflies in his garden when she thought he was going to kiss her. His lips had kissed her all right... on the cheek when he'd walked her to her door at the end of their date. Even now she wondered what it would be like to really kiss him?

"Audra, are you listening?"

"What? Huh? Sorry. My mind was elsewhere."

"On a certain man, no doubt." Olivia sent her a knowing look.

"Yup. There's something about him that has me intrigued."

"Just like Neil?"

"Ouch. That hurt."

Again Olivia's hand rested on Audra's. "I don't mean to hurt you, Audie. Truly I don't."

"I know ya don't. And I know what you're thinking." Audra leaned forward. "But there really is something about Barrett that's different. I mean, really, what kind of man has a butterfly garden? He can't be all bad, can he?"

"You can't judge a man by that, Audra," Erik tossed in.

Audra looked over at him and folded her hands on the table.

"Don't mind us, Audie," Olivia said. "We're just two friends who care about you, okay? After all, who watched over me before I met Erik?" Olivia clasped Erik's hand and gazed lovingly at him.

"Just from the little you've said, I can see you're determined to see this guy again." Erik took his phone out. "I'll make a quick note to call Daniel. He's a private investigator buddy of mine. While Daniel's running a background check on him, why don't you call this Barrett guy and invite him over for dinner this evening at our house?"

"Well, I would, but I can't. I already have a date this evening with—" Audra's phone rang. She held up a finger and glanced at the caller ID: Private

Maybe it was Barrett. Her heart skipped as she pressed the Call button. "Hello."

"Audra. Barrett here."

"Barrett," Audra glanced over at Erik and Olivia. "I'm glad you called." She pushed her chair out and walked over by the weeping willow tree where she could have some privacy.

"Why are you glad?"

"'Cause my friends and I were just talking about you. They'd like to meet you, and they wondered if you'd like to have dinner this evening at their place." Even though she knew she wouldn't be there, she wanted to see what he'd say.

Actually, she figured once she told him she wouldn't be there that he would back out. Now that she thought about what she'd done, she realized that was a pretty dumb thing for her to do. What if he took her up on the invitation? What would she say to Olivia and Erik? *Oh yeah, by the way, I invited him even though I knew I wouldn't be able to come.*

Then another thought cracked through that one. Why wasn't he answering her?

Audra plucked a thin leaf from off the tree and rubbed it between her fingers. "Barrett, you still there?"

"Yes. I'm here. Who are these friends?"

"Olivia and Erik Cole."

"Cole. As in Cole Speedway?"

"Yup. He owns it. Along with Cole Chevrolet. Listen, I'm sorry, but I need to tell ya something. I shouldn't have—"

Barrett interrupted her, "What time?"

"Barrett, I need to tell ya something. I shouldn't have said anything to you because I won't be there."

"Excuse me."

"I won't be there. I have a date tonight."

"A date? With who?"

"Wouldn't you like to know?"

"Break it."

Audra shook her head, feeling that pull again. "I don't think so."

"I'll expect you to be there at your friends'." With those words, he hung up.

Audra stared at the ended call. Just who did he think he was to order her around like that anyway?

Her phone rang.

Private caller.

She punched the Call button, ready to blast him about bossing her around, but one look at her friends, and she decided she didn't want to make a scene in front of them.

"What time?"

"I don't know. Just a sec." Audra pulled the phone away from her mouth. "What time's dinner?"

"Six," Olivia answered, looking over at her husband. Erik nodded.

"Six." Audra relayed the time to Barrett.

"Where's this place at?"

Audra gave him the address.

"Okay. Then I'll see you there."

"Maybe you will and maybe you won't." This time she hung up without giving him a chance to say another word. This evening ought to be pretty interesting.

Barrett followed the directions on his Mercedes's navigation system. He turned onto a lane lined with maple trees. Rounding a corner, a large white house with dark blue trim came into view. He looked around for Audra's motorcycle. Parked in the driveway was a pink MG midget with white stripes on the hood. He searched his memory to see if he'd noticed that car at Audra's, but he came up short.

What if she didn't show up? What if, indeed, he was left here to dine alone with her friends?

The evening could end up very awkward.

He parked his car next to the MG and walked toward the house feeling awkward and out of place. He wasn't at all used to this feeling, and he fought to out maneuver it. *Just stay cool, Barrett. This is no big deal.*

Standing at the front door, he rang the bell. While he waited for someone to answer, he checked out the place.

Someone sure liked blue.

In the shade of a birch tree were red rocks in the shape of a monster truck. Barrett shook his head. The man must have a thing for monster trucks. Well, at least the two of them would have something to talk about because Barrett liked them too.

The door opened, and an attractive woman with turquoise eyes and caramel colored tresses that flowed freely to a small waist answered the door. "Hi. You must be Mr. Camden. Come on in. I'm Olivia. Olivia Cole." She extended her hand, and Barrett shook it, noticing how his hand engulfed hers.

A tall man with dark hair and brown eyes, dressed in a light blue Polo shirt and designer jeans strode up behind her and extended his hand. "You must be Mr. Camden." His voice was neither friendly nor hostile, but his firm, strong handshake spoke volumes.

Barrett returned the grip with equal pressure as he was not one to kowtow to any man. He was more than able to hold his own. Years of working out in the gym had built up his muscles. His arms were like guns, and his stomach a solid six pack.

The man's grip sent a silent message to Barrett. Barrett admired the guy who was obviously very protective of Audra. "Please, call me Barrett."

"Barrett it is then." Erik released his grip, stood back and motioned for him to enter.

The foyer opened into a large room with cathedral ceilings and several skylights, giving the room a nice look and feel. Expensive furniture in blues and white were accentuated by the large marble fireplace. "Nice place."

"Thank you. We like it." Mrs. Cole smiled lovingly up at her husband who smiled down at her the same before turning sizing-up eyes back onto Barrett.

Clearing his throat would signal unease so he didn't though he wanted to. "Audra here?"

"Yes, she's out back helping Mickey and Virgil."

Barrett frowned. Mickey and Virgil? He thought it would be just the four of them.

"Mickey and Virgil work for us, but they're more like family." Olivia answered the question he hadn't voiced. "Normally, they don't work on Sundays, but Mickey insisted on making her famous fried chicken and slaw for tonight's dinner. We'll make sure they get time off during the week to make up for it."

Barrett nodded and followed them through the house and out onto a large patio.

There stood Audra, placing silverware on a glass table with an umbrella over it. When she looked up, she did a double take. She set down the silverware she had in her hand, said something to the older woman who he figured to be in her early fifties, and strolled over to him. Audra's white cotton dress swirled around her calves as she did.

"I need to talk to you for a moment." Audra looped her arm through his and all but dragged him over to a large tree out of the earshot of others. Her lemony perfume floated around her and right into him.

Man, she smelled nice.

She stopped, and before he could even say hello or anything, she blurted out, "Don't think you can boss me around like this all the time. The only reason I'm here instead of being with my date is because of Olivia."

"Well, hello to you too." He couldn't keep the mirth from his voice. The woman was as feisty as an ornery feline, and he loved it.

"Never mind that. Did ya hear me?"

"Loud and clear. But I make no promises. I usually get what I want."

One of her dainty brows came to a point.

"And I want you."

"Don't be so sure of yourself, Hotrod. I'm not planning on being caught."

"Not yet anyway." He bounced both eyebrows at her.

"Ech! You're incorrigible." She rolled her eyes and shook her head.

"Yes, Ma'am, I am." He smiled down at her. His eyes snagged onto hers, and his brows dipped into a frown. "Thought your eyes were hazel-gray."

"They are."

Barrett stared into them and shook his head. "Not now, they aren't."

"How observant," she said with a hint of sarcasm in her voice.

He tipped his head. "Sarcasm becomes you."

"You bet it does."

"You wear glasses?"

"Nope."

"Contacts?"

"Yup. Not 'cause I need them, but because I love changing my eye color."

"Why?"

"'Cause I can. And 'cause there's so many beautiful colors in this world, and I want to enjoy them all, even on my eyes. I used to dye my hair all kinds of colors too. But to maintain a more professional persona at my salon, I no longer dye my hair neon pink or purple or neon yellow or neon green or fire red."

His eyebrows arched. Thank the good Lord for that.

"Hey, you two joining us or what?" Erik called from the table.

Barrett leaned in closer to her, liking the warmth of her skin near his. "We're being summoned." Straightening, he offered her his arm.

She glanced at it, and without taking it, she strode back to the table.

With a shake of his head and an exhale, Barrett hustled to catch up to her. "Be nice."

"I'm always nice," she retorted.

He shot her a look that said, *yeah right*.

"I am." She frowned.

"You're what," Olivia asked, coming up alongside her.

"Nice."

"Who said you weren't?" Olivia's gaze shot up to Barrett, an inquisitive frown pulled at her face.

"No one. Barrett— Never mind. Let's eat."

Without another word about it, the four of them sat down at the table.

"Barrett, would you do the honors and pray?" Erik's eyes locked onto his.

It wasn't a question, it was a challenge. One he could handle. Barrett closed his eyes and bowed his head. "Heavenly Father, we thank You for this beautiful evening and for the food that has been lovingly prepared for us. May we always be truly grateful and always acknowledge that You are the One Who provides all things for us. Bless our time together this evening, and may every word we speak minister grace to the hearer. In Christ our Lord's name, amen." He raised his head, and when he opened his eyes, he found Audra gawking at him. Her open mouth curled into a smile, right along with her eyes.

Olivia handed Barrett a heaping platter of Southern fried chicken.

"So where are you from, Barrett?" Erik asked.

"From all over." He placed a chicken leg on his plate and handed the platter to Audra. At Erik's frown, Barrett reiterated, "My father was in the military so we traveled all over."

"You don't have a place you call home then?"

"I do now. Here in West Virginia." Experience had taught him that Erik was fishing for information. Well, he could fish all he wanted because all he was going to get were vague answers. His peace, sanity, and anonymity were at stake here, and they were too important to let his guard down even for a second.

"I see. How long have you lived here? I don't remember seeing you around."

"That's because I live in the next county over."

Erik nodded. "What is it you do?"

"I'm retired."

Erik's head cocked sideways. "Retired? You can't be more than thirty."

"Thirty-three to be exact."

"So, what *did* you do before you retired?"

The man was persistent, that was for sure. Barrett glanced over at Audra. Judging by the look on her face, she too couldn't wait to hear his answer. She held a plate of slaw toward him, not once taking her eyes off of him.

Well, they could just wait. He'd worked hard to conceal his identity. And nothing or no one, including Audra would change that. He refused to tell them what he used to do before…

He swallowed.

Before the worst nightmare of his life happened.

Crystal clear images of his wife's and parents' bodies haunted him even to this day. It was so incredibly unfair the odd moments those memories chose to attack him.

He masked his feelings from the battle going on inside him, reached for the slaw, put a scoop on his plate, and handed it to Olivia. He had yet to answer Erik's question, so he did with his years of practiced responses. "I raced motocross cycles."

"You like to race then?" Erik asked.

"Used to."

"You don't anymore?"

"No." Stop with all the questions already.

"Whose team were you with?" Erik picked up his glass of fresh lemonade and took a drink, never taking his eyes off of Barrett.

He might as well answer him and get it over with or he had the feeling that Erik would keep hounding him until he did, so he named the team. A team he left because he'd come close to being recognized.

That seemed to satisfy Erik for the moment as he dug in to his food. "I'm thinking about having motocross races here. You wouldn't be willing to come out of retirement and help me get it started, would you?"

"I'll think about it and get back to you." The idea did intrigue Barrett. After all, he used to love motocross racing; however, even as he said it, he knew there were too many ways it could end in disaster. No, retirement was much safer for everyone.

"How's the butterflies today?" Audra's sweet drawl snagged his attention.

Barrett's gaze shifted and rested on hers. The look on her face let him know that she was changing the subject for his sake. He smiled, one that he hoped showed her just how much he appreciated what she'd done. "Fine."

"Audra told us you have a butterfly garden. Just what is that exactly?" Olivia asked as she dabbed at her mouth with the cloth napkin.

Barrett explained to Olivia what it was, and Audra chimed in and told her all about it. He loved listening to her describe his garden with such compassion and pride.

"I'd love to see it sometime." Olivia's voice was wistful.

"That can be arranged." Barrett took a bite of the crunchy, juicy chicken leg, and when he finished swallowing, he said, "This is the best fried chicken I've ever eaten."

"Mickey will be thrilled to hear that." Pride floated across Olivia's face. "I wish they would have stayed and eaten with us. They're such wonderful people. It would have been nice if she would have heard your compliment for herself."

"Next time I see her, I'll tell her."

Olivia smiled at that.

Conversation at dinner flew by. They talked about everything from monster trucks to motocross racing to what church they attended and even what foods they liked.

Around nine o'clock, Barrett glanced at his watch. "Well, I'd better get going." He stood. "Thank you, Erik and Olivia, for dinner and for your hospitality."

Audra looked up at him. "You don't have to leave. The evening's just getting started."

"As you know, it's a forty-five minute drive to my place, and I have an early appointment tomorrow."

Erik, Olivia and Audra scooted their chairs back.

Barrett held up a hand. "Don't get up. I can see myself out."

Erik stood anyway. "Y'all stay here." Erik looked down at Olivia and Audra. "I'd like to talk to Barrett alone. Guy talk."

Barrett had a feeling he knew what Erik wanted to talk to him about. A certain little lady named Audra. He said goodnight to her and to his hostess, and he and Erik walked out to his car.

When they reached the driver's side door of his Mercedes, Erik faced Barrett. He spread his feet and draped his arms across his broad chest. A pose to no doubt intimidate him. What Erik couldn't know was that very little intimidated Barrett these days. In a way, a part of him had grown hard, part of him knew how cruel people could be, and he had put up thick, impenetrable walls to make sure words, gestures, and even actions could never get across them. "Look, Barrett, I want you to know up front that Audra is like a little sister to me. If you hurt her in any way, you'll have to answer to me."

"Don't plan on it."

"Good. Just wanted you to know that."

They shook hands, and Erik turned around and left. Barrett got in his car and headed for home, thinking the only way Audra would ever possibly get hurt by him was if she found out about his past. About who he really was, and about what he had really done for a living. For seven years now, he'd kept his real identity a secret. It was important that he kept it that way, otherwise things could turn deadly.

"So, what did you talk to him about?" Audra asked Erik the instant he got back from walking Barrett out to his car.

"I told him if he ever hurt you he'd have to answer to me."

That touched Audra more than words could say. Her heart smiled. Having Erik around made her feel less lonely for her big brother Josh. Josh had always been her protector, her hero, her rescuer. When she got home this evening, she needed to give him and the rest of her family a call. She missed them terribly since moving here to Charity and opening her salon. She now had a chain of salons. Well, a two-link chain anyway. One in Wheeling and now one here. Thinking of salons, she needed to get home and get some sleep so she could meet her client bright and early tomorrow.

The next morning Audra arrived at her salon two hours early. She had an early appointment with a new client. No one else was here yet because her salon normally didn't open on Monday until nine. This person had offered to pay extra if she'd be willing to make an exception. She agreed, not because of the extra money, money she wouldn't take anyway but because she liked to help people.

Doing hair, makeup, nails, and pedicures was her way of helping to make women feel special and pampered.

Her favorite thing was going to the local women's shelter and doing those things for the ladies and girls there - free of charge. Seeing their faces light up when they glanced in the mirror or seeing them relaxing while she did their nails brought a lot of joy to Audra, more importantly to them.

She got to work at her station, setting everything out that she needed for the day. It only took her a few minutes. She glanced at the neon pink clock with the neon green scissor hands. 7:15. Her new client should be arriving at any minute now. Before they did, she headed back to the espresso machine, measured out the ingredients, and turned it on. Coffee steam drifted under her nose, she inhaled deeply, loving the fresh, delicious aroma. When it finished brewing, she poured herself a cup and took a sip.

Someone knocked on her shop's door.

She set her cup down and hurried toward the front of the store.

When she got to the door, there stood Barrett, holding a white pastry bag and a beverage holder with two tall cups in it. He looked so handsome in that V-neck gray hoodie with the sleeves pushed up. The man had huge biceps. Black jeans showed off his muscular legs too and gave him that bad boy look that most women found appealing. Including her. Only she wanted nothing to do with bad boys. Thinking of… What was he doing here?

"Hello," he grinned from the other side of the glass. "You letting me in or what?"

She blinked, gave herself a mental shake, then reached inside her pocket, pulled the keys out and unlocked the door. "What are you doing here?" She peered outside, looking up and down the sidewalk, searching to see if her client was anywhere around. Seeing no one, she gazed up at Barrett. "I'm sorry, but ya can't stay. I'm expecting a client at any moment now."

His smile was maddening. "I know."

Audra's mouth twisted sideways as she pondered his words. "Wait. How would you know?"

Barrett held the bag and cup holder out. "Because I'm it."

"You're it? You're it what?"

"Your client."

He had to be kidding, right?

His smile didn't look like he was kidding.

She frowned. "Funny, you don't look like an Alice."

"Alice Winslow works for me. I didn't want her to tell you the appointment was for me, so she used her name."

"Sneaky," Audra drawled, unable to hold back her smile. "So-o-o this was the appointment you mentioned last night."

"Yes."

Now it all made sense, why he had to leave so early last evening.

Well, if he wanted a haircut, she'd give him one. The idea of running her hands through his sandy blond hair sent shivers up her arms.

She stepped out of the doorway and let him in. Much as she didn't want to be, she was pleased Barrett was her *special* appointment.

"Hope you haven't eaten yet. I brought breakfast." He nodded toward the bag and tray he was holding.

"Nope. I just fixed myself a cup of espresso."

"Well, now you have two."

"No. Now *you* have two."

Barrett smiled. "I can handle that."

"I bet you can. C'mon back and you can tell me what ya want. A pedicure. Manicure. Perm perhaps." She lifted one side of her mouth into a smirk of a grin.

"No perm. A pedicure doesn't sound bad if you're the one giving it." His hazel eyes sparkled with mischief.

She whirled and looked up at him. When she had mentioned the pedicure and manicure, she'd only been teasing as he didn't seem like the type of man who normally got them. The very idea of giving Barrett Camden a pedicure didn't feel right to her. Even though she had many male clients who often wanted pedicures, this one somehow was just too intimate for her. Besides, her other male clients weren't... they weren't... They weren't someone she was extremely attracted to and had dated. Okay, one and a half dates. But still.

Her hand went to the base of her throat and she rubbed it.

He cupped her chin and tilted it up. "Don't worry your pretty little head off. I'm not here for a pedicure. I just came to spend time with you."

"You didn't have to come to my salon for that."

"Oh? Didn't I?" He shot her a questioning look.

She knew exactly what he was getting at. He said he got what he wanted and she told him she couldn't be caught. And now, she'd fallen right into his trap. Truth was, she didn't even mind.

Audra girl, you'd better watch it and take things real slow with this one. You don't know anything about him.

He may end up being just like Neil… or worse. But what if he wasn't? Ech! Lord, help!

The thoughts were making her crazy. She didn't want to think about Neil and Barrett and if Barrett was anything like Neil. She didn't want to think about any of that. Filling her growling stomach with food, now that was something she could think about and with pleasure. "Okay, you made your point. Now, it's time to make mine. What's in the pastry sack?"

A grin slowly curled those masculine lips of his into full-blown smile. And land sakes, what a smile. Right about now, Audra wished she had a fan to flutter her face with. She sure did need one because that smile of his was about to cause her to have a case of the vapors. Whatever the vapors was. She'd seen that on a movie once, and it seemed to fit this moment.

"You're staring."

Audra blinked, and her eyes came up to his. "Was not," she huffed, a bit miffed that he'd caught her and had brought it to her attention. Putting her back to him, with a wave of her hooked finger, she said, "Walk this way."

"Can't."

She whirled around. "Why not?"

"Can't walk as cute and as feminine as you do."

"Huh?" She tilted her head, and his only response was a hiked eyebrow. The second she realized what he meant, that he was a man and not a woman and couldn't walk like one, heat rushed into her cheeks. "Smart aleck." She whirled around. "Follow me."

"To the ends of the earth."

"Schmoozer."

Barrett stepped up alongside her. "By the way, lavender eyes look nice on you, but hazel-gray is much better." He winked. Before she had a chance to respond to him about her lavender contacts, he added, "Nice place."

"I like it." They made their way through her salon toward the lounge area. Each step she took, her zebra striped heels clicked on the mosaic cream and beige porcelain floor.

She tried to see the place through his eyes. Three sides of the large room had light blush-pink chairs at each station along with a round mirror set in a white metal, abstract circle that went from the ceiling to the floor. Each resembled a figure eight. The top circle was smaller than the bottom one. The bottom portion had a mirror. In the center of the room stood what looked like a bare tree with the limbs made out of white metal strips that curled outward at the ceiling, and the trunk had a bench surrounding it. She'd had it specially designed just for that spot, but now she wondered about his impression of the art.

The fourth wall had an archway that led to the waiting section, which was where she and Barrett were heading to now. Audra loved the fuchsia and gray abstract design that started on the right side of the wall and ended in a curl over the purple-lighted archway.

They walked under the archway and into another large room with a marble fireplace, surrounded by two tapestry couches with carved wooden legs and two matching chairs in the center of the room. In the center of them was a long coffee table with white metal legs and a glass top. A bouquet of fresh pink roses and greenery sat in the center of it.

Each side of the room had two cream colored, tan and silver-blue paisley designed chairs. An end table sat between them with a small bouquet of fresh flowers on them.

"Woo wee. Sweet."

Audra looked up at Barrett. "I tried to make a place for women to come and feel pampered with a touch of class."

"This place has class all right. And so does the owner. Remind me to tell her that when I see her."

"Ha. Ha. Very funny. Remind me to laugh. Now show me what's in that sack before I send your backside out the same door you came in."

"Now who's being pushy?"

"Me. What of it?" She smiled.

"Nothing."

They sat down at one end of the room.

Audra moved the flowers back, took the drinks from Barrett, and set them on the end table. "Oh, we need some napkins and plates. Be right back." She hurried to where the cappuccino machine was and grabbed a couple of plastic plates, two forks, a handful of napkins and the espresso she'd set down earlier. Everything in hand, she scurried back to Barrett.

Barrett put a chocolate covered strawberry, a blueberry fruit tartlet, a mini cheesecake, and a cream cheese horn on each plate.

Her mouth watered just looking at the feast.

"You like pink?"

"Doesn't every woman?" She took a bite of the tartlet.

"No. My w— Most of the women I've dated didn't."

Audra thought he'd been about to say wife, but she was mistaken. She had to be, right? "Women?" she said around her food, then swallowed. "How many women have you dated?"

"Enough. How many men have you dated?"

Okay, he had her there. Enough. She had dated a lot of men. None of which had been her Mr. Right.

"You ever been married or engaged?" He took a bite of chocolate covered strawberry, his eyes never leaving hers as he did.

"No. Came close once. But thank God I discovered his true colors before that happened." She set the tartlet on her plate and wiped her fingers. "How about you? You ever been engaged or married before?"

Barrett chastised himself for letting his guard down and getting into this discussion. He couldn't believe he'd almost said his wife. From now on, he needed to be more careful. He didn't want Audra or anyone else to discover who he really was and what he used to do. His life and his sanity depended on it.

Rather than risk letting his guard down again, perhaps he should just walk away from Audra now and end his chase.

Only problem was, he wasn't sure he could anymore.

Audra had gotten under his skin the moment he'd laid eyes on her. She was the first woman since his wife's death who had even remotely interested him.

God, show me what to do.

Chapter Four

It had been six days since Audra had last heard from Barrett. Ever since he'd evaded her question about whether or not he'd ever been married or engaged, she'd felt uneasy, and when he'd disappeared altogether, she wasn't sure that was a bad thing.

The pastor's sermon earlier in the morning was about not judging another because of someone else's actions or mistakes. That was a hard pill for Audra to swallow, especially where men were concerned. Because of Neil, she now had a hard time trusting men, and that wasn't fair to Barrett. Still, the lack of trust was there and probably always would be despite the pastor's message. And the truth was Barrett's evasiveness wasn't helping her heart and head settle the matter.

Sitting on a poolside lounge chair in her back yard, Audra looked over at Erik. "Did your detective friend find out anything about Barrett yet?" Never taking her eyes off of him, she rubbed the sweet coconut scented sun lotion over her bronzed skin.

"Barrett Camden has no criminal record. No dirt. Nothing. The guy's so clean he squeaks. And just like he said, his father was in the military, they traveled around a lot, and he used to race motocross cycles. Barrett does a lot of fundraisers and donates thousands to various charities. As far as Daniel could tell, he has no girlfriend, no wife, and no children."

That bit of news put Audra's mind at ease, the rest was only a mild surprise. She screwed the lid on the suntan lotion tube, dropped it on top of her towel, and settled back on the chair, enjoying the sunshiny day.

"Do you like Barrett?" Olivia asked softly from beside her.

Audra brushed a bug off her leg and looked over at Olivia. "Yes and no. I'm not sure how I feel about him. He has an air of mystery to him and that makes me nervous."

"After what you've been through, I can see why. But, if there was anything bad about him, Daniel would have found it out. He's very good."

"He might be good, and that might be true, but I'm still not sure if I am ready to pursue a relationship with Barrett or any other guy for that matter. I don't mind going on a date or two, but that's it. And really, I'm not even sure I should do that because it's not fair to Barrett because I think he wants more."

"What makes you say that?" Olivia asked, sliding the shoulder strap of her purple one-piece bathing suit back onto her shoulder.

"Because he said so. He said—"

"Excuse me. I heard voices back here, so I let myself in the gate. Hope that's all right."

Audra's pulse sped up, and she yanked her attention toward that voice, a very masculine voice that sent liquid heat rushing through her.

Barrett stood there only yards away, wearing a white short-sleeved shirt and tan shorts that showed off his physique and bronze skin.

She wondered how long he'd been standing there and just how much he'd overheard or if he'd overheard anything at all.

Audra shifted her legs to the ground and slid her feet into the neon orange, green, and pink striped flip flops that matched her two piece skirted-bottom swimwear.

When she looked up at Barrett, even though his eyes only discreetly floated over her body as she slipped her sheer pink poncho cover up on over her head, she noticed him looking just the same.

She couldn't blame him, she herself had checked out his muscular legs, broad chest, trim waist, and large biceps.

Erik rose from his lounge chair and extended his hand. "Barrett."

Barrett walked over and shook Erik's hand. "Nice to see you again, Erik. Olivia." He shook Olivia's hand, and then his attention shifted back to Audra. "May I have a word with you, Audra?"

She glanced at Erik and Olivia.

"Y'all go ahead," her friend said with a dismissal flick of her wrist. "I'm ready for a dip." Olivia turned toward Erik. "You want to join me, Honey?"

"Love to." Erik helped her up. Hand-in-hand, they headed over to Audra's pool and dove in.

Audra turned toward Barrett. "What are you doing here?"

"Hello to you too."

Audra rolled her eyes. "Hello. There. You feel better now?"

"Much." He flashed her that grin that was both charming and infuriating.

"What are you doing here?"

"You ask me that a lot."

She planted her hands on her hips. "Don't change the subject. Just answer the question."

"Bossy."

"Just like someone else I know." She wrinkled her nose up at him and smiled.

He grinned again, only this time it wasn't charming or infuriating, it was just in acknowledgement to what she'd said. Being agreeable didn't become him. Was that weird or what? "I'm here because I came to see if you'd like to have dinner with me."

She bunched up her lips and shook her head. "Nope, don't think so."

"Well, I think so. I'll pick you up at six." He turned and made it two steps before Audra grabbed his arm and stopped him.

"Oh, no, you don't, Hotrod. You did that to me before."

"And it worked, didn't it?"

He had her there.

"Well, it isn't working this time. Listen." She glanced over her shoulder. Satisfied that Erik and Olivia were busy swimming and tossing a beach ball back and forth in her pool, she turned back to Barrett. "I like you, Barrett, but I need to be honest with you. I don't wanna lead you on or give you any false hopes. Right now, I'm just not interested in having a relationship with you or anyone else."

"Who said anything about a relationship? It's just dinner."

"That's how all relationships get started. Dinner. Coffee. Pastries. Trips to butterfly gardens. Those kinds of things usually lead to a relationship, and I'm just not interested, okay?" In spite of his squeaky clean report, she was afraid of getting hurt again. And she had a sneaking feeling that Barrett Camden had the power to do just that.

"Nope. Not okay." He took her hands in his and gazed down at her with those beautiful hazel eyes that were almost gold in color today.

The confidence she saw in them briefly flashed from that to a vulnerable hopefulness before switching back to the confidence she was used to seeing in them. That brief moment of vulnerability, however, got to her and she found she couldn't say no. "Oh, all right." One more date and that was it.

"Great. Pick you up at six. Wear your best dress," he said with a wink.

"Wait." Audra leveled her gaze at him. "Where are we going?"

His smile was at once both teasing and mysterious. "You'll see."

"No, Barrett." She clucked her tongue. "I need to know so I know exactly what to wear."

"Just told you. Your best dress."

She held her palms upward and narrowed her eyes at him, trying her best to show him how frustrated she was. "Best dress as in best summer dress or best formal dress?"

"Formal." He leaned in and kissed her cheek. "See you at six." With a wave of his hand, Barrett said goodbye to Erik and Olivia and headed toward the same gate he had just entered.

Audra stared at his retreating back until he disappeared, wondering what she had just gotten herself into.

Olivia climbed out of the pool and was at Audra's side in an instant. Water pooled around her feet soaking Audra's too. "What'd he want?" Olivia rubbed her wet arms.

"Dinner." Audra walked over to the stack of beach towels, grabbed one off the top, and handed it to Olivia.

Olivia draped it around her shoulders. "What did you say?"

"Yes." Audra put her head back, frustrated with herself. "Ech! I shouldn't have."

"Lands 'O Goshen, girl. Why not?"

Audra gave Olivia that look. "You know why."

"But what if he isn't like every other guy you've dated? You heard this morning's message at church. You can't compare every guy to Neil. I know it's hard. Boy, do I know how hard it is. But not all men are like Neil. Look at Erik."

"Erik's one in a million."

"Maybe Barrett's two in a million." Livvy's cold hand settled on Audra's arm. "Why not give him a chance? What if this one is the one God has for you?" She removed her hand. "Have you even prayed about Barrett?"

Audra shook her head, ashamed that she hadn't even really thought to pray about Barrett. She figured since she hadn't heard from him all week that she had nothing to pray about where he was concerned. "What happened to you? I didn't think you thought it was wise that I had gone out with a man I barely knew."

"That was before he prayed and we spent time with him. He seems like a really nice guy, Audie. And the detective found nothing negative about him. In life, sometimes you have to take risks. Even if those risks hurt. I know. And I'm so glad I did." Olivia looked over at Erik. His arms were crossed on the concrete ledge. The rest of him dangled in the pool, his feet kicking out behind him, as he watched and listened. The love they had for each other was obvious in their tender gazes.

Someday maybe, but not right now, Audra hoped to find someone to love her like that. Her chances were pretty slim and next to none as it seemed all the Prince Charming's were gone and only lumpy, wart covered toads remained.

Barrett's handsome face popped into her mind. Was he a toad too? Or a prince? Even more importantly, did she even want to find out? One thing she did know for certain was, she'd better get serious and start praying about him. And hard. Being completely wrong again was more than she could bear.

Six o'clock that evening the doorbell rang. Audra peeked out her bedroom window and saw Barrett's Mercedes in the driveway. Rushing to the top of the stairs, hoping Barrett could hear her, she hollered down, "Come on in, Barrett! Door's unlocked." As soon as she saw him open the front door, she rushed back into her bedroom and closed the door. She quickly shed her robe and it fell into a heap on the floor.

Audra slid her champagne silk and tulle, empire waist ball gown over her head and struggled to zip it up. "C'mon now." She wiggled and tugged until she got it zipped. Navy lace covered the sweetheart bodice and shoulder straps. And navy lace embellishments cascaded down the gathered skirt.

She quickly slid her feet into her navy, T-strap, peep toe, chunk pump high heels with the faux diamond bows. Long diamond earrings and a diamond bracelet finished her ensemble.

Behind her ears and on her wrists she dabbed on her favorite perfume. A quick glance at the clock and she moaned. Eleven minutes late. Why couldn't she ever be on time? Didn't matter how soon she started out, she still always ended up running late. "So frustrating," she mumbled as she snatched up her navy clutch purse with the synthetic diamond hummingbird clasp and headed down the stairs.

Barrett stood in front of her fireplace mantel with his back to her, picking up one picture after another and setting them down.

"Sorry, I kept ya waiting." She hurried to him as fast as her heels would let her.

He turned, and her breath hitched.

"Wow. You look great." His approving eyes raked over her, and his lips curled into the handsomest smile ever.

She didn't think the man could look any better than she'd seen him before, but boy was she mistaken. In that black tuxedo and pastel blue shirt, he looked like he had just stepped out of a photo shoot for the world's most prestigious men's magazine or something. "You don't look too bad yourself." Her voice was breathy, but she didn't care.

"These are for you." He handed her a beautiful bouquet of roses.

She buried her nose in them and breathed deeply. "Thank you. I *love* pink roses."

"I know, and you're welcome."

She was about to ask him how he knew until she remembered she had told him that the day he'd come to her salon. "I'll just put these in some water and be right back." She strode to the kitchen, feeling Barrett's eyes on her all the way there. His comment that day at her salon about not being able to walk as cute and feminine as she did flitted through her mind. She shoved the bouquet behind her back, low enough to cover her backside.

Barrett chuckled.

Heat rushed into her cheeks as soon as she realized what she'd done. They flamed even hotter when she realized that Barrett had caught on to what she was doing.

"You're late," he hollered after her.

"I know. I know. Story of my life. Get used to it."
She raised her voice over the sound of the running water.

"I'm holding you to that."

"To what?" she asked without looking at him. She
quickly added the roses to the vase, arranging them the
best she could, and headed back into the living room.

"You said 'get used to it'. In my book that means
you plan on seeing me again."

"Dream on, buddy."

"I do."

Something about the way he said it not only stunned
her but left her speechless, and rendering her speechless
wasn't easy.

When he said "I do," did he mean that he dreamt
about her or what? Whatever he meant, she surely wasn't
going to ask him.

She set the roses on her coffee table and made her
way to the door. Audra grabbed her lacey wrap and
draped it over her arm.

Outside her air conditioned home, heat and humidity
greeted her, along with rose, honeysuckle, vanilla-
raspberry, nutmeg, musk, tarragon and sweet scents from
her blooming flowers.

Barrett settled his arm on the small of her back and
led her to his car. She stood near the passenger's side
and waited while he opened the car door for her. Sitting
down, she swung her legs inside, gathered the bottom of
her skirt, and tucked it in around her ankles.

Barrett closed her door and went around to the
driver's side. When he slid in behind the wheel, she

looked over at him and asked, "So, where are we going?"

"You'll see. Buckle up."

"What? And ruin my dress?"

"You ride with me, you buckle up." The gruff tone in his voice caught her off guard.

"Lighten up. I was just teasing. I don't go anywhere except on my motorcycle without wearing a seatbelt."

"Good. And buckling up is something I'll never lighten up about."

She arched her eyebrows. "Care to share with me why?"

"I have my reasons."

Another vague answer. If Barrett's background check hadn't come out as well as it had, she would hightail it back into the house. Maybe she should anyway because some secrets had the power to hurt and destroy others.

There was no need for her to worry about that with Barrett because she had no plans of getting involved in a relationship with him. This was a one-last-time date and nothing more.

Barrett knew he should apologize to Audra for snapping at her. She had no way of knowing how deep his pain went. He knew only too well the price a person paid for not buckling up. Even so, if he apologized, it would lead to more questions. Questions he couldn't answer.

Audra's light perfume, a mixture of lemon and flowers, settled in the interior of his car.

He looked over at her.

One word described how she looked in that elegant, modest, yet extremely feminine gown.

Ravishing.

Her long wavy hair flowed down her back all the way to her small waist. The sides were pulled back, held in place by diamond hair combs. Her full lips were a pearly soft pink, almost natural in color. Her eyelashes were long, and her eyes were more of a grayish blue than their normal hazel brownish-gray. He could tell she wasn't wearing colored contacts, and he was glad. She looked amazing. And beautiful.

Any man would be proud to have Audra on his arm. Tonight, she'd be on his. And he couldn't be any more proud than he was at this very moment of that fact. He wasn't proud of her because of her outward beauty and appearance but because despite her sassiness toward him, Audra had a real sweetness about her. He'd seen it when she'd given her funnel cake to that young boy. How gentle she'd been with the butterfly in his garden. And how she treated her dog Louey.

He reached over and clasped her hand with his and gave it a light squeeze. "I'm glad you came tonight." His eyes darted from the road to her.

"Thanks for inviting me. I think."

"You think? You're not certain?"

"No. Especially since I have no clue where you're taking me."

"You'll have a good time. Trust me."

He would make sure he did whatever it took to see that she did because he wanted to see her again and again and again.

Her comment earlier about not wanting a relationship with him or anyone else sent uncertainty drifting through him. Since he was afraid of getting involved with anyone, why couldn't he stop chasing her?

Chapter Five

Forty-five minutes later, they pulled in front of a posh country club. The large tan brick building with white pillars and white arch trimmed windows resembled a mansion more than a country club. Lush green grass surrounded the front and sides of the building and a good-sized lake set behind it.

Audra glanced down at her evening gown. Though her dress was very elegant, and her diamond earrings and bracelet were genuine stones, judging by the outward appearance of this place, she was sorely underdressed.

Valets opened Audra and Barrett's doors.

Barrett was at her side instantly, looping her arm through his. His arm was as hard and solid as the diamonds gracing her wrist.

As he led her toward the front door, he leaned down. "Did I tell you how beautiful you look this evening?" His breath brushed against her ear, sending shivers rushing up and down her spine.

She gazed up at him and whispered, "Great, yup, beautiful, nope," she said with a teasing smile. "Thank you."

They stepped inside and Audra's eyes roamed the enormous room dotted with tables covered with linen tablecloths, crystal goblets with gold rims, fine china, gold colored silverware and crystal and gold chandeliers.

"Hey, Barrett. Good to see you again." A man as tall as Barrett and dressed in a black tuxedo strolled up to him with his arm extended. The two of them shook hands and then pulled each other into a bear hug.

A lovely woman with beautiful red hair and an exquisitely done hairdo stepped up with him. She was wearing a black velvet gown and smiling at Audra.

Audra returned her smile. Before Audra could introduce herself to the woman, the man next to the redhead spoke.

"I see you didn't take my advice." Ocean blue eyes peered down at Audra.

Advice? What advice? She didn't even know this man. She frowned, trying to place him but couldn't come up with how she knew him or more importantly how he knew her. She gazed up at Barrett, hoping he could enlighten her.

"This is my friend—"

"Captain Anderson Marlowe," the man finished for Barrett.

"Oh, oh. Captain Marlowe." Audra looked at Barrett than back at the captain, extending her hand for him to shake. "Nice to meet you."

Captain Marlowe clutched her hand and gave it a hardy shake.

"In response to your comment about not taking your advice, you see, Captain Marlowe, it's like this, I tried to run, but he kidnapped me," Audra said as conspiratorially as she could even as she put her hands back around Barrett's arm.

The captain ducked toward her. "You want me to arrest him for you?"

"Hmmmm." She placed her fingertip on her chin and gazed up at Barrett. A smirk covered his face. "Nah, not right now. Maybe later, okay?"

Captain Marlowe chuckled, and the woman next to him cleared her throat. He draped the redhead's arm through his. "Forgive me for being so rude. This is my wife, Keera. Keera, this is Audra Darron."

"Pleased to meet you, Keera."

"Likewise."

Audra and Keera shook hands.

Keera looked at Barrett. "We're so glad you invited us to join you this evening."

"Glad you could make it." Barrett narrowed his eyes toward the captain and pointed his finger at him. "Behave yourself, Marlowe."

"Me?" Anderson pointed his thumb toward his chest. "I always behave. It's you I have to worry about." That same laughter Audra had heard before on the phone that day flowed out of the captain now as he turned and led his wife over to a table by the window and away from the orchestra.

Barrett hooked Audra's arm through his and followed them.

As soon as Audra sat down, Keera spoke, "I love your dress. Wherever did you get such a beautiful gown?"

Audra told her the name of the place. "It's one of my favorite places to shop."

"I'll have to check them out."

"You'll love them. They have the cutest shoes too."

"I love shoes."

"Me too."

"Oh, no," Captain Marlowe groaned. "Another woman who loves shoes as much as my wife. Don't *even* get her started on shoes, Audra."

Audra glanced over at the captain who didn't look the least bit upset. "Sorry to disappoint you, Captain—"

"Andy," he interrupted.

"Sorry to disappoint you, Captain Andy—"

"Just Andy. No captain in front of it."

"Sorry to disappoint you, Just Andy—"

Andy looked at Barrett. "Is she always like this?"

"Afraid so."

Audra scrunched her face at him. "Be nice."

"You know you love it, Honey." Keera smiled at her husband.

"You're right, Sweetheart, I do." Andy smiled tenderly at his wife.

Keera picked up her black velvet clutch bag. "I need to use the powder room. When the waiter comes, would you order a tonic water with lime for me?" she asked her husband.

"Mind if I go with you?" Audra asked.

"I should have known."

Audra's attention swung to Barrett. He wasn't looking at her but at Captain Marlowe.

"Women never go to the lady's room by themselves. There's got to be some sort of conspiracy or something that goes on in there."

Audra shot him a smirk. "You're right. We go in there to plot our revenge against men who complain about women and their shoe fetish. So you'd better behave. Or you may find a high heel upside your head." She winked and snatched up her clutch bag. "I'm ready when you are," she told Keera, and the two of them strolled toward the powder room.

"She's a feisty one. And beautiful."

Barrett agreed with his friend.

Andy glanced around the room before leaning closer to Barrett. "Did you know someone recently ran a background check on you?"

Barrett frowned. "Do you know who it was?"

"Not yet. I'm still working on it."

"You don't think it was him, do you?"

"No. As far as I can tell it was someone local."

"Audra."

"You think she did it?"

"Maybe. After all I told her I ran one on her." Barrett ran his finger around the brim of his water glass.

"What?" At Andy's raised voice, Barrett glanced around the room to see if anyone was paying attention to them. No one seemed to notice.

"Hey, cut me some slack here. I like her, Andy. A lot."

His friend lowered his eyes. "So why the background check then?"

"Simple. To find out where she lived and to get her phone number."

"You know, you could have gotten that from the phone book."

He hiked a shoulder. "True enough, but I wanted to learn a few things about her before I pursued a relationship with her."

"So, this is where this is heading, huh?" Andy folded his hands on the table. "It's nice to see you going out again. It's been seven years since Felicia died."

The thought hit him like a punch. Amazing after all these years how just the mention of her name could still take his breath away. "Still can't believe it's been that long ago. Have you had any leads on her killer yet?"

"No, but I haven't given up." Andy glanced around again. Lowering his voice, he asked, "Have you thought about what it's going to be like when we find him?" Andy took a drink of water and set his glass back on the table.

"All the time. Since everyone believes I'm dead, you don't think I'll have to go to court or anything, do you?"

"I don't think so. One more thing…" Andy looked less than excited about whatever it was he was going to say next. "If this relationship continues, do you think you'll ever tell Audra who you really are?"

Like a snap, Barrett's eyes widened. "Are you crazy? Of course not. Why would I?"

His friend's nod was both concerned and understanding. "If you ever do, how do you think she's going to take the news when you tell her?"

"I don't know. But, I have a feeling she's been lied to by guys in the past." Although he wasn't technically lying to her, keeping secrets from her—especially ones this big—felt like a lie. He loosened his tie to get more air into his system. "Truth is, I'm hoping she never finds out who I really am."

~♥*~*

"Oh dear. What am I going to do? Just look at this, Elsa."

Inside the powder room, standing in front of the large vanity mirror, Audra's attention went to two elderly women who looked so much alike they had to be sisters.

Keera excused herself and headed into one of the bathroom stalls.

"Why'd you let Lisa do your hair, Ingrid? You know she always messes it up. And why'd you wait until the last minute, until it was time to leave, to make an appointment?" the woman with the perfect hairdo asked.

"Because I forgot, okay, sister. My mind isn't what it used to be." Wrinkled hands with age spots blotted at the tears glistening under her eyes. Her designer dress and diamond jewelry were exquisite, but her hair….

Shame on the hair dresser who left gaping holes in that poor woman's petal curl hairdo, exposing a rat's nest underneath.

Without giving it a second thought, Audra marched over to where the women stood. "Excuse me, I couldn't help but overhear your conversation."

Both of them turned and looked at her. The one called Elsa narrowed her blue eyes at Audra. The other lady, Ingrid, lowered her head.

"What were you doing eavesdropping on our conversation, young lady?" Elsa's hands fisted on her ample hips.

Ingrid's eyes snapped up to Elsa. "Elsa, where're your manners?"

Elsa ignored her. "Well?"

A soft hand rested against Audra's wrist. "Please excuse my sister. Did you need something, dear?" Ingrid's soft voice sounded so motherly. It made Audra think of her own mother and grandmother. How she missed them, missed her whole family. She really needed to give them a call.

Before she answered Ingrid, Audra glanced over at Elsa. The woman crossed her arms over her abundant bosom and glared at Audra. Well, she could glare all she wanted to. Audra could help her sister and she aimed to do just that, with or without Elsa's approval.

"Listen, I just wanted to let ya know that I own a salon—"

"This is no place to solicit business, young lady," Elsa huffed.

"Elsa, really. Behave yourself, sister, and let the woman speak."

Elsa narrowed her eyes even further. Could the woman even see out of those tiny slits?

"I'm not here to solicit anything, Ma'am." Audra's attention never strayed from Elsa. "I don't even live around here. I just wanna help your sister."

"And just *how* do you plan on helping her?" Skepticism oozed through Elsa's question.

"I can fix her hair. That's how." She smiled to soften her words.

Elsa glanced at Audra's clutch purse. "With what? You certainly don't have a comb or a can of hairspray in that purse." A smug look overtook her wrinkled face and her blue eyes turned to a smoky color.

"I can take care of those holes and cover up the rat's nest."

That brought a tongue-cluck out of Elsa. "Oh, I don't think so."

Ingrid laid her aged-spot hand on Elsa's wrist. "Elsa, please. I would like her to try. Anything has to be better than this. I don't want to go back out there and take even more ridicule from Mrs. Vandersmithe. She already thinks I'm an eccentric old hag who's gone in the head as she calls it. Just because I forget things here and there doesn't mean I'm crazy." The woman sniffed.

Audra kept her eyes from widening. Whoever this Mrs. Vandersmithe was, Audra would like to give her a piece of her mind about respecting your elders and about not saying anything if you can't say anything nice.

Elsa's eyes softened, she looked over at Audra. "Are you sure you can fix this mess?" She pointed to her sister's hair. "And that you won't make it worse?"

"I'm positive." Audra sent her a reassuring smile.

It took a moment before Elsa nodded. "Okay."

"Thank you, sister." Ingrid smiled at Elsa, then looked at Audra. "I'm Ingrid. And this is my sister Elsa."

"Nice to meet you, Ingrid. Elsa. I'm Audra." Audra clutched Ingrid's hand and patted it. She did the same with Elsa's who grudgingly let her.

"Why don't we go over there and you have a seat, okay?" Audra pointed to the lounge chairs off from the powder room.

Ingrid nodded.

Keera came out of the stall, and Audra told her to go on back to the table that she would be there shortly. Keera looked at her and then at the ladies and with a questioning nod left the powder room.

Audra slowed her pace to match the older woman's. The two of them shuffled their way to the glass door. Audra held it open for Ingrid and Elsa.

Ingrid sat in the mauve chair and Elsa in the paisley patterned chair.

Audra removed the hair pic from out of her clutch bag and the miniature can of hair spray she always carried with her. She did a quick work of manipulating the stiff curls until each and every hole was covered and Ingrid's lopsided hairdo was even. She sprayed her hair, using up all of the small canister.

"There. All done. Would ya like to see it?" Audra grabbed the little hand mirror she carried with her from out of her purse and handed it to Ingrid.

Ingrid took it, but instead of looking in the mirror, she looked over at Elsa.

"It's lovely, Ingrid. Simply divine." Elsa's tone was soft and filled with kindness. Her gaze slowly came to Audra's. "I owe you an apology for my behavior."

Audra waved her comment away. "You were protecting your sister. I would have done the same thing."

"Thank you for doing this for Ingrid."

Ingrid rose and walked over to the vanity. With her back to the large vanity mirror, she held the small mirror up and off to the side. Switching sides, she twisted her head slightly to the right and then to the left. "Oh my. It is lovely, sister." She lowered the mirror and looked at Audra. "You don't know what this means to me. I don't know how to thank you."

"No need to thank me. I'm glad I could help."

"What do we owe you?" Elsa asked.

"Nothing. Nothing at all. The pleasure was all mine."

"We need hairdressers like you around here." Elsa's voice turned all business like. "Would you be willing to move your shop here?"

Touched by the woman's kindness and enthusiasm, Audra fought back her own tears. "Thank you, Elsa, but I'm happy where I am. If you and Ingrid ever come to Charity, look me up. I'd love to give ya both the full treatment. Free of charge, of course." She smiled, tossing her things back into her purse.

"We sure will. Won't we, sister?" Ingrid's question sounded more like a statement.

Careful not to crush their red roses and babies breath corsages, Audra hugged both of them. She held the door open for Ingrid and Elsa and followed them out of the powder room. Ingrid's stooped shoulders were no longer stooped, and her chin was poised an inch or so higher than when Audra first saw her. Audra smiled. She lived for times like this.

Barrett kept looking toward the lady's room, waiting and watching for Audra to come out. He glanced back at Andy and Keera. When he looked back, two gray haired ladies, who he immediately recognized, stepped out of the room. Audra was holding the door for them. They stopped and talked for a minute. With a wave of their hands, they headed the opposite direction of Audra.

Audra rounded the maze of tables, heading straight toward him. A smile covered her beaming face. When she reached their table, he and Andy stood.

Barrett held Audra's chair, waited until she was seated, and gazed down at her. "Didn't know you knew the Johansen sisters."

She twisted in her chair, looking up at him with a question mark on her face. "You mean Ingrid and Elsa?"

He gave a short nod and sat down.

"I don't. We just met."

Barrett frowned, not really understanding.

"I fixed Ingrid's hair."

His frown deepened. "You did what? I'm confused."

"I can see that." She smiled. "Look, it's like this… Ingrid was crying because some Vandersmith or Vandersmithe or," she flicked her wrist, "whatever the rude woman's name was, had humiliated her because of her hair. So, I fixed it." She hiked a shoulder as if that wasn't any big deal. But little did she know it was a very big deal.

In fact, Audra had no idea what she had just done. The Johansen sisters were on the top 100 wealthiest women in the world list. Things would never be the same for her after the service she had just done for them. Ingrid and Elsa were just like that.

"Are you ready to order?" Barrett eyed everyone.

"I'm starving." Audra picked up her menu and flipped it open.

Barrett chuckled, opening his menu. "You're always starving."

"Yup, I sure am. Ya gotta problem with that, Camden?" The twinkle in her eyes softened her words.

"Are you two always like this?" Andy asked.

Barrett winked at Audra. "Pretty much so."

Audra wrinkled her nose at him. She looked so cute when she did that.

She studied the menu. "What do you recommend?"

"Do you trust me to order for you?"

"Uh, no." Audra grinned and winked at him. The simple action caused his stomach to do a backflip. "Sure, why not. What do I have to lose?"

"Thanks for the vote of confidence."

"She's right not to trust you," Andy interjected, grinning.

"Marlowe, you're cruisin' for a bruisin'. To think I set this up so Audra could meet you. So she could see that I'm not a psychopath or anything."

"Who said you weren't?" Andy had his serious face on. The one he used against perps.

Barrett knew he was kidding, but one look at the confusion on Audra's face told him she didn't. "Marlowe," Barrett growled.

"I'm just teasing you, Audra. There's not a better guy around, and I mean that." This time Andy's face not only had a seriousness to it, but it was also filled with brotherly love. The feeling was mutual. Barrett owed the man his life. Literally.

"I'll just have to find out for myself whether he is or isn't." She smiled, but there was more behind that smile than she was letting on. She was sending him a message. What that message was exactly, he wasn't sure yet, but it was there nonetheless.

"Does that mean you plan on going out with me again?" He dared to hope.

"Does that mean you're asking again?"

"Yes, Ma'am, I am."

"We'll see."

"That's it?" He expected more and was sorely disappointed when he didn't get it.

"Yup." She smiled with an air of mystery.

Well, at least she didn't say no. That was enough... For now.

Minutes after they finished eating, Audra watched as Andy and Keera headed to the dance floor.

Barrett stood and gazed down at her. "Would you do me the honor of dancing with me?"

"My, aren't we formal?" She resisted the urge to bat her eyelashes at him and offer him the top of her hand to kiss.

"You complaining?" The challenge was there in his eyes.

"Nope. I'd love to dance."

He smiled and held her chair as she stood. With his hand on her back, he led her to the floor.

Once there, he held his arm straight out from his side. Audra laid one hand in his and the other rested on the back of his shoulder blade. He waltzed her around the floor, turning one way, then another, and spinning her in a circle every so often. He was so poised and so graceful, he made Audra feel like a princess at a ball. When he dipped her, his eyes came down to hers. He even looked like a prince. In the next second, she was upright again, swirling and twirling around the floor. When the song ended, the orchestra switched gears to a slow song.

Barrett pulled her up against him, his arms wrapped around her. As if it were the most natural thing in the world, Audra slipped her arms around his neck and gazed up at him.

He gazed down at her and smiled.

Audra smiled back at him.

As they swayed to the music, his soft woodsy-after-a-spring-rain masculine scent wafted into her nostrils. "Tell me, Barrett Camden, where did you learn to dance so beautifully and so gracefully?"

"Dance lessons."

She tried to mask her shock but wasn't very successful.

"I get that same shocked reaction every time I tell someone that I took dance lessons. Believe it or not, when I was younger, I was pretty klutzy. Always tripping over my own two feet. Someone told my mom that dance lessons would help me. At the time, I felt pretty stupid taking them though."

"Why?"

"Because there were only two boys in my dance class. Boys just didn't take dance back then. Especially armed forces brats. If they did, they caught thunder and were called sissies. And no boy wants to be called a sissy. Especially in front of girls." He smiled. Every time he smiled, her heart did a funny little flip.

"How old were you when you started?"

"Ten. I was sure glad when we moved to the Air Force base in Hawaii. The teasing finally stopped then along with the dance lessons.

"You've been to Hawaii?"

"Yes. Lived there for four years. Loved it. Loved the beach and loved surfing. Loved the sound and the spray of the surf smashing up against the rocks. The salty air. The feel of the surfboard under my feet while riding those curls. Loved it all."

His eyes lit up with each word he'd spoke. Audra could almost picture him surfing. "You're a surfer, then?"

"Was." He gazed down at her. "Haven't surfed in years."

The light in his eyes dimmed. Audra wondered what that was all about.

He drew her closer, his hand on the back of her head, rocking and swaying to the beat of the music. "How about you? Where'd you learn to dance so well?"

"I took ballroom from the time I could walk. Well, I was five."

He pulled back, dropping his hands to her waist. "Didn't walk until five, huh?" His hazel eyes twinkled as he twirled her again.

"Ha ha. Very funny." She popped him on the shoulder.

"Did you compete?" He pulled her close again, settling her head on his shoulder. Her arms ran up his arms, ending on his shoulders.

"I did for a few years. It really wasn't for me. Don't get me wrong, I love dancing, but I found I enjoyed the more outdoorsy stuff." His heartbeat rhythmically tapped against her ear, tuning out the music from the orchestra.

"Like what?"

"I love camping, hiking and fishing."

He set her from him, and his eyes raked over her before he clasped her hands and pulled her into his arms. "Can't picture you camping."

"But you can picture me fishing and hiking?" She sent him a smirking grin.

"No, Ma'am. None of those things." He weaved his head.

"Don't underestimate me, Barrett Camden. There's more to me than what meets the eye."

"Can't wait to find out what makes you tick, Audra Darron. And I plan on doing just that."

Audra's heart gave a flutter.

He let go of her hands and settled his at the sides of her waist again, and she splayed her hands over his biceps.

As much as she hated to admit it, she wanted to find out what made Barrett Camden tick too.

Barrett continued to sway her back and forth.

"Hey, you two, music's over." Andy's teasing voice sounded from beside her.

Audra glanced over at Andy and Keera. The orchestra might have stopped playing, but music was still playing and dancing around inside her heart. With a dreamy sigh, she reluctantly stepped back, wishing the orchestra would play another slow song and another and another.

Chapter Six

Audra really liked Barrett's friends. Andy was a riot, always making them laugh. And Keera, well, she was so easy to talk to. They talked as if they'd known each other for years instead of merely hours.

She'd been surprised when she discovered that yesterday evening's dinner had been a fundraiser. There was nothing to indicate that fact. The benefit's she'd attended had silent auctions with tons of tables loaded with the things or pictures of the things that were up for auction.

She wished she had known, she would have written a check.

Barrett told her that the club held one every third Sunday, each one was for a different charity, and monies and reservations were done in advance. So maybe next time she'd be able to write a check.

Monday morning. Time to go to work. Audra finished getting dressed and headed to her shop.

All morning long every time Audra worked on an elderly woman's hair, her mind strayed to Ingrid.

Even now, sitting in her office chair, paying bills and filling out spreadsheets before her next client showed up, Ingrid's sad face popped into her mind.

Something about that sweet woman tugged at Audra's heart. Could it be because her sister seemed to control her and to speak for her? Or was it because the woman seemed lonely? Whatever it was, Audra couldn't seem to shake the feeling that she was supposed to do something concerning Ingrid.

If only Audra had thought to get the woman's phone number, she'd give her a call just to check on her and perhaps invite her to dinner or tea or something.

"Audra, there's a delivery for you." Angela, one of her hairstylists, cheery voice broke through Audra's thoughts.

"Can you sign for it, Angie?" She jotted down a few more figures. "I'm kinda busy right now."

"No, I can't."

Audra looked up at her, frowning. "Why can't you?"

"You'll have to come see for yourself."

What could have possibly arrived that Angie couldn't sign for? Audra shoved away from her chair and followed Angela.

At the front, Audra suddenly stopped, and her mouth dropped open.

There, standing near her salon door, stood Ingrid, dressed in an elegant beige pantsuit with a wide white stripe around the bottom of the sleeves and jacket and a thin stripe up the front. Dangling from her wrist was a matching purse.

Next to Ingrid stood a man wearing a white chef's hat and a white coat. Next to him were two women dressed in white coats. Four long carts, covered with linen tablecloths, filled a corner of her shop.

Delicious food aromas overrode the perfume, hair dyes, and perm solution scents that normally filled the air of her salon.

Thrilled to see Ingrid, Audra yanked herself out of her stupor. Smiling, Audra rushed to her, and without thinking it through, she pulled Ingrid into her arms and gave her a big hug before releasing her. "I'm so happy to see you, Ingrid." She hugged the woman again. "I've been thinking about ya all morning. To what do I owe this pleasure? How'd the hair hold up?"

Ingrid laughed, and what a pleasant laugh it was. One filled with joy, putting Audra's troubled heart about the woman at ease. The sadness from the night before was gone, replaced with a genuine smile. "As you see, my hair is still holding up quite nicely." She patted her petal curls. "And, I'm doing fine, dear. As to why I'm here, well, I brought lunch for everyone." Ingrid glanced about the room. "We have plenty, and if not, Pierre has more in his kitchen van." Ingrid pointed outside.

Parked in front of Audra's salon was a big white truck with the name – Pierre's Gourmet Catering – across it, along with a picture of Chef Pierre wearing a chef's hat and holding a steaming, delicious looking, dish.

"I don't know what to say. What—? How—"Audra knew she was stuttering, but this was such a huge surprise that she was actually speechless.

A soft hand rested on Audra's wrist, and Audra covered it with her own. "I wanted to repay you for rescuing me last night."

"You didn't have to, Ingrid." She gazed into the woman's kind blue eyes. "I did it because I wanted to help."

"I know. That's what made it so special. Usually people always want something from Sister and me. That's why Elsa was so protective last night. When she realized you didn't have a clue who we were and that you genuinely wanted to help, she let you. Anyway," she waved her hand in the air. "Enough of that. There's food a plenty here for everyone."

"How did you accomplish this in such a short time?" Audra asked, still awestruck over the whole thing.

"I have my ways." Ingrid winked and giggled. "Actually, I called Pierre last night, and he said it was no problem that he and his staff would get right on it. And they did." Though more wrinkles lined her mouth, her smile took ten years off her face.

"Thank you, Ingrid. I'm sure my clients will enjoy this delightful blessing." Audra turned, raising the tone of her voice, she announced, "Everyone, listen up." When all eyes were finally on her, she continued, "My dear friend, Ingrid, would like to treat y'all to lunch. When you can, please feel free to come up here and help yourself."

While the men and women lined up to fill their china plates, Audra took Ingrid off to the side. "This is really sweet of you, Ingrid. How did you find me? I never said my last name."

"Simple, my dear girl. I called Barrett and asked him."

Barrett. Just his name brought a sigh out of her. She'd have to remember to thank him because the sad Ingrid of last night was gone, replaced with a smiling, happy version. "Well, I'm glad you did. Not because of the food, which is very nice, but I'm glad to see you."

Ingrid smiled. "I'm glad to see you too." Her eyes took in the room. "This is a very lovely place you have here. Sure you won't consider moving out to our neck of the woods?"

"I'm sure, but thank you. Hey, while you here, would you allow me the privilege of doing your hair and nails?"

"Oh, I'd love for you to. But let's eat first, all right, dear? I haven't had anything since breakfast and those divine smells are causing quite a stir in my stomach."

"Mine too." Audra hooked Ingrid's arm through hers. On the way to the line, Audra slowed her pace to match Ingrid's, which surprisingly wasn't nearly as slow as yesterday evening's.

They filled their plates and strolled to the lounge and ate.

Audra took a bite of the grilled Brie, peach and smoked pork sandwich. "This is heavenly."

"Chef Pierre is the best there is." Ingrid took a sip of hot tea, holding her little pinky up when she did.

"How do you know Barrett?" Audra asked, taking another bite.

"We met at a fundraiser a few years ago. Mrs. Vandersmithe, a woman who is always pointing out my flaws," Ingrid sighed before continuing, "was saying some very cutting remarks to me. Barrett stepped in and rescued me. Just like those knights of old." She covered her mouth and giggled like a school girl. "Ever since that night, Barrett makes it a point to come and see me at least once a month. Bless his heart. He is such a kind boy."

Boy? There was nothing boyish about Barrett. He was all man. Audra wanted to ask Ingrid more about just how he'd rescued her, but her mind took a turn of its own with thoughts of Barrett. A man, who in her book, was turning out to be quite a hero. A very well liked one.

While they ate, Ingrid regaled Audra with stories from her past. When they finished, Audra led Ingrid to her station. When Audra finished with her petal style hairdo, Ingrid once again oohed and aahed over it. She offered to pay Audra, but Audra refused and told her to come back anytime. Ingrid left with a promise from Audra that she would come with Barrett the next time he went to visit Ingrid.

Later on that day, when everyone else had gone home, Audra sat alone in her salon with her legs stretched out and her ankles crossed drinking a Diet 7-Up with a slice of lime, wishing she had Barrett's phone number. If she did, she would call him and thank him for telling Ingrid where her shop was.

Ingrid was a lot stronger than Audra had originally believed her to be. Audra had a sneaking suspicion it was due to the fact that Elsa wasn't there to take control.

Audra's cell phone rang. Without looking at the number, she lazily answered it. "Hello."

"Hi, gorgeous."

Audra quickly shifted positions, settling her feet on the floor and pressing the phone closer to her ear. "Well, hello there, handsome."

"Handsome, huh?" Barrett's light rumbling chuckle tickled her.

"Gorgeous, huh?" she retorted back in their playful banter.

"How was your day?"

"Great." She brushed a stray strand of hair off her face. "You'll never believe who came to see me today."

"Let me guess. Ingrid. And…" he paused. "She brought her favorite chef along with her."

"How did you know? I mean I know you gave her the address to my shop and all, but how did ya know what she did?"

"Simple. She told me. In fact, she invited me to join all of you."

"Why didn't you?" Oh how she wished he would have.

"I had business to take care of, or I would have been there." The mysterious, disappointed way he said it made Audra wonder what kind of business. Wasn't he retired?

"I see." She tapped her finger against her chin. "Oh, before I forget, thank you for telling her how to find me."

"I wasn't sure if you'd be angry or not." A hint of concern edged those words, and she wondered at that.

"Why would I be angry? Ingrid's a lovely woman."

"I know. But most people don't appreciate it when someone gives out private information."

"My shop isn't private." She put her legs back up on the couch, stretching them out in front of her, and crossing her bare feet.

"You know what I mean." The sigh came over the phone as if he were standing in front of her instead of miles away.

"Yeah, I do." There was dead air for a few seconds until Audra finally spoke. "Ingrid told me how the two of you met."

"Oh she did, did she?" Humor accompanied his question.

"Yup. She thinks you're like one of those knights of old." So did she, but she wouldn't tell Barrett that.

"And you? What do you think of me?"

He had to ask. Since he did, she would go ahead and tell him. "Truth is, I'm beginning to agree with her."

"Well, that's nice to hear. It's about time." The deep rumble in his chest came over the air loud and clear, putting a smile on Audra's face.

"Oh, just so you know," she blew sideways at the same stray strand that had tickled her face just moments ago. "Ingrid made me promise to come with you next time you go to see her."

"She did, huh?" He chuckled again.

"What's so funny about that?"

"Oh, you've got to know Ingrid. She's back to her matchmaking tricks again."

"Matchmaking tricks?" she asked, intrigued.

"Yes. For years, she's been trying to set me up with the single ladies. Not just any single ladies either, but someone she is 'extremely fond of'. Her words, not mine."

"Oh. And just how many females that she is extremely fond of has she tried to set you up with?"

"Enough. Why, you jealous?"

"Nope. Just curious."

"Curiosity killed the cat."

"Well, I'm safe then because I'm not a cat." Audra took a sip of her 7-Up and set it down. "Now that we got that out of the way, is there a reason for your call? Did you want something in particular or was this just a general, see-if-you-can-get-a-rise-out-of-Audra call?"

"Yes and, yes."

Audra chose to ignore his remark even though it sent a thrill of excitement rushing through her veins. "Okay, so what did you want?"

"Erik and I met today and talked about starting motocross races at his speedway."

"You and Erik got together?"

"And Olivia."

"Livvy was there?" She uncrossed her ankles.

"Yes, ma'am."

Why hadn't her best friend said anything to her about the meeting? Then again, in all fairness to Liv, Audra hadn't had a chance to talk to her the night before or today.

"And I learned some pretty interesting things about you." Barrett's voice had a teasing quality to it.

"Oh yeah. Like what?"

"Like how you're scared to death of snakes and bees, and how you insist on confronting all your fears."

"Livvy has a big mouth," she mumbled.

"What's that?" Barrett asked.

"Nothing."

"You think Livvy has a big mouth." The smirk was there hidden underneath his question.

"If you heard me, why'd you ask?" she retorted.

"Just wanted you to see if you'd repeat it."

"You're incorrigible."

"So you keep telling me."

She loved hearing that throaty rumble of his when he laughed.

"Back to the reason for my call. Erik wants to meet at his Speedway tomorrow evening, and I wanted to know if you'd like to go with me. We can grab dinner afterward."

The idea of spending more time with him sent excitement rushing through her veins again. "What time?"

"Pick you up at six?"

"I'll be ready."

"Yeah right."

"Hey, be nice."

"I am being nice."

"No you aren't."

"I speak the truth as I see it."

"Oh, you think so. Okay, buddy boy, I'll make you a deal."

He hesitated just slightly. "What kind of deal?"

Good. Finally he was the one left fumbling and unsure.

"If I'm ready on time you have to promise to do something that I've wanted to do for a long time," she said, purposely leaving just a hint of mystery in her voice.

"What's that?"

She cocked her head coquettishly even though she knew he couldn't see it. "I'm not telling."

"Then I'm not promising."

"Okay, fine." She rushed the words out. "Have it your way."

"I usually do."

He said it with so much confidence that she wanted to shoot a retort back at him, but what would be the point? "If I'm on time, you have to go parasailing with me."

"Parasailing?" His voice raised an octave. "You serious?"

"Yup. It's on my list of things to do."

"Your list of fears to overcome?"

"That would be the one."

"Whew, I thought it was going to be something terrifying like shoe shopping, or something equally as bad." She heard the shudder in his voice.

"Ha. Ha. Very funny. Remind me to laugh. On second thought," she placed her finger against her chin. "I've changed my mind. Shopping for shoes sounds much, much better."

"No."

Wow, that was quick.

"No, it doesn't sound better?" She swallowed her giggle.

"No, as in, no way am I going shoe shopping with you. I have my limits. And shoe shopping exceeds those limits." There was no humor whatsoever in his voice this time.

"Ah, c'mon now. Where's your sense of adventure?"

"It does not stretch to shoes. Parasailing, yes. Shoe shopping, no."

"Okay. Well, you can't blame a gal for trying." Audra's other line beeped. "Listen, I gotta run, my other line's beeping. I'll talk to you later. See ya at six. Sharp." She emphasized the word sharp.

His only response, laughter.

Chapter Seven

B arrett showered and shaved, then slid on a pair of black jeans, a black t-shirt, and his black boots before heading out the door to pick up Audra to go to Cole's Speedway to meet up with Erik.

The humidity reminded him of home. A home he'd never see again. He shook off that depressing thought and headed toward Audra's place.

Forty-five minutes later, he pulled into her driveway, and glanced at the dash clock. 5:45. He sent up a quick prayer that this would be one time Audra wouldn't be ready on time. Weird, he knew, but a dreaded shoe-shopping trip might be at stake here. After all, women changed their minds as often as they changed their shoes. It definitely had him concerned that Audra would be ornery enough to change her mind about parasailing and insist that he go shoe shopping with her instead. One look at her pleading eyes, eyes he couldn't refuse, and he knew he'd say yes and then live to regret it. The very idea of sitting for hours while she tried on one pair of shoes after another made him shudder with repulsion.

Before he got too worked up over the idea, he climbed out of his roadster, and took the six porch steps two at time.

Movement at the big picture window snagged his attention. With his rear feet on the back of the chair, his front paws on the window ledge, Louey stood there, barking and growling, and glancing back and forth between the front door and him. For such a tiny thing, the dog sure had guts.

He raised his hand to ring the bell when the front door suddenly opened. The screen door almost nailed him, but he jumped back out of the way before Audra caught him in the face with the thing. "Hah, hah, you lose," she said standing in the doorway, grinning from ear to ear.

Hopping around Audra's feet, Louey yapped menacingly up at him, baring his teeth. Louey could yap all he wanted, Barrett only had eyes for Audra.

Man, she looked good. Smelled good too. Like sweet lemon tea if he wasn't mistaken. "Hello to you too."

"Never mind that." She looked down at Louey. "Louey, hush, and go lay down." With his tail tucked tight against him, he let out another bark and a growl before he turned and left. "You have to go parasailing with me now. You promised." A smirk curled those lips of hers.

He was so relieved she hadn't changed her mind about going shoe shopping with her instead of parasailing that he wanted to yank her to him and kiss her senseless. Now he wouldn't have to worry about trying to resist her pouty face.

Audra rose on her tiptoes and kissed his cheek. "Thank you." She whirled and slung the screen door open, barely missing him again, and flew through the door with a spring in her step.

Barrett stood on her porch. He couldn't believe she'd kissed him on the cheek.

Seconds later, Audra stepped outside, keys in hand. Her white skirt with the burgundy hummingbird scene down one side of it swirled around her calves as she whirled around and locked her door. She shoved her keys into the pocket of her burgundy three-quarter length sleeved sweater, looped her arm through his, and all but dragged him toward the steps. "You look nice," she said, her gaze scanning him from head to toe.

"So do you." He scanned her from head to toe as well, stopping to admire her cheerleader legs, as he called them. Every cheerleader he'd ever known had nice shaped legs. "Nice skirt."

Cupping the fabric on the hummingbird side of her skirt, she held it out for inspection. His or hers, he had no clue, nor did he care he just admired the woman wearing it. "Thanks. I like it." She released her skirt, and it brushed against her trim figure like a gentle spring breeze.

On the way to his car, he asked, "You sure you're okay with eating a late dinner? Or would like to grab a quick bite first?"

"Afterward is fine with me. I ate a late lunch. How about you?"

"I'm good too."

If he wasn't mistaken, he thought he heard her say, *You sure are.*

At his car, Barrett opened her door, waited for her to be seated, then shut it. Settling his arms on the top of the door, he leaned over and gazed down at her. "You,

Audra Darron, are one beautiful woman." He pressed his lips to her soft cheek, wishing she'd turn her face so that his lips would *accidently* kiss her mouth instead. He stood, winked at her shocked face, and headed over to the driver's side, whistling *The Temptations* song *My Girl*. He knew she wasn't his girl - yet. But he could always hope.

Could you do that again, but this time on the lips, Audra wanted to ask after he'd kissed her on the cheek. She still couldn't believe she'd kissed him on the cheek. It was such an impulsive thing with her, and that always seemed to get her into trouble.

"You're awfully quiet. What're you thinking?"

"About you."

"Good."

She glanced over at him. "I'm not so sure it is."

His frown showed his confusion and his concern. "Why?"

She shifted in her seat as much as the seatbelt would allow. "You're a man of mystery, Barrett Camden."

"And this is bad, because...?" He turned right at the traffic light and glanced over at her.

Audra wasn't sure how she should answer him or how much she should tell him. "You know how some women like bad boys?"

"Only too well," he muttered.

"Excuse me?"

"Nothing."

"No. No 'nothing' here. What did ya mean by you know only too well that some woman like bad boys? Is this experience talking? Were you, or are you a bad boy?" she asked the question even though she knew he wouldn't answer. Who would?

"Not really. Let's just leave it at that." His tone said he was finished and that nothing she said would change that fact. Well, she'd leave it alone. For now.

"Tell me, what kind of man do you like?" His eyes caught hers before he looked back at the road and made a left turn taking them closer to Cole Speedway.

"Unfortunately, I'm drawn to men of the mysterious sort."

"Good for me then." His smile curled her toes as his hand reached over and clasped hers.

"No, not good." She removed her hand from his and held it with her other one.

"I don't understand."

"Let's just say that the last man I dated was very mysterious. With good reason. He was hiding something." Boy was he ever.

"Did you pray about the others before dating them?"

Whoa, she hadn't seen that remark coming. One minute they were talking about the men she'd dated hiding something and the next about her praying about them. "Yes, I prayed about him."

Another frown came her way.

"When it comes to men and God, obviously my ability to hear clearly from either one is sorely lacking."

"So, I take it that you haven't prayed about me then."

Heat rushed up her neck and settled into her cheeks. She quickly looked out at the scenery, brushing her windblown hair off her face.

She loved how green everything looked and how the thick trees and brush that lined the curvy road almost encapsulated them.

"You didn't, did you?"

Why couldn't he just leave it alone?

No, she hadn't prayed about him. She'd meant to. But when it got right down to actually doing it, she had chickened out. A part of her was afraid God would say no. But her biggest concern was she wouldn't know if it was God talking to her or her own spirit trying to get its way. Finally, without looking at him, she shook her head.

"Well, I can assure you, I've prayed about you."

She yanked her attention toward him, stunned to hear that he'd prayed about her. "Oh yeah, and what did the Lord say about me?"

"I'm here, aren't I?"

That was his only answer, and she wasn't sure how to feel about that. Neil, the last man she'd dated, had said the very same thing to her.

He lied.

In fact, their whole relationship was based on nothing but lies and secrets. None of which she'd known about at the time.

Barrett's hand covered hers again, shattering her line of thinking. Something she was extremely grateful for as she didn't want to relive that pain again.

"What's going on in that pretty little head of yours? Talk to me."

Audra looked over at him but refused to answer his question.

What if Barrett was lying to her too? That question blew through her brain like a piece of straw caught up in a tornado. Though his background check had come back squeaky clean, those checks didn't have the capacity to reveal every hidden secret a person carried. She should know.

Her chest expanded with the weight of her heavy sigh.

Secrets.

How she despised them.

Feared them even.

A fear she wasn't sure could or would ever overcome. Once trust was severed, it was hard to trust again.

She knew her next question was futile, but she had to ask it just the same. "What are you hiding, Barrett?"

Whoa. Barrett hadn't seen that one coming. Just how would he answer her? There was no way he could reveal the things he was hiding – his past and his true identity. If word got out who he really was, nothing would be the same for him ever again.

Only a handful of people, agents mostly, and Andy knew his birth name. If it wasn't for Andy, Barrett shuddered to think where he'd be right now. Andy had taken care of everything. If anyone did a background check on Barrett, the only information they would ever find would be on Barrett Camden. Nothing connected him to his other two identities. Nothing.

"You're stalling, and that makes me nervous." Her fingers swirled fast circles over the hummingbird picture on her skirt and beads of sweat dotted the end of her nose. Something he'd discovered happened when she was nervous or upset. "Okay, that's it. Turn this thing around and take me home. Now."

That wasn't going to happen. "Let me ask you something." It was a statement not a question. "What are you hiding?"

"Me?" She pointed to herself, and her eyebrows spiked at the same time. "I'm not hiding anything."

"How do I know that?" He checked his rearview mirror and switched lanes.

"Because I'm telling you it's so, that's how." She crossed her arms over her chest. "You, however, haven't even done that."

She had him there. "Point taken. Listen, Audra, all I can say is there are things in my life that are best left in the past. That are too painful to talk about. And that are really no one else's business." Everything inside of him rebelled at speaking his next words. "If that's something you can't handle, then yes, I will take you home now. I don't want to, but I will." He checked his rearview mirror again, turned his blinker on before changing lanes and pulling off to the side of the road. Angling his upper body toward her, he looked her square in the eyes and said, "Your call."

~♥*~*

Audra clasped her hands together, formed a church steeple with her forefingers, and rested them against her lips.

Should she have him take her home this instant? Or should she trust him and stay? More importantly, did she dare?

Something about Barrett made her want to stay, but on the other hand, something about Barrett made her want to have him turn this thing around and hightail her back home. She wanted to pray about him like she did about everything else in her life, but for some reason when it came to praying about the men in her life, her ability to hear from God regarding them was almost nonexistent.

"Make up your mind, Audra." His thumbs tapped against the steering wheel as he gazed at her. "I don't want to leave Erik waiting or be late."

She flicked her fingernail on her bottom teeth as her mind continued to rush through whether to go back home or not. Finally, she came to a conclusion she could live with. "I'll go with you to the speedway. While you're talking with Erik, I'll decide if I wanna continue seeing you again or not."

Barrett nodded. "Fair enough." Checking his side mirror, he put his roadster in gear and continued heading out to Cole Speedway. The rest of the way there neither spoke.

At the speedway, they drove past the bleachers, the concessions stands, and through the contestant pits, until they pulled up in front of the large metal shop. Barrett shut the engine off and bowed his head. "Father, Your word says, *But, if any of you lacks wisdom, let him ask of God, who gives to all generously and without reproach, and it will be given to him.* Lord, You know Audra's been hurt, and You heard her fear about not being able to discern Your guidance where men are concerned. I'm asking You for that to change from this moment on. Not for my sake, even though You know I want to get to know her better, but for her sake alone. In Christ's name, amen."

Like a Popsicle left out in the hot sun, Audra's heart melted into a pool of liquid sentiment. To think that a man would pray so unselfishly for her touched her deeply. Neil had never prayed for her even though he'd gone to church with her. She learned rather slowly that just because a person goes to church it doesn't mean they're who they profess to be.

Why hadn't she seen the signs earlier?

Were there even any?

She ran their whole relationship through her mind so many times that she'd worn a path in her brain. She needed to stop doing that. What was done was done. Right now, she wanted to concentrate on thanking Barrett for praying for her. "Thank you," she said softly. "Would you please tell Olivia I'll be over at the stands and to please give me a few minutes? I want to be alone and pray." She quickly opened her door and scurried toward the bleachers.

She climbed all the way to the top. Tucking her skirt under her, she sat down, crossed her leg over the other, and stared out into the empty parking lot. A moment passed before she bowed her head and closed her eyes. She silently prayed about the concerns invading her mind where Barrett was concerned.

She must have sat there for thirty minutes or so praying her heart out before Olivia came up and joined her.

"You okay?" Olivia asked, sitting down on the seat next to her.

She faced her friend. "I'm not sure."

"What's wrong?"

Audra's fingers traced the design on her skirt. "I like him, Liv."

"And that's a problem because…?"

Her eyes came up to her friend. "Because I don't know if I can pursue a relationship with Barrett. I'm scared." She nibbled at her lower lip.

Olivia pulled both of Audra's hands into hers. Compassion filled her eyes. "You've always confronted your fears, Audie." She spoke softly. "This is just one more for you to confront and to conquer."

"I thought about that earlier, but I'm not sure I'll ever be able to confront this particular fear."

"Sure you can. You don't want it to keep you from finding true love. Barrett may or may not be that person. If you're waiting for a guarantee that you'll never be hurt, well that isn't going to happen. There no guarantees in this life. I of all people know that. Just think, if I had never taken a chance on love again I would have never met Erik. I have you to thank for that."

"Me?" Audra thumbed herself. "God did it."

"Yes, but you encouraged me and were there for me the whole time, reminding me how much Jesus loves me. Everything I went through, Audie, I would go through again to be where I'm at today. All of those things have made me stronger, and I'm happier than I've ever been. Take the risk. If it doesn't work out, God has something better for you then."

"I'm not sure my heart can take it."

"I didn't think mine could either."

"But look how yours turned out."

Olivia cocked her head and frowned. "What's really going on, Audra? This is not like you. You usually are the one to tell others to trust God, and that he'll take care of everything. Where is that woman now?"

"I'm still here. I'm just struggling is all."

"We all struggle. There's more going on here than just Barrett. Spill, girl."

Audra withdrew her hands and once again stared straight ahead of her. She played with the back of her hair, raising a handful and dropping it. Finally, after several minutes, she settled her hands on her lap and gazed over at her friend. "I know this sounds crazy, Liv, but..." She swallowed and closed her eyes for a split second before opening them. "I think he might be the one."

"The one what?"

Audra tilted her head and hiked a questioning brow.

"Oh. Oh." Dawning widened Olivia's eyes. "You mean the one as is *the* one."

"Isn't that what I just said?" Wasn't Olivia listening to a single word she was saying?

"Lands O' Goshen, girl. You got all that by praying just now?"

"No." She shook her head. "God was silent on the matter. But," she held up a finger. "I feel peace about him deep in my gut."

"Do you love him?" Olivia asked.

"I didn't say I loved him. I said I think he might be the one. Besides, you know I never believed in love at first sight, and Barrett is no exception. In fact, the first moment I laid eyes on him, love was the last thing I felt for him. Annoyance, yup, love, no."

"What changed?"

"When we were at his butterfly garden and I saw all that beauty he'd created and watched how gentle and tender Barrett was with those beautiful, fragile, winged creatures," she sighed. "Well, the enchantment of it all lured me to him just like the butterflies were being lured to the blooming flowers there." Confusion and doubt rushed in on the wings of those words. "But I'm scared, Liv, because he's so secretive."

"You can't keep comparing every man you meet with Neil."

"I know. But I have to use discretion too."

"So what are you going to do about Barrett? It wouldn't be fair of you to keep seeing him and lead him on. He obviously is smitten with you."

"I know. He said as much."

"So, why not give it a chance?"

"Because, what if his secrets turn out to be as devastating as Neil's?

"What if they don't?"

Good point. Still… Was she willing to risk putting her heart out there and pursue a relationship with Barrett?

An hour and half later, Barrett finished his meeting with Erik. "Thanks for all your help. Sure you won't change your mind and join Livvy and me for dinner?"

"Thanks, but no. I have reservations at Luigi's. If you two would like to join us, I can change it to four."

"Not this time. Mickey has dinner waiting. A rain check?"

Barrett nodded, and they shook hands. Erik was quickly becoming a good friend to him. A nicer guy he'd never met, except for Andy.

"Shall we go find our women?" Erik asked, as the two of the headed out the shop door.

Barrett liked the sound of that – our women.

However, in the very next thought, uncertainty pounced on him. Audra wasn't his woman. And after their conversation, he wasn't sure she would ever be.

The closer he and Erik got to the bleachers, the tighter the knots in his stomach twisted.

What would he find when he saw her?

What if it wasn't the answer he hoped for?

What if she sent him away forever?

Could he change her mind?

Could he change his own?

Determination rose up inside him. He'd figure out some way to keep her.

Barrett and Erik's footsteps echoed against the aluminum steps as they climbed their way up the bleachers to Audra and Olivia.

As soon as Audra saw him, she and Olivia stopped talking. They both looked guilty as all get out, and Barrett didn't like that one bit.

"Hi, Sweetheart." Olivia stood and greeted Erik.

"What time is it?" Audra rose, looking everywhere but at Barrett.

That wasn't good. Not good at all.

Chapter Eight

B arrett twisted his wrist and looked at his Rolex. "Ten after eight."

"Thanks." Audra still hadn't looked at him.

"Are you two joining us for dinner?" Olivia eyed him and Audra before turning her hopeful gaze up at Erik. "You did ask them, didn't you?"

"Of course I did."

"And...?"

"And, I said not this time," Barrett answered for him. "We already have plans."

"Oh." Disappointment seeped through Olivia's voice. "Okay. Well, maybe next time." Her gaze went to Audra, and a look he couldn't decipher passed between them.

"Well, you two have fun. We're going to run along now." Olivia hooked arms with her husband. On their way down the stairs, every other step or so, Olivia glanced back up at him and Audra.

Erik tugged on her, and Olivia yanked her attention forward. They climbed into Erik's blue Chevrolet pickup, and within seconds, the truck's taillights disappeared around the corner of the shop and out of sight.

Suddenly alone and not knowing if she'd prayed or not or if this was the end of their relationship, Barrett slowly faced her, willing his nervous stomach to calm down. "You didn't say no."

Audra cocked her head. "Huh?"

"You didn't say no when I mentioned us having dinner plans. Does this mean you're going to go with me?"

Lowering her eyes, she scuffed the toe of her sandal against the aluminum floor and nibbled on her lower lip.

Barrett hooked his finger under her chin and tilted her face up about as far as it would go. With her eyes closed, Barrett found himself lowering his face to hers. His lips touched hers.

She gasped, and her eyes flew open.

He stared into her eyes, questioning her with them as to whether or not he could continue and hoping she was getting his message.

Her eyelids drifted shut, and her lips parted.

Barrett took that as a yes.

Gently, he captured her lips with his own. Their softness along with the impact of the electrical current that flowed from her lips to every part of his being yanked the breath right out of him.

She matched his every move with kisses that nearly drove him to his knees. The need to be closer to her pressed through him. Not wanting to scare her, he cupped her face and deepened the kiss. When she didn't balk, he slowly lowered his arms around her and pulled her toward him, closing the gap between them even more.

Her arms tentatively and slowly slid around his neck. Within seconds, with their lips locked in a breathless kiss, using a gentle force, he pulled her even closer until they were locked together in a strong embrace. How long they stayed like that, he didn't know, but what he did know was, he wanted this kiss to last forever.

Audra held on tight to Barrett, fearful her legs wouldn't hold her up and that she'd fall to the floor into a heap around his feet. His lips were strong yet incredibly soft, and his kisses were unlike any she'd ever experienced before. They were both possessive and gentle. She knew she should pull away, but she didn't want to. She wanted to continue kissing him. To continue the amazing connection with his soul that his kiss offered.

Moments later, Barrett ended the kiss, his lips still hovering over hers. "Wow," he whispered, his spearmint breath brushed against her lips.

"Wow, is right." She waited for him to kiss her again, but he raised his head.

"As nice as this is…" His voice rasped, and he immediately cleared it. "It's getting late. I have reservations at Luigi's for 8:45."

Too overcome with emotions, emotions that scared her half to death, Audra could only nod.

Barrett stepped back and clasped her hand. Hand-in-hand, they headed down the steps, and neither of them spoke.

When they got to his vehicle, he led Audra to his side of the car and opened the door for her. She sat down and scooted across the seat, leaving just enough room for him behind the wheel. Their shoulders brushed as he climbed inside. Their eyes met, and once again, he cupped her chin with his large hand and kissed her gently and tenderly before he pulled back, started his car, and drove toward the restaurant.

The whole way there, Barrett's arm anchored around her shoulder, and her head nestled into him.

Twenty minutes later, they pulled up to the restaurant, and even though she was famished, Audra wished they hadn't. She didn't want to leave the closeness of him.

"Shall we go in?" He kissed her.

She kissed him back. "No."

"I don't want this to end." His lips touched hers only briefly.

"Neither do I?" she responded, their breaths mingling together.

Were they talking about the same thing? Was he talking about the kiss or their relationship or both? All questions vanished when he wrapped his strong arms around her and kissed her until every part of her melted. All too soon, he raised his head, opened the door, hopped out, and held his hand out to her. She settled hers into his and smiled up at him.

They strolled toward the front door of the Italian restaurant, barely taking their eyes off of each other until they stepped inside the air-conditioned building. Normally at this time of night, she'd need a wrap, but she was still all warm and fuzzy inside, and therefore didn't need one.

The scent of freshly baked rolls, Italian herbs and spices, including garlic filled the air. Her stomach rumbled.

Her eyes took in the room. Little Italy or a Tuscan villa came to mind, complete with tables and chairs and imitation trees with rubber grapes and lanterns hanging from the branches.

A small wrought iron balcony with grape vines lingered above their heads, reminding her of the movie Romeo and Juliet.

Wine bottles of various shapes, sizes and colors sat on a long ledge that ran the length of the terracotta wall.

A beautiful blonde woman with long legs, spiked, bling-toed heels, and black sequenced mini-dress that revealed a little too much cleavage strolled up to them. "May I help you?" The woman's blue eyes landed on Barrett and never once strayed to Audra. They did, however, glaze over Barrett's left hand tucked against his chest. The very one Audra had her arm looped through.

"Camden, reservations for two."

"Yes, Mr. Camden. Your table is ready."

Audra mentally rolled her eyes at the woman's syrupy voice. Did she really have to be so obvious that she was flirting with him with his date standing right beside him? If Audra was the jealous type, she'd be jealous right now. But her philosophy was that if a man didn't want her, then she didn't want him.

"Follow me." Miss Leggy Blonde scooped up two menus. When she walked, her hips had a little bit too much sway in them. All for Barrett's benefit, no doubt. She led them to a table near the window, overlooking the lake.

Barrett held out Audra's chair and waited until she sat down before he took his own seat.

"My name is Lisa," she said looking directly at Barrett who seemed totally unfazed by the woman's charms. In fact, his eyes weren't on Lisa, but on Audra instead.

Audra sent him her sweetest, warmest smile, and allowed her affection for him to be evident in her eyes.

"I'll send your waiter right away."

"Please do," Barrett said, dismissing her without so much as a glance her way.

That tickled Audra and made her feel special. She reached across the small table and offered him her hand, which he took with a big smile. "Thank you."

"For what?"

"For making me feel special." Audra ignored the puzzled look on his face, and her attention shifted out to the lake. "What a beautiful view. Don't ya just love sunsets over lakes?"

"I watch them often."

She yanked her attention to him. "You do?"

He nodded. "There's a lake on my property."

"There is?" Where? She didn't remember seeing one.

"Yes, and you sound like a parrot." Humor laced his voice.

"Never mind that." She waved his comment away. "Where's this lake at on your property?"

"Would you like to see it when we're finished here?" He moved the wine glass to the edge of the table.

"I'd love to."

"Excuse me." A man wearing a white shirt with black pants and a black vest hovered next to their table. "My name is Antonio, and I am your waiter this evening." His Italian accent fit the atmosphere. "May I get you something to drink? Wine perhaps?"

"None for me," Barrett answered. "You?" He looked at Audra.

"None for me either, thanks." Audra added her wine glass to Barrett's. "I would like a glass of sweet tea though."

"Very well, madam. And you, sir?"

"I'll have the same."

He turned their glasses over and filled them with iced water. "Are you ready to order, or do you need more time?"

"More time, please," Barrett answered.

"Very good. I will be right back with your drinks." Antonio spun on one heel and walked away.

"Guess we'd better look at the menus before he gets back."

"Guess you're right," Audra agreed.

They perused the menus.

Antonio returned with two glasses of sweet tea and set one in front of each of them. "Are you ready to order?" He held his tablet and poised his pen above it, looking at her then at Barrett.

"Audra?" Barrett sent her a questioning look.

"Yeah, I'm ready. I'll have the shrimp tetrazzini dinner. What kind of salad dressing do you have?" she asked, looking up at Antonio.

"We only have one kind. All salads come with the house special."

"That'll work." Audra handed Antonio her menu.

"And you, sir?"

"Steak, medium rare, baked potato loaded, and instead of the salad, a side order of spaghetti."

"You can do that?" Audra asked.

"Just did." Barrett smiled at her. "Would you like spaghetti instead?"

"No, salad's fine."

"Will that be all?"

"We'll have spumoni ice cream for dessert. One bowl, two spoons." Barrett winked at Audra before looking up at the waiter.

The waiter took the menus Barrett handed him and left.

Barrett reached across the table, taking both of Audra's hands in his. "I'm so glad you said yes and that you're here with me."

"I am too."

Barrett frowned. "This is too far." He scooted his chair next to hers and moved his water, silverware and napkin in front of him. "There. That's better." His eyes drifted to hers. "So tell me, Audra, what made you say yes?"

"Say yes?"

"Yes, to coming to dinner with me? To seeing me."

Oh that. How could she have forgotten so soon? He'd just mentioned it only a minute ago. "Olivia."

"Olivia?" He sounded disappointed.

"Now who's being a parrot?"

"Never mind that," he quoted the same words she'd said to him. "What did Olivia say to convince you?"

"It wasn't what she said as much as what I said to her." There was no way she was going to tell him that she had revealed to Olivia that she felt he might be the one. That thought scared her. Because of what happened with Neil, love now frightened her in ways it never had before.

Barrett had to know. "What did you tell Olivia?"

"I'll never tell." Audra cocked her head, batted her long eyelashes, and smiled that playful smile of hers before she leaned back in her chair and gazed out the window.

Barrett let it go for now, but he would definitely be asking her later on at his lake.

He looked out the window and watched as the sun slipped away. Purple sky sliced with ribbons of gray and red reflected in the water. The beauty of God's creation stole his breath from him. That and the beautiful woman sitting beside him. His chest expanded with a sigh of contentment.

Barrett's cell phone vibrated in his pocket. Who would be calling him this late? He pulled it out of its belt holder and checked the caller ID. Marlowe. "Excuse me,

Audra, I need to take this." He punched the green phone icon. "Marlow, what's up?"

"We might have a lead on the killer."

Barrett's heart slammed against his ribs, and he forced himself not to leap to his feet or to let his emotional shock show. "Hang on." He looked over at Audra. "Be back in a sec. Don't go away."

Her brows puckered, but she nodded.

Barrett headed outside and around the building. Making sure he was alone, he asked, "Did the lead check out?"

"We won't know for a couple days. But I thought you'd like to know."

"You got that right." Any and every little detail he wanted to know about. "Thanks."

"You know what this means, don't you?"

"I do," he said, swallowing back the lump of dread stuck in his throat. "Call me if you find out anything more."

"Will do. Tell Audra hi."

"How'd you know I was with her?" A grungy white cat darted in front of him and headed into the alley.

"Because you told someone you'd be right back and to not go away. Who else would it be since she's all you ever talk about anymore?" Andy chuckled.

"Smart man." Barrett watched the cat jump on boxes and things until it landed inside the dumpster. He felt bad for the poor skinny thing and wished he could take it home and fatten it up.

"You've got it bad. I'm happy for you, buddy. It's time you get on with your life and find love again.

Felicia would want that." Barrett heard Andy suck in a sharp breath. "Oh man, I'm sorry, Barrett. I shouldn't have said that."

"It's okay, Andy." He put his back to the alley. "It's been seven years. God has healed my heart. I'm ready to move on... hopefully with Audra. But before I get ahead of myself I need to get to know her better to see if she can handle what may come."

"Do you think she can?"

"Not sure yet. I'm hoping so." He raked his hand through his hair.

"We'll just have to pray about that, won't we?"

"I have been."

"Well, whatever you decide, you know Keera and I are behind you one hundred percent."

"Thanks, man." What would he do without them? He shuddered just thinking about it.

"Anytime. Well, I'll let you get back to Audra. I'll keep you posted. Love you, my friend."

"Love you too, brother." Barrett ended his call. Gratefulness swelled his heart. Andy had become the brother he never had.

Barrett headed back inside and sat down. A basket of bread sticks set in the middle of the table along with a salad and a side of spaghetti. "Sorry to keep you waiting. You should have gone ahead and started."

"I'm fine." Her forehead creased. "Is everything okay with you?"

"Fine." He smiled. "That was Marlowe... Andy. He said to tell you hi."

Her lips curled upward. "He's such a nice man. I really like his wife too. Keera and I had such a good time."

"We'll have to get together again with them sometime. I think I'll have a barbeque at my place and invite them and Erik and Olivia, if you think they'd come."

"I'm sure they would. Unless it's a race day, then Erik wouldn't be able to."

"Well, we'll just have to plan it when it isn't a race day."

Audra smiled at Barrett's thoughtfulness. "Sounds good to me."

"Well, shall we pray?"

They bowed their heads, and he said the blessing over the food.

"So how's Andy doing?" She forked a bite of salad and chewed while she waited for his answer.

"You fishing for information again?" He uncovered the bread and placed a garlic stick on her plate and one on his before he took a bite of the bread.

How did he do it? How did he know she was hoping to discover what they had talked about? "Yup. You bitin'?"

"Nope."

Audra frowned. The less he said about himself the more nervous that made her. "So, tell me about your family. Are they from around here?"

"Tell me about yours." He twirled spaghetti noodles around his fork and ate them.

There he goes again, changing the subject.

"I will if you tell me about yours." She watched as he took his time chewing what was in his mouth.

After he swallowed, he answered her. "Fair enough."

That response took her by surprise. She had figured he would probably change the subject again or something. "My mom and dad live in Wheeling." Audra proceeded to tell him. "They'll be celebrating their thirty-fifth wedding anniversary next month. Both of my parents are lawyers. My brother Josh and his wife Marissa are expecting their second child. Josh is a pediatrician. He has his own practice. And Marissa is a stay at home mom now. She was a nurse." She forked a piece of shrimp and a slice of mushroom and chewed them.

"Let me guess. At your brother's practice."

"Yup." She smiled.

"Any more siblings?" He sliced a chunk of his steak off, never taking his eyes off of her.

"Yup, my sister Riley. She's doing missionary work in Thailand."

"That's cool." He slid the meat from his fork into his mouth.

Audra took another bite of her shrimp tetrazzini. "Yeah, she loves it."

"So what about you?" He set his knife and fork down. "What made you want to do hair?"

"When I was fifteen, a high school football player who constantly picked on me thought it would be fun to chop a big chunk of my hair off. I was mortified. It looked horrible, and at the time, I just knew my world had ended. I ran home and told my mom. My aunt Mayce was there. She took one look and said she could fix it.

"She wasn't a beautician or anything, but she loved messing with hair. Mom offered to take me to a regular salon, but Aunt Mayce begged my mom to let her do it and promised she could fix it up real cute like. Mom asked me if it was okay, and I told her yeah. At that point, I didn't figure I had anything to lose.

"Somehow my aunt was able to turn that chopped up mess into the cutest hairdo I've ever had. Everybody at school loved it and wanted to know who'd done my hair. I remember how good it made me feel, and well, I wanted to make other people feel that good too.

"I worked hard and earned enough money to open my own shop. I lived upstairs in a tiny apartment and saved every penny I could. After Olivia moved, I missed her something awful, so when she told me they needed a good hairdresser here, I decided to open a salon here. It's really taken off and grown into a very profitable business. But honestly, I don't care about the money. I care about making people feel good. And that's probably way more information than ya wanted to know."

"I enjoyed hearing about it. And you've obviously succeeded in what you set out to do. To make people feel good. Ingrid can definitely vouch for that."

"She's such a sweet lady. I'm so glad I could help her."

"I bet she was too judging from what Keera had said Ingrid's hair had looked like."

They laughed.

Audra bit off a small chunk of the chewy bread stick. "These are really good." She spoke around the morsel in her mouth.

"They make really good ones here. Lots of butter, garlic, and parmesan and mozzarella cheeses."

"And lots of fat." She laid hers back down onto her plate and wiped her buttery fingers off on her napkin.

"Like you have to worry about that."

"I may not have to now, but I wanna keep it that way." As if to prove her point, she forked a huge bite of salad and shoved it into her mouth and sent him a cheeky grin. Her cheeks bulged, and now she wished she hadn't been so silly. She held her hand over her mouth and chewed. When she finished, she set her fork down and leaned toward him. "So, tell me about your family. And don't you dare even think about changing the subject."

"Wasn't going to. I don't have any."

Chapter Nine

"I don't know how much longer I can keep skirting around the subject of my family," Barrett told Andy. He switched to his Bluetooth in order to free up his hands and started pruning the shrubs in his butterfly garden. The morning sun had already started to heat up the place. Good thing the temperature was on a regulator. Sweat soaked his shirt and face. He wiped the sweat with his forearm. Humidity was the one thing he didn't much care for in the garden.

"Don't."

"You know I can't tell her." So why was Andy even talking like this?

"You can tell her about them. What they were like."

"Every time I talk about them, I remember what that crazed man did. If only I would have taken those threatening notes more seriously. Why would anyone do something like that?" He sent the question into the void, not really expecting an answer, as there could be no logical answer for any of it.

"Who knows what goes on in the mind of a killer? Or I should say killers?"

Barrett stopped pruning and shot up to his feet from his squatting position. "What do you mean *killers*?" He turned the volume up on his Bluetooth.

"That's why I was calling. He wasn't working alone."

"How'd you find that out?"

"My buddy, Jeremy, at the secret service. He said an anonymous tip came in. The man wanted to keep his identity a secret, but he was digging through a dumpster in an alley in New York. When he heard voices, he hopped in the dumpster and covered himself up with newspapers. He overheard these two men bragging about killing Gage Lincoln's wife and family and how smart they were that even the FBI couldn't find them."

"Did he get a good look at them?"

"No. He was afraid if they knew he was there that they'd kill him too."

"Did your buddy trace the call?"

"Of course he did, to a pay phone. By the time they got an agent out there, the man was long gone."

Barrett's heart sank. "So we're back to square one again then?"

"Not really. They're starting to slip up and get sloppy. Something that happens often. They're proud of what they did and the fact that no one has caught them and can't catch them. When they start getting cocky like that, they start getting sloppy, and start boasting about it. Which is exactly what we want them to do. Not only that, we now know that there is more than one killer and that they are in New York."

"Have you ever been to New York? Looking for them there is like looking for an eighth of a carat diamond at Delray Beach in Florida."

"True, but its way more than we had before."

"You're right." He snipped a dead flower off and sighed. "This whole thing is so hard."

"I know. I wish I could do more."

"You've done more than enough."

"No. More than enough is when the killers are behind bars."

Barrett didn't know how to respond to that, so he remained quiet.

"Hang in there, Barrett. I'll talk to you later, okay?"

"Thanks."

"Anytime."

The ramification of what he'd just heard made him feel weak all over. Barrett ended the call, walked over to the fountain, and sat on the ledge.

Images of his wife and parents' dead bodies bombarded his mind. His stomach churned, and he was certain it would heave its contents at any moment. He swallowed hard several times to keep that from happening.

Needing a reprieve from where his mind kept wanting to go, he tossed his shears on the pile of greenery and branches and headed toward his house. He quickly showered and headed toward Charity.

Audra's MG sat in the driveway along with her Harley. He hoped that meant she was home. He needed to see her cheery, smiling face.

Louey barked as Barrett climbed the porch steps and the Chihuahua's familiar face peered through the window.

Audra swung the door open. "Barrett." She opened the screen door. "What're you doing here? Did we have a date and I forgot about it?" She brushed the part of her arm that wasn't covered with her wet rubber glove across her forehead. Her long hair hung down her back in a ponytail, and she had on an apron. He hadn't seen a woman wear one of those since his grandmother.

"Can I come in?"

"Oh, yeah, sure. If ya don't mind the mess. I'm scrubbing my windowsills and walls, and I have everything all over the place."

"Maybe I should come back later. I didn't mean to interrupt anything."

"Don't be silly." She stepped back and motioned for him inside. "I'll just put ya to work."

"You think so, huh?"

"You come in, you clean. Make up your mind. And hurry so I can shut the door. You're letting the cold air out and the heat in. July is a miserable month for heat."

Before either one of them could react, Louey darted out the front door and tore down the street after a tabby cat.

"Louey! Come!" Audra took off down the street after the dog.

Louey ran in circles chasing the cat.

He was heading right into Barrett's path when a fast moving car rounded the corner.

"Louey! Heel!" Audra yelled.

The dog stopped, and Barrett snatched him up.

Tires squealed on the pavement.

Barrett's heart slammed against his ribs as the car came to a stop only within inches of hitting him in the knees.

~♥*~*

"Carson Jones." Audra slammed her hands on her hips while her heart thumped like a jackrabbit's foot. "How many times do I have to tell you to slow down on this street? There are children who live around here. And animals. You're gonna hit somebody someday if you don't stop driving like you're on a racetrack."

Carson leaned his head out his car window. "I'm sorry, Miss Audra."

"You should be. Ya almost hit Louey. If Mr. Camden hadn't scooped him up you would have. Then how would you feel?"

Carson's eyes lowered. "Pretty bad."

"Exactly. What are we gonna do with you? We've had this conversation at least thirty times already this summer."

Barrett stepped up alongside her.

Audra took Louey from him. "You naughty dog. Don't you ever do that again." She hugged her trembling dog and kissed the top of his head.

"So, you like to race huh?" Barrett stood back and crossed his arms over his broad chest as he scanned Carson's maroon '55 Chevy with the chrome blower on the hood. "454 with a dual four barrel Edelbrock carburetor, right?"

Audra couldn't believe her ears. What was Barrett doing? Carson had almost hit him and Louey, and he was talking about racing and the size of engine Carson had under his hood?

Audra stood there, tapping the toe of her red slip-on sneakers against the pavement.

Barrett looked over her and winked.

She hiked a palm upward and sent him a what-are-you-doing frustrated look. He just smiled and winked again before turning his attention back onto Carson.

Carson got out of his car, leaving the muscle car idling in the middle of the street, and popped the hood. The two of them leaned over the engine, talking about what all it had in it.

Audra stood there watching them and shaking her head in disbelief. Barrett didn't need to encourage the nineteen-year-old anymore than he already was. She opened her mouth to say so, but Barrett started talking.

"If I can arrange it, what do you say we take this thing to a race track and see what it'll do?"

"Are you kidding me?" Carson's sky blue eyes widened, and his blond eyebrows disappeared under his long bangs.

"No. I know someone who owns a track, and he just might let us use it to see what this thing can do."

"Wow, that's awesome, dude."

"We need to get your parents' permission first."

"Dude, I'm nineteen. I have my own place. And my parents don't even live around here. I'm from the west coast."

"Okay. Well, if I can work it out, we'll do it. But there's a stipulation that goes with you racing."

Carson's shoulders slumped. "What's that?" he asked, skepticism marched across his face.

"You have to stop flying down not only Audra's street but any other as well. And you have to listen to instructions and follow them. Do we have a deal?" Barrett held out his hand.

"Can I race it there more than once?"

Barrett hiked a brow at Carson and sent him a serious are-you-kidding-me look.

Carson lowered his head and scuffed the asphalt. "Okay. I promise." The two of them shook hands. "When can I race?"

"Give me a second." Barrett pulled out his phone and walked several yards away from them.

"Can you believe it, Miss Audra?" He gave her a double-thumbs up.

"No. No, I really can't," she groaned.

Barrett strode up to them. "Okay, it's all set. Are you free now?"

"Yeah. I don't have to be to work until five."

Barrett turned to Audra. "How fast can you change? Not that there's anything wrong with your attire or anything," he rushed on to say with mirth dancing across his eyes and his lips twitching.

Carson shot him a look as if to say *Are you serious, Dude*? before looking back at her, and scanning her from head to toe.

She knew she looked a mess. What did they expect? She'd been cleaning house all morning. "Give me ten minutes, and I'll be ready."

"See you in twenty." Barrett smirked.

"Wager you a shoe shopping trip."

"I'd rather be tossed into a snake pit filled with poisonous snakes."

Carson rocked his gaze between her and Barrett, no doubt wondering what was going on.

"Chicken."

"Yes, Ma'am, and I have no problem admitting it either when it comes to shoe shopping."

"Dude, I don't blame you. I wouldn't take that wager either." The teen shuddered, and his face scrunched with repulsion.

Audra couldn't help but laugh. "I'll hurry as fast as I can." With those words, she sprinted to her house, Louey running and hopping at her side. Twenty minutes later, dressed in a pair of blue slim fit jeans, a pastel green cotton blouse, and pastel green slip on tennis shoes, out the door she flew.

On the way to her driveway, she overheard Carson say to Barrett, "Dude, you were right. It took way more than ten minutes."

Barrett smiled at Carson and strode over to her. "Ten minutes, huh?" He tapped his watch.

"Get over it." She winked. "You know I'm always late."

"That I do." With those words, Barrett told Carson to hop in his '55 Chevy and follow him.

She and Barrett hopped in his roadster and headed to Cole Speedway.

When they pulled into Cole Speedway, Erik and Olivia were waiting for them at the drag strip section of the speedway.

Carson rapped up his engine before shutting it off. He strode over to them with his hands buried in the front pockets of his baggy jeans.

"So, you want to race?" Erik asked Carson.

"Yes, sir, I do." Carson held out his hand. "Name's Carson. Carson Jones."

Erik shook Carson's hand. "Erik Cole. Nice to meet you, Carson." He shifted sideways and motioned to Olivia. "This is my wife Olivia."

Olivia stepped forward and shook the boy's hand.

Carson slipped his hands back into his pockets.

While Barrett and Erik prepped the boy on the rules, Olivia and Audra headed to the stands to watch. On the way there, Olivia asked, "So, how'd your evening go last night?"

"Great. We had a really nice time at dinner. We were gonna go see the lake at his house, but it was getting late, and I asked if he minded if I saw it another day. He said that was fine. We talked a little about my family, but when I asked him about his, he said he didn't have any."

"Oh, he's an orphan, like me."

Audra tipped her head. "Never thought about it that way, Liv. I just figured it was his way of saying he didn't want to talk about them."

The sound of revving engines drew their attention toward the strip. "Barrett's running his roadster up against Carson?"

Olivia shrugged. "Sure looks that way."

Seeing him sitting in his roadster all smoking hot, with his arm resting on the window ledge, sent goose bumps rising all over her arms and down her spine. Audra sat on the edge of her seat. She had no idea when Barrett said race at the speedway that he meant he would be the one doing the racing.

"Okay, what gives?" Olivia pointed to the sweat beads on Audra's nose. "What are you so nervous about?"

She wiped the sweat from off the top of her nose. "He's racing Carson."

"So?"

"Carson's never raced before, and he's only nineteen."

"Erik and Barrett know what they're doing."

Those words were meant to calm her down, but they didn't. What if something happened to Barrett? That thought dropped dread into her heart.

Carson and Barrett lined up side-by-side.

Audra watched as the light switched from red to yellow to green. Her heartbeat increased with each switch of the light until she was certain that it would burst out of her chest.

Both cars took off, but not as fast as Audra thought they would. In fact, if she had to guess, she'd say they were barely going twenty or thirty miles per hour.

She looked over at Olivia relieved, yet confused.

"They're just letting him get used to feel of the track and having someone beside him."

"Oh." That made sense, she relaxed a little.

After they did that several more times, increasing the speed each time, Audra felt more comfortable about the situation. From what she could tell, Carson controlled his car a lot better than she thought he would for someone so young.

They took off again. Only this time they flew down the strip. Carson hit the finish line before Barrett.

Audra and Olivia rushed to the strip, waiting until they pulled their cars in front of them and shut them off.

Carson jumped out of his car and trotted over to Barrett's. "Wow, what a rush, dude. That thing of yours sure is fast."

"Thanks." Barrett clasped him on the shoulder. "You did a great job of handling that car and listening to instructions. Good job."

Carson pressed his shoulders back, beaming under Barrett's praise.

Audra stepped up alongside Barrett. She looked at Carson. "You did great, Carson."

His face glowed even more.

"And you're gonna keep your promise to Barrett now that you've gotten to race where racing belongs, right?"

"I sure am, Miss Audra. Besides, I'll be doing more racing here, thanks to Barrett and Mr. Cole." Carson looked at each one, his admiration for them was evident.

Audra looked up at Barrett, questioning him with her look.

"Barrett talked me into hiring Carson," Erik jumped into the conversation.

"That way Carson can race whenever he wants as long as Erik is around the track and approves it."

Audra smiled at Barrett. He'd taken a potentially hazardous situation and turned it around to where it benefitted everyone. Her appreciation and admiration for him went up a notch. Two actually, because she knew without a doubt that Barrett had let Carson win the race. Barrett really was a nice guy. So why did she still have the uneasy feeling that taking a chance on him might turn out to be a huge mistake?

"Well, I'd better get. We have a lot to do to get ready for the races tonight," Erik said.

"Anything I can do to help?" Barrett offered.

"No, but thanks for offering. We pretty much have it all lined out who's going to do what."

"I'd offer to help, but I have to work this evening." Carson looked genuinely disappointed.

"You sure you want to give up your job, Carson?" Erik eyed the boy.

"To work here? Are you kidding me, Mr. Cole?" His eyes brightened.

"You can call me Erik."

"Cool." Carson nodded his head like a bobbing chicken. "This is so awesome. I've been praying for God to give me a different job. Something I would enjoy. I love racing and cars. Thanks for hiring me, dude. Er, um, I mean, Mr. Cole."

"You're welcome." Erik didn't say anything about Carson's slip up in calling him dude or 'Mr. Cole'.

Carson said his goodbyes, shook hands with the men and headed out of the speedway without spinning his tires or burning rubber or speeding.

"That's the first time I've seen him drive slow." Audra watched until Carson drove out of sight.

"It worked then."

Audra gazed up at Barrett. "We'll see. Time will tell."

"He'll be just fine, Audra." Barrett sounded so confident she believed him.

"Great idea you had there, Barrett." Erik grasped his shoulder before releasing it. "Better to have the kid drag racing out here than on the streets and getting in a wreck and hurting himself or someone else."

"True," Audra admitted, realizing just how important Barrett's quick thinking had been. She would never have thought of it even though she had the same connections with the track that he did.

"So, are y'all coming to the races tonight?" Erik asked.

Audra glanced over at Erik, then up at Barrett.

Barrett turned to Audra, his gaze hopeful. "What do you say?"

She hiked a shoulder. "Sure why not."

"I have a better idea," Olivia spoke up.

"What's that?" Erik asked.

"How about you let Barrett use one of your derby cars and compete in the men's demolition derby tonight?"

"Great idea, Sweetheart." Erik put his arm around Olivia and drew her close to his side. "How about it, Barrett?"

Barrett looked at Audra, this time with more skepticism and possibly hope she might talk him out of it.

"I'm competing in the powder puff tonight. So, why don't ya join us?" Audra sent him what she hoped was a please say yes look.

"Okay, then. Sounds like fun."

"Great." Audra could hardly wait.

"Sure you don't mind me using one of your cars?"

"Are you kidding? He loves taking old junkyard cars and making them into derby cars." Olivia winked up at Erik, and Erik smiled down at her.

"Anything I can do to help get them ready?"

"Nope." Erik gave Barrett a quick shake of his head. "They're already ready and rearing to go. Just show up around five."

"Yay, this is going to be so much fun. Thanks, Erik." Audra gave him a hug.

"Hey, what about me? It was my idea."

Audra playfully rolled her eyes at Olivia before pulling her into a hug.

"It's all settled then. We'll see y'all here around five." They turned to leave but Erik stopped and turned around. "Hey, Barrett, since this is your first time competing here, we require all racers to wear gloves, a mouth guard, a safety helmet and eye protection gear. If you don't have any of those, we could probably scrounge some up around here somewhere."

"I have all of that. I'll bring them with me. Thanks again."

Erik nodded before he and Olivia left.

The evening couldn't come fast enough for Audra. Thoughts of competing again sent bubbles of joy floating through her stomach. Thoughts of Barrett competing, that sent an explosion of bubbles erupting inside her.

Chapter Ten

"Is this your first demolition derby?"

Barrett looked over at Audra. "Yes." He didn't think he'd be this excited about competing in a demolition derby as they'd never seemed all that thrilling to him before. But after watching Audra race, he was.

"You'd better hurry, they're lining up in the arena."

"How about a kiss for good luck?"

Audra cocked an eyebrow. "How about not. Just go."

He crossed his arms over his chest. "Not until you give me a kiss."

"Well, then you're just gonna have to plan on missing the derby, because ya aren't getting one."

Stubborn woman. He yanked her to him, kissed her, and set her away from him.

She smacked him on the arm, but before she had a chance to say anything more, he kissed her again and hurried to the '71 Dodge Dart Erik had ready for him.

He hauled himself through the window and slid behind the wheel. As he fired up the car, he glanced over at Audra, who was standing in the same place he'd left her, staring at him. He gave a quick wave. She shook her head and waved.

As instructed, he drove into the arena, backed his car along the fenced-in arena wall, and jogged to the other side of the track. He scanned the crowd for Audra and found her standing near the gate.

The announcer's voice over the loud speaker said it was time. Barrett listened for the count of three. As soon as he said it, Barrett ran to his car, slid inside and put all his protective gear on, harnessed himself in, then lowered his flag.

Drumming his fingers on the steering wheel, he watched the flagger. As soon as the flagman waved the green flag, Barrett fired up the car. Adrenaline rushed through his veins as his competitive side took over.

It was game on.

He quickly found his first victim and rammed his right front bumper on the front end of other man's Impala, spinning the guy around. Another car came and hit the Impala from another direction, head on. Metal crunched against metal. Steam rolled from both of the competitors engines. Their flags went up.

A quick look and he saw Audra on the sidelines, hollering and cheering him on.

The competition continued, Barrett dodged many direct hits, and rammed several more competitors until there was only him and another guy left. They played chicken back and forth a few times, finally Barrett decided to end this thing. Whether he won or lost, this time he wasn't chickening out. He spun a cookie, leaving a trail of dust and dirt and headed straight for the front end of the red station wagon with the big number one on the doors.

"Well, let's just see if you really are number one, buddy," Barrett said even though he knew the guy couldn't hear him.

He gunned the car, racing directly toward the other man.

This time neither one of them swerved.

Crash.

Crunch.

Even though Barrett's body barely moved, he felt the impact nonetheless. His car died. He tried to restart it, keeping his eye on the other guy to see if he moved. Though steam rolled out of the engine, the '71 came to life. Barrett quickly backed up, ready to bash the guy again. His derby wobbled, spit and sputtered yet Barrett was able to gain some speed as he headed straight for the guy again.

Only yards away now, right before he was about to hit the station wagon, the man reached outside and raised his flag.

Barrett yanked the wheel hard to the right to avoid hitting him, barreling through the dust that encompassed the world around the stalled cars.

Just as he cleared the chaos behind him, much to his horror, only three feet ahead of him appeared Audra running after a small child.

Barrett's heart gave a lurch.

He slammed on the brakes.

The car died.

Audra fell to the ground.

"Audra!" he screamed. "God no! Please!"

People started running out into the arena.

Barrett quickly undid his harness, tossed his helmet off, slung the mouth guard away from him, and yanked his body out of the car and was at the front of his car within seconds.

Audra was lying on the ground almost in a fetal position, cradling a small girl in her arms.

A redheaded woman came running from the gate and dropped to her knees in front of Audra. "Penny, are you okay, baby? Are you okay, ma'am?" Panic filled the woman's voice.

"Don't worry about me."

Relief poured through Barrett the second he heard Audra's voice.

The little red haired girl wiggled out of Audra's arms.

Her mother plucked her up and coddled her to her. "Thank you for saving my baby. If you hadn't been there..." The woman closed her eyes as tears streamed down her face.

Barrett dropped to his knees beside Audra. "You sure you're okay?"

"I think so." She started to move, but Barrett gently pressed her shoulder down, holding her in place.

"Don't move," Barrett ordered. "Stay there until the paramedics check you out."

"I'm fine." She gazed up at him. "You can let me go now."

"Maybe, but for me, stay still, okay?"

Audra huffed out a breath and stayed put much to Barrett's relief. "I don't know how you do it," she mumbled.

"Do what?"

"Talk me into doing things I don't wanna do."

Did he? Was that a good thing?

Erik and Olivia pushed their way through the crowd. "Please move back, everyone. Give us some room." Erik motioned to one of his workers wearing a fluorescent orange vest. "Get them out of here so the ambulance can come in."

"You okay, Audie?" Olivia's voice trembled as she dropped to her knees on the opposite side of Barrett.

"I'm fine."

Erik turned to the woman whose daughter Audra had saved. "Is your daughter okay, ma'am?"

"She's shaken up, but she seems fine. I'm so sorry." Her gaze was on Erik, then it turned to Barrett. "I only looked away for a second. When I saw her, she had just squeezed through that small gap between the fence and gate. If this woman," the mother's gaze dropped to Audra, "hadn't ran after her and put herself between my baby and your car..." The woman's voice broke into sobs.

A commotion yanked Barrett's attention away from the woman and Audra.

"Let me by. That's my wife and daughter." A man tried forcing his way through the barricade of people. The people cleared a path like the parting of the Red Sea scene in the movie *The Ten Commandments*.

Barrett could understand why when he saw a tall man with a build like a Mr. Universe body builder rushing toward the woman and child.

Barrett tuned them out and put all of his focus on Audra. His eyes raked over her body, stopping midway between her thigh and knee.

Blood.

Any time he saw blood, images of his wife and his parents' bodies invaded his mind. This time was no exception.

He immediately masked his emotions, something he'd learned to do for survival, and concentrated on forcing the bloody images of his loved ones from his mind. He swallowed hard to keep his stomach from lurching.

When he finally regained control, his attention shifted to the front of his car, what was left of it anyway, and there he saw a piece of metal protruding out with blood on it. He yanked his attention away so the images of his family wouldn't invade his mind again. He had to concentrate on the here and now. Audra needed him. "Where are those paramedics?" Barrett yelled.

"Here."

Barrett hadn't even heard them drive up.

One of the two men and one of the two women medics carrying medical supplies rushed up to them, the other two concentrated on the woman and her daughter.

Erik helped Olivia to her feet and back away from them.

Making sure Audra couldn't hear him, Barrett made Audra's injury known to the one of the paramedics.

"We'll take care of her. Your wife is in good hands."

Wife? "She's not my..."

"Please, sir, you need to move."

Erik laid a hand on Barrett's shoulder. "They'll take care of her, Barrett. Let them do their job."

Not feeling any part of him, Barrett stood. He, Olivia and Erik watched from just a few feet away, waiting while the paramedics worked on her. When they cut the pant leg of her jeans, Barrett got a glimpse of the jagged wound. He quickly forced his attention away from it and set his mind to praying before the gruesome images of his loved ones bodies dared to invade his mind again.

Several agonizing minutes later, they finally had Audra loaded on the gurney.

Right before they put her into the ambulance, Audra held up her hand. "Wait." She raised her head, and her eyes came to Barrett's. "You're coming to the hospital, right?" He'd never seen her look so vulnerable.

Barrett wanted to reach out to her, to touch her, to comfort her. He might not be able to physically, but his eyes held her just the same. "Nothing could keep me away."

"You're coming too, Liv and Erik, aren't you?" As she asked, she winced.

"I'm coming." Olivia patted Audra's foot under the white sheet. "Erik has to take care of things around here."

Audra nodded and lowered her head, looking rather groggy. A second later, she jerked it up again. "The little girl is okay, right?"

"Thanks to you she is." Barrett sent her a look to let her know how proud of her he was.

"Good." She winced again, and that set his heart hammering.

"We have to go now, ma'am," the female EMT said to Audra.

Audra nodded and settled her head back down onto the white sheeted pillow.

"Can Olivia ride with you?" Erik asked from beside Barrett.

"Of course."

Erik peered down at Olivia. "She'll be fine, Sweetheart."

"I know she will be. It's just so hard seeing her being wheeled off in an ambulance." Olivia snuggled into him as Erik wiped the tears off of her cheeks. "I know. I just hope her leg's okay and that they give her a tetanus shot."

"What do you mean?" Erik asked.

"She had blood on her leg," Barrett supplied the information so Olivia wouldn't have to. She was already upset enough as it was. "There was a piece of metal sticking out on the car."

The ambulance started to pull away. "Let's go, Olivia." Barrett rushed out the words.

After Erik kissed his wife, Barrett and Olivia ran to his car.

Emotions swamped emotions making Barrett's hands shake as Olivia gave him directions to the hospital. Why couldn't he outrun those images of the past now mixed and mingling with Audra lying there bleeding?

When they pulled into a nearby emergency room parking spot, the paramedics were just wheeling Audra inside.

Together, Barrett and Olivia hurried into the hospital. When he stepped through the doors, the instant the antiseptic and cleanser odors reached his nostrils, memories of spending months in a hospital, going through one excruciating surgery after another, rushed through his mind. It took every ounce of willpower he possessed to dash the painful memories of the past from his mind and to concentrate on Audra.

By the time they stitched Audra's leg up and she filled out all the necessary paperwork at the hospital, three and half hours later, she and Barrett pulled into her driveway. Feeling a bit woozy from the shot of pain medication the ER nurse had given her before stitching up her leg, Audra clung to Barrett's arm for support as she slowly made her way in the dark to her front door.

As soon as they stepped inside her home, Barrett flipped the light switch on for her.

Louey pranced and hopped around Audra's feet, whining and wanting her to pet him. "Can't hold you right now, Louey."

Barrett reached down and picked up Audra's Chihuahua.

"Wow, that's a shocker. He doesn't let just anyone hold him." She gave her dog a quick rub behind the ears and a kiss on top of his head before Barrett set him down.

Louey darted to the window and peered out into the darkness, glancing back at her and then back at the window, tail wagging.

Audra looked up at Barrett. "Thank you for helping me home. There's no way I could have driven myself here."

"You're right, especially since your car's already here." His eyes twinkled and his lips twitched.

Even tired, she could get annoyed with him. "Smart aleck."

"Seriously, how you feeling?" Barrett asked as he slipped his arm around her and escorted her to the sofa.

"Other than feeling a bit woozy from the pain meds, I feel fine."

Keeping a hold of her, he helped balance her as she settled her right thigh against the back of the sofa, leaving her wounded side out and free from anything touching it. Even with the pain medication, every so often a stinging, sharp pain thrust through her leg, and she fought not to wince.

Barrett placed a few throw pillows under her back and neck. "I'm going to grab you a glass of water. As soon as you start to feel anything, take two of these." He set her prescription on the coffee table and turned to leave.

"Ya don't have to wait on me, you know."

"I know. I want to."

"I'm sure glad that little girl didn't get hurt," Audra said to his retreating back.

Barrett stopped and turned around. "I am too." He rubbed the back of his head as pain swiped across his face.

"Barrett, none of this is your fault. There's no way you would have known that a child would run into that arena. I'm still surprised she could even squeeze through that small slat between the gate and the fence post. Erik worked hard to make sure everyone would be safe at his track. But things can and do happen no matter how careful you are. So, stop blaming yourself, okay?"

He stood there, staring at her, saying nothing. Finally, he gave a nod, a very unconvincing one at that, then turned back around and strode into the kitchen.

Lord, help Barrett to see that none of this is his fault.

A minute later, he returned with a glass of water, set it on the end table next to her prescription bottle, and sat down on the coffee table, facing her. His gaze went to the site where her bandage was. "They gave you a tetanus shot, right?"

"Yup."

"How many stitches?"

"Ten."

"Sorry I wasn't in the room with you."

Audra put her hand on his knee. "Barrett, what happened back there?"

"What do you mean? Don't you remember? Did you hit your head when you fell?" He reached his hand toward her head.

Audra caught his hand and lowered it, resting both of their hands on his knee. "No. I didn't hit my head. I remember exactly what happened to me. What I wanna know is, what happened to you back there?"

His brows furrowed. "I'm not following you. You mean how did my derby hit you?"

Audra shook her head. "No, not that." She rubbed her thumb across the back of his hand. "Your face got real blotchy, and you looked like you were gonna throw up. What happened? And don't say it had anything to do with me because I'm not buying it."

Barrett turned his face away from her. Seconds later, when he looked back at her, pain etched his face. "Audra, there are just some things too painful to talk about. What happened back there is one of them."

"Something from your past?" she asked softly, treading gently.

He closed his eyes and nodded.

Audra squeezed his hand and let it go. Whatever had hurt him so badly caused her heart to go out to him, but at the same time, it also scared her. She detested secrets. Secrets hurt people. As she knew only too well. Question now was, what to do about Barrett and his secrets.

Should she trust that whatever secrets he harbored weren't anything like Neil's?

Or should she end whatever was happening between her and Barrett now?

God, show me what to do. And make it clear. Please?

Chapter Eleven

B arrett hated leaving Audra alone. He'd stayed until way after midnight when she'd finally fallen asleep on the couch. He'd covered her with a blanket and locked the door behind him on his way out.

On the drive to his place, he thought about Audra and the none-too-pleased look on her face when he'd basically told her he didn't want to talk about his past. He just hoped that wouldn't be the end of their relationship. If the look on her face was any indication, it just might be. Oh sure, she was cordial to him the rest of the time he was there, but there was a distance he couldn't deny that wasn't there earlier.

Barrett pulled into his drive around 1:00 AM.

He was too wound up to go inside and go to sleep, so he headed to his butterfly garden. Floral and earth scents mingled in the air. He sat on a bench near the waterfall.

Resting his arms on his legs, he clasped his hands together and lowered his head. "Father, I really like Audra. In fact, I think I might even be in love with her. Show me what to do. You know why I can't reveal my past to her or to anyone else. But I'm afraid if I don't, and she finds out who I really am, that she'll walk out of my life completely.

"I hate that my life has become such a farce. Nothing more than a masquerade." He sighed. "But what other choice did I have? They wouldn't leave me alone, wouldn't let me forget that someone murdered my wife and my parents." Anger bolted through him.

Anger over the merciless killing of his family, and that he wasn't there to save them.

Anger that he had to live in constant fear of being found out, and that people didn't mind their own business and just leave him alone.

Anger that he might lose Audra because of all those things.

He pushed himself off the bench and paced through the butterfly garden that normally brought him the tranquility he so desperately needed. Even the sound of the running water over the rocks didn't have its usual peaceful and calming effect on him. Nothing seemed to soothe the restless unease boiling inside him. All because he'd seen it in Audra's eyes and in her actions that she wasn't sure she wanted to pursue a relationship with him.

"Lord, how do I make this right?"

"Honey, where are you?"

"Felicia, is that you, my darling?"

"Of course it's me, who else did you think it was?" His wife cupped his face and kissed him before she went limp in his arms and slid to the floor.

"Felicia, what's wrong?"

Blood pooled around her. Barrett dropped to his knees, blood soaked through his jeans.

"You're next."

Barrett squinted. The fog was so thick he couldn't see a thing, couldn't find the source of the chill-binding, hair-raising voice.

Through the haze, he spotted movement. He struggled to make out what it was.

A form?

A figure?

Or what?

The image slowly came toward him, forming a shadow of man, holding two machetes.

Before Barrett could react, the man ran toward him like a banshee, screaming wildly, waving and crossing the machetes like some crazed lunatic.

Suddenly, from out of the darkness, his parents stepped directly in between Barrett and the madman.

"No! Get out of the way! Run!" Barrett screamed, squirming to reach them, but his feet wouldn't move. They were firmly cemented in a block of concrete.

Crack!

Boom!

Barrett bolted upright, panting like an overheated dog.

His gaze flew about the dark room, lit up only by the lightning flashing through the sky like a jagged scar.

Hail pelted his windows.

When he realized he was alone, that it was the same nightmare that had plagued him off and on for seven years, he fell back against the pillow on his bed, and glanced over at the clock. 4:17. He groaned. He'd only been asleep a little over an hour.

His bedroom lit up again as another flash of lightning pierced the sky. Thunder followed within a second, indicating it was close.

Crossing his arms behind his head, he stared up at the ceiling. It had been a while since he'd had that dream, and he knew exactly what had brought it on - seeing Audra's blood-soaked pant leg the day before.

Would there ever be a time when he saw blood that it wouldn't cause the nightmare to come or that he wouldn't see the images of his families' bodies?

The back of his eyes stung. Tears slipped over his bottom eyelids and trailed down his cheeks as the pain of loss buried him in a cocoon of agony. It had been years since he'd cried actual tears and mourned the loss of his loved ones. He usually masked his grief like he had so many of his emotions and actions. Right now, however, there was no masking his grief.

No burying his pain.

He felt free to let it out because there was no one here to witness it. He was alone. Something he was tired of being, especially since meeting Audra. She'd breathed life into him again.

He couldn't lose her. He just couldn't. The pain would be more than he could bear.

Audra woke up with a start and a sudden urge to pray for Barrett. She glanced at the clock on her nightstand. 4:15.

Earlier, when sharp, stinging pain had awakened her around one AM, before she took another pain pill, she made her way up the stairs to her bedroom, thanking the Lord each step she'd taken that she had been able to climb the steps on her own. If the laceration had been on her ankle or her knee, she wouldn't have been able to do that. For some reason, even as she'd climbed, the doctor's words about that had given her comfort even when the pain had tried to tell her it was impossible.

Lightning lit up the sky, and thunder loud and fast boomed outside, giving her the willies.

Louey burrowed himself under her cover, whining. She reached under the blanket and rubbed his ears, something she knew soothed him, and she began to pray.

"Father, I don't know why You're having me pray for Barrett, but whatever it is, I ask for You to cover him with Your mercy and Your grace. Wrap him in Your loving arms and comfort him. Give him the strength to overcome whatever it is he's going through. Shield his mind, his spirit, his body, and his emotions from the onslaught of the enemy. Surround him with Your peace. Touch him everywhere he hurts, Lord." She continued to pray for him until she felt a release in her spirit.

Another glance at the clock revealed it was 5:02. Audra closed her eyes. She couldn't wait to talk to Barrett, to find out what had happened to him.

Unable to sleep, worrying about him, she lay there awake, staring at the ceiling and talking even more to God about Barrett. Thirty minutes later, her leg started to throb, so she downed another pain pill. Shortly afterward, she found herself finally drifting off to sleep.

Sunlight filtered through the curtain sheers covering Audra's window, shining directly onto her face. Audra squinted against its brightness.

Louey lay curled up on her other pillow. Her dog raised his head and yawned before he settled his head on his front paws again.

Audra looked at the clock on her nightstand. 8:35. Her first thought was to call Barrett until she remembered that she didn't have his phone number.

Tossing the covers aside, she swung her legs onto the floor. Immediately the pain in her thigh reminded her that she'd been hurt, something she'd managed to forget all about as her mind had been on Barrett and what could possibly have happened this morning that God had woken her up to pray for him.

Audra grabbed the prescription canister and the bottled water from off her nightstand. With her leg throbbing, she unscrewed the water bottle lid and quickly downed the pill.

She shuffled her way to the bathroom and looked in the mirror. Her hair was a mess and her makeup was half gone. Using a washcloth, she gave herself a sponge bath, washed her face in the bathroom sink, and pulled her hair back into a ponytail.

Since she was still wearing the same shorts that Olivia had gotten for her the day before after they had finished stitching her up at the hospital, Audra gently removed her clothes and put on her light teal, loose fitting, summer dress.

Holding onto the handrail with one hand, her other clutching her cellphone, Audra made her way down the stairs, and headed into the kitchen.

Louey followed her, his toenails tapping against the floor as he did. He stood on his hind legs and did his little mariachi dance thing he did every morning when he wanted to be fed. Only thing missing from his dance was a sombrero.

She no sooner fed and put fresh water in his bowl when her phone rang. "Morning, Liv."

"Hey, I just called to see how you're doing and to see if you need anything? How's the leg feeling? Are you in a lot of pain? How late did Barrett stay?"

Audra grinned at the onslaught of questions Olivia tossed out at her. Her friend tended to do that when she was excited, nervous, or scared. "Uh, hello. Questions overload, girl."

"Get over it, Aud, and just answer them."

"Pushy." Audra leaned her good hip against the counter and crossed one foot over the other.

"Quit wrinkling your nose and rolling your eyes and answer them already."

Olivia knew her only too well. Those two things were exactly what she'd done.

"One: I'm doing pretty good, considering. Two: No, I don't need anything." She mentally ticked through Olivia's questions and marked them off as she answered them. "Three and four. My leg is stiff and sore this morning. And five, I fell asleep on the couch and woke up early this morning and he was gone. There. I think I answered all your questions."

"You did. I'm so glad Barrett was with you. I wanted to be there, but Barrett was right. He thought I needed to go be with Erik because he knew Erik was upset over the whole thing. He sure was. This morning he's got a crew out there checking over the whole place and taking care of any holes or any places that a child or anyone else could get through."

"Poor guy. He tried so hard to make sure it was safe."

"And it is. This was just a fluke. I still can't figure out how that girl squeezed herself through that small slot."

"Me neither. How's she doing? Have you heard?"

"Erik called them this morning. She's fine. I'm not so sure she would be if you hadn't run in after her. You're a real heroine, Audra."

"C'mon now, I'm no heroine. I did what anyone else would've done. I just happened to be standing there is all. I'm surprised I didn't see her before she made it through that crack. But then again, I was watching and rooting Barrett on. Speaking of Barrett, the strangest thing happened this morning." Audra told Olivia about being woken up and about praying for him.

"Wonder what that was all about."

"I don't know. I wish I could call him, but I don't have his number."

"You don't?" Olivia asked as if that was highly strange, which Audra was trying not to admit to herself.

"No, I just never thought to ask for it because I didn't really want it until I knew more where this thing between him and I were heading. I wish I had it now though."

"I can get it for you."

"You can?" Audra pushed herself off the counter and instantly regretted the sudden move as pain shot through her leg. She stifled the ow because that would only cause Olivia to worry.

"Yeah. Just a second and I'll get it from Erik. Honey, could you give me Barrett's phone number so I can give it to Audra?" Audra heard everything even though Olivia's voice sounded muffled as if she had covered the speaker on her phone. "He's getting it for me. He's such a sweetheart."

"You are a blessed woman, Liv. But then again, he's blessed to have you."

"You ready?"

"Just a sec." Audra opened the Contacts on her phone and typed in Barrett's name. "Ready."

Olivia ticked the numbers off slowly and clearly as Audra put them into her cell.

"Thanks, Liv. If you don't mind, I'm gonna let ya go and give him a call."

"No, I don't mind at all. But before we hang up, I want you to know that I'll be bringing lunch and dinner over for you so you don't have to cook today."

"You don't have to do that. I'm fine, really."

"Lands O' Goshen, girl. I know I don't have to, I want to. No arguing with me. See you around eleven." With those words, she hung up.

Audra stared at her phone and shook her head. How blessed she was to have such a special friend as Livvy.

Anxious to find out what was going on with Barrett this morning, Audra called him. She leaned her good leg against the counter again and waited while it rang once. Twice. Three times. After the fourth ring, it went to his voicemail. "This is Barrett Camden. Leave a message, and I'll get back to you."

Audra debated whether or not to wait for the beep and leave a message. Finally, she decided to just hang up, hoping he would call her back soon, and praying with all her heart that he was all right.

Barrett left the bakery and drove over to Audra's house. He knew he should call first, but he didn't want to give her a chance to tell him not to come.

He turned his Mercedes into her driveway and shut it off, yawning for the twentieth time since leaving home. He purposely brought his Mercedes because it was quiet. Something his roadster wasn't.

Again, he yawned. He needed sleep, but it would have to wait. Right now, he wanted to make sure Audra was well taken care of.

Gathering everything he'd brought with him, he strode to Audra's door and rang the doorbell with his elbow.

As usual, Louey was in the window with his paws on the window ledge, his nose pressed against the glass, barking, growling and wagging his tail.

The front door opened, then the screen door. "Barrett, am I ever glad to see you. Come on in." She held the doors open for him as he stepped inside. "Here, let me help ya with that."

"I've got it." He turned the sacks away from her, walked into the kitchen, and set the bags on the counter. When he turned, she was right there, and a sight for sore eyes.

The urge to pull her into his arms and hold her, drove through him, but knowing her leg was injured, he didn't want to risk hurting it or causing her pain. Instead, he drank her in and held her with his eyes.

"Are you okay?" she asked, and concern dashed through her eyes.

He forced himself to stop his virtual embrace. "Why do you ask? It's me who should be asking you how you are."

"I'm fine. But I wanna know how you are." Worry creased her brows even further. "This might sound strange, but God woke me up this morning and had me pray for you."

Shock rippled through him, shaking him like a massive California earthquake. He'd never heard someone say that God had awakened them to pray for him before. He had to admit, it blessed his socks off and comforted his distressed soul. "What time was that?"

"4:15. Why? What was going on then?"

Barrett braced his hip against the counter, his knees suddenly felt weak, and he feared they wouldn't hold him up.

"You better sit down. You don't look very good." Audra tugged on his arm, but he pulled away from her grasp.

"I'll be fine, just give me a minute. It's the shock of hearing it, is all."

"What? The shock that God woke me up to pray for you?"

"That and the time. I—I—" He rubbed the back of his neck trying to figure out how to answer her question. If he told her what had happened to him at that time, then she'd bombard him with questions. Questions he couldn't answer.

God, show me what to say here and how to handle this. And thank You for laying me on Audra's heart. You know how desperately I needed Your help then.

Louey put his paws on Barrett's pant leg. Grateful for the momentary distraction, he picked Louey up, reached inside his pocket and handed him a dog treat. Louey gently took it, then squirmed, wanting to get down. Barrett put him down, and when he looked up, he found Audra watching him, her arms over her chest, her lips pressed together, and her brows puckered.

"You're not getting out of it that easy. Now spill, mister. What was going on this morning? And don't even think about not telling me."

His chest heaved with a sigh. "I'll tell you what I can, but not until after I've had my coffee." He pulled one cup out of the cardboard holder and handed it to her, then grabbed one for himself. "Where's your plates?"

"What for?"

"I brought breakfast. You haven't eaten yet, have you? And shouldn't you be sitting down?"

"I have a cut, I'm not crippled. And no, I haven't eaten yet."

"Good. You may not be crippled, but you need to take care of that cut so it doesn't split open. Too much stress on it will do that."

"Okay, fine, whatever. You win. But don't think because I'm gonna go sit down now that you don't have to tell me what went on this morning. It only means I'm hungry and I, too, am ready for coffee." She grabbed two plates out of the cupboard, some silverware out of the drawer, then turned and headed in the opposite direction of the living room, limping as she went.

Barrett followed her, carrying the bakery bag and diner sack, and wondering where she was going.

Off to the left of the front door, they stepped into a parlor that was something straight out of a Jane Austen movie. The only reason he knew that was because his wife loved watching Pride and Prejudice and all those other sappy chick flicks of Miss Austen's. He himself preferred to watch fast action or racecar movies.

Audra walked over to a tan fainting couch, set her coffee on a coaster on the end table, then after moving the brown and tan throw pillow out of the way, she slowly lowered herself making sure her good hip wasn't against the back of the couch.

Barrett pulled a chair up alongside her and sat down. "Why are we sitting in here? Wouldn't you be more comfortable sitting on the cushiony furniture in your living room?"

"Probably. But I just felt like sitting in here this morning. I call it my thinking room."

Uh oh. That didn't sound good. Usually when Audra got to thinking, it meant trouble. For him.

They sat in silence while they ate their biscuits and gravy and sugar-glazed croissant with thin almond slices on them.

When they finished, Audra wasted no time in asking him to tell her.

Barrett wiped his hands and mouth off and set the paper napkin he'd gotten from the diner on tcp of his plate. "First of all, let me say thank you for praying. I needed it."

She nodded.

"The truth is I had a nightmare. A reoccurring nightmare."

"About what?" she asked softly.

"It was about things that happened in my past, things…" He closed his eyes and fought to not let the memories overtake him again. "I know you want to know, but let's just say there are things I can't talk about because they hurt too much." That part was true. The other part was he just refused to say anything and risk being exposed.

She frowned, and he could see the wheels turning in her head, wanting to ask more questions. He just hoped she wouldn't.

"Does something trigger these nightmares?"

He gave a short nod. "Yes. Seeing the people I care about bleeding." That much he could tell her.

"Does this have anything to do with the seatbelt thing?"

"Seatbelt thing?"

"Yeah, you said something about buckling up was something you'd never joke about or something like that."

Oh that. "Partially. Truth is, anytime I see someone bleeding really bad, the nightmare comes."

"Who did you—"

"Audra, I don't mean to be rude, but please don't ask me any more questions. The past is the past and I am trying to forget it and move on. Please try to understand that."

"I do. But you have to understand where I'm coming from. I dated a man who did nothing but lie to me. He constantly avoided my questions and one day I found out why."

Did he dare ask her why? If he did, would she then expect him to answer her questions? Well, as bad as it sounded, she could expect all she wanted, it wouldn't change the fact that he couldn't tell her. If she knew his reasons why, she would understand. He could only hope so anyway.

Audra waited for Barrett to ask her why, when he didn't, she stood to her feet, picked up the dishes and headed to the kitchen. As much as she liked Barrett, the secrets of his past both bothered and scared her, so she had to end it.

Today.

Chapter Twelve

"Here let me carry those for you."

Audra turned them away from Barrett's grasp. As soon as she put the dishes in the sink, she turned around and found him watching her.

"Barrett, who are you? Where do you come from? And what are you running away from?"

He said nothing. Only stared down at her.

Just like Neil when she had confronted him. He said nothing to defend himself. How could he? Neil was a liar. The question was, was Barrett a liar too?

Audra understood about not wanting to talk about a past that was so painful, but at the same time she hated secrets. In order to be in a relationship, communication and honesty were key. Her parent's wonderful, loving marriage had taught her that.

She wanted a marriage like theirs. She wanted a man like her father. A man who was open with his feelings and didn't harbor secrets with the power to hurt others. And so, right there, she made up her mind. Pressing her back against the sink, she crossed her arms over her chest, and lowered her eyes as pain, far worse than the pain in her leg, sliced into her heart. "I can't do this."

"Do what?"

"This." She pointed to him, then back at herself. "Us."

Barrett was in front of her in seconds, cupping his large hands around her upper arms. "What do you mean? Talk to me, Audra."

She heard the concern in his voice, but she couldn't let it affect her, she had to be brave. "As much as I like you, Barrett, I can't see you anymore. I'd like you to go now, please."

Frustration and something close to anger bellowed into his eyes. "Whoa. What just happened? Is it because I won't tell you about my past?"

Not looking at him, she nodded. "Please go."

"Not until you talk to me."

Audra jerked his arms from off hers and shoved past him, banging her sore leg on one of the bottom cupboard handles as she did. Pain jolted through her leg, but she ignored it the same way she did the knife-gouging pain stabbing at her heart.

Once again, she'd fallen for a guy who had a secret past. She was sick of secrets. Careful to hide her limp from the pain slicing up her leg, she marched to the door, opened it, and with a hard wave of her hand, she motioned for him to leave.

Hurt flooded his eyes. Barrett stared at her for several moments before he stepped out her front door. With his hand on the screen door handle, he looked back at her. "I'm sorry I can't give you what you want. I love you, Audra." With those words, he walked to the driveway, got into his car, and drove out of sight.

Audra closed her door and slid to the floor.

He loved her.

And until that moment, she hadn't realized or admitted that she loved him too.

But nothing could ever come of it.

She placed her head in her hands and wept, soft tears filled with disappointment.

It felt like only minutes had elapsed, but Audra had no real way to gauge the time when the doorbell rang.

Afraid it was Barrett, she ignored it.

"Audra, I can hear you in there. Open up. It's me, Olivia."

With effort, Audra pushed herself to her feet and swung the door open. She threw her arms around Olivia and the casserole dish and sack she was holding.

"Aud? What's wrong? Is it your leg?"

As crazy as it sounded, Audra continued to hold onto her friend as her tears soaked through Olivia's blouse. "He's gone." She sobbed harder.

"Who's gone?"

"Barrett."

Olivia wiggled out of Audra's arms. She stepped back and looked at her. "What do you mean he's gone?"

"I sent him away, and he loves me."

"Lands O' Goshen, girl. You're not making any sense. Here, let me put these in the kitchen, then we can sit down and talk."

Audra numbly followed her friend to the kitchen, swiping and wiping at the tears she couldn't get to stop.

Olivia set the casserole dish and bag on the counter. She put her arm around Audra's shoulder, led her into the living room, and sat down on the sofa. "Now, start at the beginning and tell me what happened."

Audra relayed all that had happened since Barrett's arrival, including how secretive he was and the little odd things like not giving her his phone number right away and his insistence on not talking about the past.

While she waited and watched for her friend's reaction, Audra grabbed a tissue and wiped her eyes and nose, then tossed it in the trashcan beside the couch.

Olivia nodded and nipped at her lip. "I can understand why you're concerned. I wonder if Daniel can see if he can find out anything more about Barrett."

Audra shook her head. "No, Liv. Don't bother. Communication and honesty are important in a relationship, and Barrett's just not willing to give those things. I shouldn't have to file for a background check to get to know a guy, and I won't pursue someone who makes me feel like I need to. No matter how much I love Barrett."

"Love? Oh, Audie. When did you realize you loved him?" Olivia asked quietly.

"Today. When I asked him to leave, when he told me he loved me." She shrugged. "It about killed me to make him leave, but I knew I had to." She lowered her eyes to her lap and plucked at her fingertips.

"I see."

They sat there, neither one said anything. What could they say? There was nothing to say. She and Barrett were finished.

Kaput.

Over.

Just like that.

"Oh no."

Audra turned concerned eyes on Olivia. "What? What's wrong?"

"Look at your dress."

Audra looked down and saw a big spot of blood pooling on the front side of her dress between her thigh and knee.

"You must've torn your wound open or something. We'd better check."

Audra raised her dress up far enough to see the wound. Her bandage was soaked with fresh blood. Immediately her mind went to Barrett and what he'd said to her about the nightmares he had whenever he saw blood. Her heart went out to him even though she didn't want it to. She wanted to forget him, just like he wanted to forget his past. But both were obviously easier said than done.

"We need to go to the bathroom and take that bandage off to see what's going on."

Nodding, Audra stood being careful not to put too much pressure on the wounded leg, and the two of them made their way to the bathroom. There, Audra closed the lid on the stool and sat down.

They carefully peeled the bandage off. Two of the stitches had come out, leaving a gaping hole. "It must've happened when I banged it on the kitchen cupboard handle."

"When did you do that?"

"When I told Barrett to leave."

"Oh." Olivia nodded as understanding brushed across her face. "I'm taking you to the hospital."

Audra laid three sterile pieces of gauze over the wound and off they headed once again to the ER.

"Are you okay?" Erik asked Barrett. "You seem distracted.

"Sorry, I am. I'll try harder to concentrate." Sitting in Erik's office at Cole Speedway, Barrett struggled to keep his mind off of Audra and onto mapping out the final details of getting the motocross races underway.

Erik set his pen down and leaned back, his navy leather chair squeaked as he did. "Is it anything I can help with?"

Barrett never got a chance to answer because Erik's cellphone rang.

Erik sat forward and picked his phone up off his desk. "It's Olivia." He held up a finger. "Just a minute." He tapped the phone. "Hi, Sweetheart, what's up?" Five seconds into the conversation, Erik's forehead furrowed, and he looked over at Barrett. He grabbed his pen and started rapidly flicking it against the table.

The constant tapping was about to drive Barrett crazy, especially since his nerves were already on end. He wanted to snatch the pen out of Erik's hand and toss it across the room.

"Will she be okay?"

Will who be okay? Barrett wanted to ask.

"Do you want me to meet you at the hospital?"

Hospital?

Was he talking about Audra?

Barrett held his breath, waiting.

"Okay, if you need me, call. Keep in touch and let me know what's happening, okay?" A short pause, one that seemed to go on forever before Erik spoke again, "Okay, Sweetheart. I love you too. Tell Audra I'll be praying."

"Audra?" Barrett shot to his feet as Erik hung up. "Is Audra okay? Is she at the hospital again?"

"Whoa, hold on there, buddy. Sit down and relax and I'll tell you."

"I don't want to sit down and relax," he said with more calmness than he felt. "What's wrong with Audra?"

"A couple of stitches came out of her leg. Olivia took her to the hospital to get it re-stitched."

"I'm going." Barrett yanked his jacket off the back of the chair and flew out the door.

"Wait," Erik hollered after him. "I'm going with you."

"You'd better hurry then." He tossed the words over his shoulder, not bothering to take the time to look.

Erik caught up to him. "We'll take my truck. You're in no shape to drive."

"I'm fine," he said even though he felt anything but fine. Worried yes. Fine. No.

"Yeah right, and I'm a pro-football player." Neither of which were true.

Erik strode toward his truck.

Barrett knew Erik was right. He was in no shape to drive. His heart and mind were racing at a hundred and ten miles per hour. "You're right. But let's take my car.

184 | Debra Ullrick

You drive. That way I'll have a ride home and you won't have two vehicles there."

"That'll work." Erik switched directions and headed toward Barrett's car.

The seven-mile drive to the hospital felt more like ninety. When they finally walked inside the ER, Erik stepped up to the desk before Barrett and asked if Audra Darron was still in being seen.

"I'm sorry, unless you're a relative, I can't give you that information." The young brunette clerk sent them an apologetic look.

"What a dumb rule," Barrett mumbled as the distinct scent of rubbing alcohol and disinfectants slipped into his nose.

"Not really. Privacy and all that." Erik looked at Barrett sympathetically. "Why don't you go sit down over there? I'll let Olivia know we're here." He removed his cell and walked to the opposite side of the room.

Barrett sat down, laid his arms on his legs, and clasped his hands together. He lowered his head and prayed for Audra. Even though she never wanted to see him again, it didn't stop him from caring about her, or stop him from loving her.

He hadn't realized he was definitely in love with her until she said she didn't want to see him again. In that moment, the deep ache in his chest let him know loud and clear that he was. Only one other time in his life had he felt that way, and that was with Felicia. The minute he'd laid eyes on his wife, he was a goner. It took him a long time to win Felicia's heart. When he finally did, all his efforts were worth everything he'd gone through.

If only he could win Audra's heart.

But he wasn't stupid. His past stood between them and always would because there was no way he could ever reveal his secrets.

"They're almost finished." Erik sat in the chair next to him.

"How's Audra?"

Erik didn't answer, making Barrett's anxiety increase. He waited forcing himself to be patient even though everything inside of him was screaming for the answer. One grueling second after another ticked by as Erik stared at Barrett as if he were looking for some clue or something. "You got it bad, don't ya?"

Barrett wanted to pretend that he didn't know what Erik was talking about, but one thing he learned about Erik was he was an honest, God-fearing man, and he could spot a liar a mile away. Barrett also knew he could answer him honestly and his answer would go no further than between the two of them. He briefly closed his eyes and gave a nod. "For all the good it does me."

"What's that supposed to mean?"

"Means she doesn't want to see me again."

Erik frowned. "I know it's none of my business, but what happened between the two of you?"

Barrett glanced in the direction of the ER rooms, then back at Erik. "What happened to Audra that she doesn't trust men?"

"That's something you should ask her."

"It sure is."

Barrett jerked his face up.

Audra sat there in a wheelchair, a nurse standing behind her, staring over at him with obvious disapproval. "What are you doing here?"

Barrett stood. "Came to make sure you're all right."

"As you can see, I am."

His focus shifted to her dress and the big red stain on it. Her hand splayed across it as if to cover it, the caring gesture wasn't lost on him. His gaze went to hers holding a questionable look.

"Let's leave them alone." Erik cupped Olivia's elbow.

"Audra?" Olivia sent Audra a silent look meant to both ask if that was all right and to tell her she wouldn't leave if her friend didn't want her to.

All of which Barrett had no trouble deciphering. That look also asked if it was even okay with Audra to leave her with him. Audra must have told Olivia that she didn't want to see him again and why. What other reason would she have for hesitating and sending her that silent question?

Audra nodded to her friend.

"Okay." But Olivia didn't sound at all convinced. "We'll wait outside for you." With a quick look of compassion to both Barrett and Audra, they went out the Emergency Room's automated door.

Audra looked back at the nurse. "I left my purse back in the room, would you please get it for me?"

The nurse looked over at Barrett, then down at Audra. "Sure, I'll be right back." The nurse headed toward the direction of the room Audra had just been in.

Making sure no one else was within earshot, Barrett turned to Audra and asked, "What happened that you no longer trust men? I know you overheard me ask Erik, now I'm asking you." He shot up a quick prayer that she would give him another chance even though he knew he didn't deserve one. But that didn't stop him from asking just the same. He loved Audra and he would fight for her, just like he had Felicia. He just hoped the outcome of the chase ended in him catching her.

Chapter Thirteen

Sitting in front of Barrett in the wheelchair at the hospital waiting room, Audra gazed over at him. Her heart was tugging her toward him, but her head was dragging her the other direction.

Should she tell him? Or should she just walk away and tell her heart that it had to let him go?

The tug on her heart was even more persistent than a moment before, and it was getting worse.

Maybe, just maybe, if she told him about her past that would help him to open up about his. It was a thought anyway.

If she didn't at least try, would she end up regretting it the rest of her life? Finally, the decision was made. Someone had to go first in opening up, and it looked like that someone was going to be her. "I'll tell you. But not here. Take me home and I'll tell you there."

The relief on Barrett's face was evident. Not only on his face either, but in the stiffness in his spine that had now relaxed.

The nurse returned with Audra's purse. She wheeled Audra out the door.

Olivia and Erik were sitting on a nearby bench and stood when they saw them.

Olivia was the first to reach them. Questions raced from Olivia without her uttering a single word.

Erik stepped up alongside her and put his arm around her shoulder.

"If y'all don't mind, Barrett's gonna take me home."

Olivia smiled. "We don't mind, do we, Honey?" She gazed up at Erik.

"Not at all." He reached his hand out toward Barrett. Barrett took it, but instead of shaking Erik's hand, he yanked Erik to him and gave him a hug. Those two were sure becoming fast friends.

Erik handed Barrett his car keys.

Barrett went and got his car and drove it around to the ER exit where Audra and the nurse were waiting. Barrett had her settled inside before the nurse went back into the ER.

Back at her house, while she changed into a clean dress and got comfortable on her living room sofa, Barrett was in her kitchen pouring them each a glass of the lemonade Olivia had brought over earlier that morning. When he came in carrying them, Audra adjusted a pillow behind her and sat up straighter. Barrett handed her a glass and took a seat across from her.

Delaying the inevitable, she took several sips of the cold liquid, savoring the tangy sweetness of the freshly squeezed lemons.

"How's your leg feeling?"

With her glass to her lips, she looked over at him. "It hurts."

"Do you need a pain pill?"

"Not now. Later."

He nodded.

Time ticked by.

Neither one spoke, nor even looked at the other.

Finally, Barrett broke the silence. "What happened?" He gave a nod toward her leg.

"I ran into the cupboard handle earlier."

"This morning? When I was here?"

"Yeah." She set her dew-covered glass down on a coaster and wiped the moisture from her hands on the throw blanket lying on the back of the couch.

"You covered it well. I didn't even notice."

"I tried hard."

"Why?"

"Because I wanted you to leave, and I knew if you found out I hurt myself, you wouldn't go."

"Audra." He reached over and clasped her hands in his.

She wanted to yank them away, but the strength and the warm feel of his large hands kept her from doing so. As much as she didn't want it to, she needed the connection to him, needed his strength when she revealed what had happened to her with Neil.

"Tell me what happened." The tone in his voice had a soft huskiness to it.

She made the mistake of looking in his eyes, hazel eyes filled with compassion and… love. Was that same love shining through her eyes right now? If it wasn't, she'd be surprised because her love for him twined through every part of her being… her mind, her soul, and her body. She wanted to reach out to the love he offered, but she couldn't. Not now. Not yet. Not until she found out whether or not he would reveal his past after she told him about hers.

Slowly, she dragged her hands from his. Disappointment shrouded his face, but understanding replaced it.

Drawing in a long breath of courage, she exhaled it slowly. "Two years ago, I met a guy at church. His name was Neil Jetts." Her gaze dropped to her lap, and she fidgeted with the fabric of her dress. "We hit it off right away. We had so much in common. He loved trying new things and with me always wanting to confront my fears, I gave him plenty of exciting new things to do, and he liked that." The memory of what she was about to tell him gushed over her in one grueling, relentless wave after another. Pain stricken faces, lies, deception, betrayal, they all crashed into her with a force of a tsunami until she could no longer hold back the tears that had dammed up behind her eyes. She dropped her head into her hands and burst out crying. "I didn't know." She shook her head. "I didn't know."

The sofa sank beside her. With a gentleness she'd never experienced before, she felt herself being shifted around and lowered onto Barrett's lap, the wounded side of her body protected with great care.

Strong yet gentle hands rubbed her back, yet he said nothing.

Words weren't necessary.

His comfort and strength were.

Both of those she received in massive doses, absorbing them into the wounded parts of her.

Finally, her sobs let up, but she remained there, with her head settled against his chest, not wanting to see Barrett's face when she told him about the most painful time in her life. The pain she felt wasn't so much about what she went through, but what the others involved had gone through.

She drew in another long, steadying breath of courage, only this one stuttered as she inhaled. She nibbled on her lip before opening her mouth to speak. "About year after I'd been dating Neil, a woman came to my door. She asked me if I was Audra, and when I said that I was, she started crying. I had no idea who she was or what she wanted, or even why she was crying. I wanted to hug her, to comfort her somehow, but something held me back. God no doubt.

"She asked if I knew Neil Jetts and if he was here. I told her I did, that his place was on the other side of town, and that he was out of town at the moment. I asked if I could help her. I thought maybe she was Neil's sister or a relative and that perhaps something had happened to his parents.

"She asked if we had been seeing each other. Right then I had a feeling in my gut that something wasn't right. I asked who she was and what business it was of hers. That's when she told me." Audra's lungs constricted as the weight of that moment drained the air from them. She drew in several short breaths until she could finally speak. "She told me her name was Ellie Jetts, and that she was Neil Jett's wife."

The heart wrenching pain on Ellie's face stared back at Audra even from the shadows of the past. "She accused me of being a home wrecker." Those accusing words still haunted Audra to this day. They still had the power to make her feel like someone who would intentionally be "the other woman" even though that was the last thing she'd ever do. She would never intentionally date a married man, or any other woman's man whether they were married, engaged, dating or otherwise.

To this day, it still sickened Audra to think about what Neil had done to his poor wife.

Audra could still see the angry tears and hateful accusation in Ellie's big blue eyes, and she didn't blame her one bit. After all, Ellie didn't know that Audra was telling her the truth about not knowing he was married.

If she looked into Barrett's eyes right now, would she see those same things in his? Accusation. Horror. Judgment.

She had to know.

Had to find out.

Audra shifted back far enough in his arms until she could see Barrett's face.

What she saw there touched that aching place in her soul.

There was no disgust.

No repulsion.

No judgment.

No condemnation.

Even more importantly, no pity.

Only compassion and understanding.

Audra closed her eyes as relief trickled out of her one tear at a time.

She loved how Barrett seemed to sense her need for silence at this moment, as he said nothing.

The silence was needed to gather her thoughts because her next words were going to be even harder to say. "There's more." She opened her eyes and once again looked up into his handsome face.

A face she'd grown to love so much in such a short time.

She laid her hand against the side of his face.

His warm, comforting hand covered hers.

His reassuring nod gave her the courage to continue. "Not only did Neil have a wife, but three small children. The man was married, Barrett, and I didn't even know it." Disgust churned in her stomach. "He had children. I can still see their tiny hands pressed against the windows of the car and their faces peering at me as their mama stood there crying. I had no idea, Barrett. None whatsoever." Her eyes caught his, begging him to understand what she herself couldn't comprehend.

Like, how God could allow this to happen to Neil's wife and to those innocent children?

Or to her for that matter. Though she was the least important person in the situation.

The pain of reliving the whole thing was almost more than she could bear.

Was that why Barrett refused to talk about his past? Or was it something else? She shook her head. She didn't know anymore. Thinking things through in a straight line just wasn't working. She didn't know what to think or how to even feel about the whole thing anymore—Neil, Barrett, the lies, the secrecy. Fighting against all of it, she shook the disturbing thoughts from her mind and continued.

"I told her that I had no clue Neil was married. She started crying and told me that she believed me. That completely blew me away until she told me Neil was seeing another woman too and that the other woman had told her the exact same thing. I felt so bad for her, Barrett. And for those children." Tears stung her eyes once again.

Barrett brushed them off of her cheeks with his thumb and gazed down at her, looking at her as if he understood.

"I felt so stupid. So used. And so angry. I felt like the home wrecker she thought I was."

"You do realize none of this was your fault, right?" Barrett asked her quietly, breaking his silence.

"Not really. Sometimes I do because I never saw the signs, but most of the time I blame myself."

"Why?"

"Because when I really get to thinking about it, the signs were all there, even though I didn't know they were signs at the time. Does that make sense?"

"Perfect."

"Now when I think back on it, they were all there. Neil was very secretive. Every time I asked about his family, or questioned his childhood, or asked about where he went to school, or where he lived, or where he went when he traveled on business, he changed the subject. Kind of like you."

~♥*~*

Now Barrett understood why she wanted him to leave. Why she wanted no part of him. He didn't blame her. He just didn't know what to do about it. He would think of something though. And something soon, so he didn't lose her. "Audra, now I understand why you have a hard time with me not revealing my past. I can assure you, I'm not married, and I don't have any children."

Her eyes studied his.

He hoped the truth of what he'd just told her was revealed in them.

Her brows dipped, then rose, before dipping again.

She squirmed, and he had no choice but to remove his arms from around her.

She sat down beside him, her wounded leg nowhere near him. "Barrett, I wanna believe you, but I'm not sure I can. Surely you understand why I can't."

"I do. I do understand. Completely. Perfectly. But what can I do to assure you that I'm telling you the truth?"

"I'm not sure. I thought knowing about your past would be enough, but when I told ya what happened with Neil, it hurt so bad that I could hardly bear it. I understand why you don't wanna talk about your past. If it's even remotely as painful as mine, I get it. I'm just not sure how I feel about anything at the moment."

"Do you love me?" he asked, feeling more vulnerable than he'd ever felt before.

She lowered her eyes and nodded.

Barrett closed his eyes. At least he had something to work with now. He hoped so anyway. "So, where do we go from here, Audra?" He held his breath waiting for her answer and dreading it at the same time.

"I'm not sure. Once something like that has happened to you, it's hard to trust again." She sighed. "That's why I'm struggling with trusting God to guide me where men are concerned. Not because of Him, but because of my inability to hear from Him where men are concerned. I've dated some real doozies. Like you." She sent him a smirk before replacing it with a serious look. "I know you say you aren't married, but how do I know that the things that lie in your past aren't equally as devastating? Can you assure me of that as well?"

His heart sank. That he couldn't do.

Audra studied him, waiting for an answer, one he couldn't give her.

Suddenly, Louey growled, then darted toward the front window, barking.

"Louey, hush."

Louey gave one more bark and jumped up on the sofa, his attention firmly fixed on the door.

A second later and the doorbell rang.

Barrett was thankful for the reprieve. "I'll get it. Stay put."

He strode to the door and swung it open. "Ingrid? Elsa? How nice to see you both again." He smiled down at the two women dressed in designer pant suits and holding purses that were almost as big as they were. He could only imagine what they had in those things.

"Told you he'd be here, Ingrid. Didn't I?"

"That you did, sister."

What were they talking about? How did they know he'd be here?

"Can we come in, or are you just going to stand there all day staring at us, boy?" Elsa tapped him with the tip of her cane. A cane she rarely used.

"He's no boy, Elsa. He's a man."

Elsa sent an airy dismissive wave her sister's way. "A moot point, Ingrid, a moot point."

"Maybe not to Barrett," Ingrid muttered.

Elsa sent her sister a glare before turning her attention back to Barrett. "We heard about Audra's heroic feat, and we came to see if she needed anything. Now, are you going to let us in, young man, or leave us standing out here in this heat all day?" Elsa's smile softened her words. Sometimes the woman came across gruff, but under that brusque exterior lay a heart of gold. There wasn't anything she wouldn't do for the people she loved and cared about. Even complete strangers she helped, as long as she could remain anonymous to them.

"Ingrid? Elsa? Come on in," Audra said from the sofa.

Elsa pushed her way inside.

Barrett stepped back and out of her way.

Ingrid followed Elsa at a much slower pace. He stepped in line with Ingrid.

Once again, Louey growled and barreled toward Elsa.

"Louey, stop! Come," Audra ordered.

Lying low, Louey growled once more before jumping onto the couch with Audra, but he never took his eyes off of Elsa.

"Elsa, what a pleasant surprise."

Barrett heard Audra say before he returned his attention back to Ingrid. "Is your arthritis acting up again today, Ingrid?"

"How could you tell?" Her blue eyes came up to his, and a twinkling smile accompanied her wrinkled lips.

"Because normally I have to take much bigger steps in order keep up with you." He smiled. "When I don't, I know your arthritis is flaring up."

"It is acting up today. Weather and all, you know. Storm's a brewing."

"You always say that, Ingrid." Elsa shook her head and rolled her blue eyes.

"And I haven't been wrong yet," Ingrid whispered to Barrett. "But Elsa won't admit it." She smiled up at him, and the wrinkles around her mouth increased in a sweet old lady sort of way.

They reached Audra, and Elsa was already making a fuss over her, insisting she cover herself up so she didn't *take a chill* as Elsa called it.

He looked down at Audra and smiled. It was sweet of her to comply with Elsa's insistence even though the room temperature was a comfortable cool temperature.

"Ingrid, it's so nice to see you again." Audra's smile lit up her face.

Ingrid put her finger to her lips and shook her head.

"What do you mean 'again'?" Elsa asked, looking back and forth between Audra and Ingrid, frowning.

"We had lunch, and it was wonderful." Audra supplied the answer, sparing Ingrid her sister's wrath. If Elsa knew the meal Ingrid had arranged and didn't invite her, Ingrid would surely never hear the end of it. Obviously Audra had figured that out and had learned really fast like which sister was in charge.

Barrett smiled at that though only to himself.

"Oh." Elsa looked at Ingrid. "How come you didn't invite me?"

"Because you were busy that day, Elsa."

"Oh." The hurt left Elsa's face.

"Well, to what do I owe this pleasure?" Audra freed her arms from the blanket, coming to Ingrid's rescue with a change of subject though not an overly subtle one.

"Like I was telling, Barrett, we heard about your heroic feat in saving that poor child, and we had to come see if there was anything we could do. We would have come sooner, but there were some appointments we just couldn't break. We are sorry for the delay. Aren't we, Ingrid?"

"Yes we are, sister."

"How did you hear about it?" Barrett asked while the two women set about fussing over Audra.

Ingrid twisted the clasp on her oversized purse and withdrew a newspaper. "This is how we found out." She handed the paper to Barrett, then pulled out a box of Godiva chocolates and handed them to Audra.

"That and it made the national news. Can you imagine our little old county making the national news?" Elsa beamed with pride.

Barrett unfolded the newspaper, and his heart sank. On the front page of a local county newspaper were several pictures. One of Audra on the ground, one of the woman holding her child with her husband standing next to her, and a close up one of him, looking up at the paramedics. He bit back the groan that almost made it to his throat.

Ever since the brutal murders of his family, including the time he competed in the motocross races, he'd been careful to avoid having his picture taken up close so no one would recognize him even though his appearance had been altered greatly. He was still afraid that there were enough of his birth features that someone might recognize him anyway. And didn't Elsa say it made the national news? His gut churned. He swallowed hard as acid burned his esophagus.

"Barrett, are you okay?" Audra's concerned voice broke through his thoughts.

He masked his alarm, a trait he'd learned to master, and smiled down at her even though he was certain his smile hadn't made it to his eyes. "I'm fine."

Audra frowned up at him. "You don't look fine."

"Oh dear, it's the article, isn't it? I'm sorry, Barrett. I just didn't think how that would affect you. Why it must bring back horrific memories for you."

What was Ingrid talking about? She didn't know about his wife and parents murders.

"Seeing the woman you love lying on the ground like that. Here, let me have that." Ingrid removed the newspaper from his hands, folded it, then shoved it back into her bag, snapping it shut.

Did she just say seeing the woman he loved?

A painless snap on his arm with a solid object, snapped the questions he asked himself from his mind.

"Snap out of it, boy. I asked you a question."

Barrett gazed down at Elsa. He hadn't heard her ask him anything because he'd been so busy asking himself questions. "I'm sorry, Elsa. Please, repeat the question."

"I asked if you've told Audra that you loved her yet?" Elsa sent him that no nonsense look of hers.

"Yes, have you told her yet, Barrett, dear?" A knowing twinkle lit Ingrid's face.

Barrett couldn't believe his ears. How did they know he loved Audra? Had he been that obvious at the charity dinner the day Audra met them? That was the last time he'd seen them.

"Don't be so surprised." Elsa tapped him on the arm again with her cane. "Anyone who looks as distraught as you do in that newspaper article has to be in love."

They got all of that from one picture?

"Are ya gonna answer them, Barrett?"

He shifted his focus to Audra, sitting there looking amused with that cheeky grin of hers.

"Why don't you?" he retorted. Two could play this game.

"Because they asked you," she tossed back at him.

"Will you two stop it and just answer the question?" Elsa slammed her hands on her ample hips.

Both of them looked over at Elsa.

Barrett smiled. "As a matter of fact, ladies, I have told her."

The two women clasped their hands.

"I knew. I just knew." Elsa beamed.

They looked so pleased that Barrett didn't have the heart to tell them that while he'd told Audra he loved her, he still wasn't sure if there was a future with her or not.

Chapter Fourteen

Audra called her clients one by one and rescheduled their appointments. Her leg throbbed if she stood for much time at all. At the rate she was going, she would have to divvy her clients up to her other hairdressers. That was not a pleasant thought.

She sat on her sofa, thinking back to the day before. Ingrid and Elsa were so sweet. They wanted to take her home with them. In fact, they were pretty adamant about it. That is, until Audra, along with Barrett's help and assurance that he'd make sure she was well taken care of finally convinced the two of them that she'd be fine. The real deciding factor, however, was Louey. Neither one thought having him in their homes was a good idea. It was so nice of Barrett to mention that fact.

Barrett. Audra placed her hand alongside her head and sighed. What was she going to do about him?

Louey let out a string of barks, ran to the window, and wagged his tail. A sure sign it was Olivia.

Audra listened for her steps. As soon as she neared the door, Audra hollered, "Doors open. Come in, Liv."

In breezed Olivia, carrying a sack and a drink carrier. "What would you have done if it wasn't me?"

"I knew it was you."

Olivia looked down at Louey, prancing and hopping around her feet. "Louey, did you give me away again?" His tail wagged harder as he gazed up her with those big brown eyes of his. Olivia set the sack and beverage container on the coffee table, then leaned over and tapped Louey on the end of his nose before giving him a quick scratching behind his ears.

"What's in the sack? Sure smells good whatever it is."

"Wouldn't you like to know?" Olivia sat down next to her on the sofa. "Chinese."

"Yum. Sounds good. I'm so hungry."

"Didn't you eat breakfast?" Olivia frowned.

"Uh, no. I haven't really moved from this spot. For some reason, my leg really hurts today." Audra lightly touched the area surrounding her wound.

"Tearing it open and having it re-stitched will do that." Olivia opened the sack and pulled the contents out, spreading them out on the coffee table. "I'll run grab us some plates." Olivia hurried to the kitchen. Plates clinked and within minutes Olivia was back in the living room. "Wontons, fried rice and sweet and sour shrimp, right?"

Audra nodded and watched as Olivia filled her plate before handing it to her along with a set of wooden chopsticks.

Olivia filled her plate, sat on the opposite end of the sofa, and tucked her foot under her. Something they did so often when they were about to have a girl chat.

Audra bowed her head and sent up a prayer of thanksgiving.

She barely got the last word out of her mouth before Olivia asked, "So, how did your talk go with Barrett yesterday? I've been dying to hear all about it." Olivia bit off a piece of wonton, keeping her eye on Audra as she chewed.

Audra took the chopsticks and devoured several pieces of sweet and sour shrimp. A quick bite of her cheese wonton and she set it back on her plate, and set her plate on top of her lap. "I told him."

"Told him what?"

"About Neil."

Olivia's mouth formed into a big O. "You did? What did he say?"

"Nothing." She shrugged a shoulder. "He just let me talk. There was no judgment or anything."

"Why would there be? Neil's the one who was at fault." Olivia popped another bite in her mouth.

"I know, but somehow I still feel guilty." She hated that, but she had no clue how to deal with it.

"Why?" Olivia put her plate on the coffee table and picked up her drink.

"You know how I always used to pray about everything?"

"Used to?" Olivia tilted her head, and her long caramel ponytail tilted to the side.

"Well, I still do. It's just my hearing abilities are off when it comes to men." She chuckled but no humor accompanied it.

"Your hearing abilities?"

"Yup. I must not have too much discernment when it comes to men. I keep picking the wrong ones. Or they keep picking me, and I end up dating them for long periods of time."

"So you've had a few bad experiences, Audie. We all have. Look at Hammond. At one time, I thought my ex-fiancé hung the moon. But when he went missing, the more we talked and the more I thought about it, the more I realized how selfish he really was. How unfeeling he was to not only me but to his twin too. Speaking of twin, I wonder how Haskell is doing."

"Last I heard he got married and has a little girl."

"Oh really? Who'd you hear that from?"

"One of my clients back in Wheeling told me. Haskell married a cousin of hers. She said that he's very happy, and so is her cousin."

"I'm so glad to hear that. I sure hated that I hurt him. I know I didn't do it on purpose. I mean I had no idea he loved me, but still, I felt bad for him."

"Well, he's happy now. So no need to feel bad."

"You're right." Olivia set a foot on the floor and leaned forward. "Now enough of that. Let's get back to your situation. If I would have let my relationship with Hammond stop me, I would have never married Erik. Everyone goes through bad relationships."

"You call dating a married man with children a bad relationship? That's a catastrophe. Those poor children. I wonder if Ellie and Neil are even still together."

Olivia shook her head. "I don't know. My point was... Not everyone is like Hammond or Neil. There are good guys out there. I believe Barrett is one of them. Erik's always going on and on about him and what a praying, Godly man he is."

"How does he know?"

"Because he's spent quite a bit of time with Erik helping him get the motocross races started at the speedway. In fact, Barrett's there now."

"He is?" That surprised her. She picked up more rice.

"Yeah."

Audra nodded half-heartedly. "That's nice."

"Anyway, back to hearing from God. Sometimes, Audra, you just have to step out in faith. You have to trust God even when it's hard. No, especially when it's hard." Olivia quirked her head sideways, gazing at Audra without blinking.

Audra knew that look.

Olivia was contemplating whether or not she should say something and whether or not it would hurt Audra's feelings.

"I know that look. Go ahead. Spill."

"You're doing what I used to do. You're wanting a guarantee that if you allow yourself to fall for Barrett that everything will be all right. That he won't hurt you. Or that something in his past won't hurt you. But there are no guarantees for any of us. Every relationship involves taking a risk. And every decision we make in life involves stepping out in faith. Faith not in our abilities, but in God's."

Audra sighed. "You're right, and I get what you're saying. But the thing that keeps holding me back is his past and him not wanting to talk about it."

"We all have a past. Look at mine. I hate talking about mine. Does that mean I've got some secret agenda or that I'm hiding something? No. It's just that each time

I talk about it, it's like reliving it again and it's just too painful sometimes. Being locked in the past isn't good for anyone. God tells us not to dwell on the past. He put that in the Bible for a reason. He knew what he was doing. There's a whole," Olivia waved her arms in a great big circle as she said the word whole, "bright future ahead of us if we just embrace it."

Audra pondered Olivia's words. She never thought about it that way before. Talking about what had happened between her and Neil had really hurt. And Barrett, well, he did say his past was just too painful for him to talk about.

Even so, she couldn't ignore that little niggling doubt that there was more to it than what he was letting on. And that's what kept her from completely pursuing a deep relationship with him.

"Audie, you aren't going to like this, but..."

Audra's attention shifted to Olivia.

"You know how the things you're afraid of you hit them head on and conquer them. Well, this is just one more fear for you to face and to conquer. Even if it doesn't turn out the way you want it to," Olivia rushed out the words so fast Audra barely caught them. "You're always saying that fear keeps people from enjoying the life that God has for them.

"And while I know we have to use discernment, this is one fear I think you need to confront. If you don't, you're never going to find your Mr. Right or get married or have children. That fear of all of them being like Neil will keep you a prisoner no matter who that person is.

"No matter what they say or do. The minute they don't want to talk about something in their past, you're right away going to assume it's something bad. And it may be." Compassion filled Olivia's face. "The question is, is Barrett worth taking that risk for? Are you willing to find that out? Or are you going to walk away because of fear?"

Ouch. That hurt. Only because Audra knew Olivia was right. Her friend had definitely given her something to think about. And think about it she would.

Barrett and Erik had just finished working on the new plans for motocross races when Olivia came strolling into the room.

They both stood until she sat down.

"How was your lunch with Audie?" Erik asked.

"Very nice. Did y'all have a good lunch?"

"We didn't eat lunch."

Olivia yanked her thumb Erik's direction "Boy is he a hard task master or what?" She gazed at Barrett with a twinkle in her eye.

"Hey, we had donuts and coffee around ten," Erik defended himself playfully.

"Ah, so now the truth comes out. Did you save a donut for me?"

"Nope."

Watching these two made Barrett jealous. Jealous for the easy love they had for each other. It was something so evident every time they looked at each or spoke to one another. Someday he hoped to have that again. With Audra. "So, how's Audra's leg doing?"

Olivia looked over at him. "She said it was pretty sore."

He shot to his feet. "I think I'll go see if there's anything she needs."

"You do that." Olivia smiled with a gleam in her eye.

Something was up. He wanted to ask what, but he also wasn't sure he really wanted to know.

"I'll get those figures to you tomorrow morning," he told Erik.

"Sounds good." Erik rose and extended his hand. "Thanks for all your help. I appreciate it."

They shook hands. "Happy I could help."

He turned to leave.

"Wait." Olivia stopped him. "My sister-in-law Camara and her husband Chase are coming this weekend. I would love it if you and Audra would join us for a little get together."

"Did you ask Audra?" He didn't want to answer for her, especially considering how he didn't really know where he fully stood with her right now.

"Yeah. She said she would love to see Camara and Chase again."

"Does she know you invited me?" He hated asking, but had to know.

"She knows I was going to."

Barrett quirked a brow toward Olivia, hoping she would continue.

"And she said that was fine." There was that gleam in her eyes again.

Fine wasn't great, but it wasn't a no, so that much was good. "I'd love to join you. What time?"

Olivia gave him the information, and he headed out the door to see Audra.

When he pulled into her driveway, he sent up a quick prayer that things would go well between them.

Louey was at his usual place at the window, barking, but this time he wasn't growling. The little Chihuahua must be getting used to him.

Barrett rang the bell.

"Who is it?" Audra yelled from inside.

"Barrett," he hollered through the door.

"Come in."

He was glad to comply. Barrett stepped inside.

Louey met him at the door, tail wagging. Barrett dug in his pocket and pulled out a small rawhide bone and handed it to the dog. Louey gently took it from him and then darted off. He found a place by the fireplace, and placing it between his front paws, he started chewing on the bone. Barrett chuckled. "Must like it, huh?"

"He loves those things. You're going to spoil him, ya know that, right?"

"You got a problem with that?" he asked using his playful tone.

"Not really. I love it." She smiled and patted the sofa next to her. "Come on in and sit down. I'd offer to get ya something to drink, but I haven't moved much today. Kinda sore." She wrinkled her nose and pursed her lips off to one side as if it pained her to mention that fact.

A fact he was already aware of. "That's what Olivia said. You sure it isn't infected or anything?" He had yet to sit down.

"I'm sure."

For the first time since he'd arrived, an awkward silence filled the room. He was the first to break it. "Listen, before I forget, Olivia said she talked to you about getting together with them this weekend. If your leg is doing better, do you want to go? With me?" He added 'with me' to make sure she understood it was a date.

"I'd love to. I just hope this thing," she pointed to her thigh, "is better by then."

"Me too."

More silence. Sitting down didn't feel quite right yet, and she hadn't made a second offer.

Not knowing what else to do, he looked at the pitcher of lemonade on a tray, along with fruit, cookies and pretzels. Her pills and Bible were within reach as well. Far as he could tell, she had everything she needed. "Well, I just stopped by to see if you needed anything and to see if we were on for this weekend. Everything seems to be taken care of, so I'll just let myself out."

"Um, do ya have to rush off now? I'm not doing anything, and I am so-o-o bored."

"Is that the only reason you want me to stay? Because you're bored?" He had to know. Had to hear it from her own lips.

She shook her head. "No. Truth is, I wanna spend some time with you."

"Why?"

"Because."

"Because why?" He wasn't letting her get off that easy.

"Okay, okay. I wanna see where this thing between us goes, all right?"

"More than all right." He strode over to her and sat down on the coffee table. He clasped her hand in his. "Thank you, Audra." He cleared the emotion from his voice.

"For what?"

"For taking a chance on me."

She waved a finger at him. "You better not let me down."

He grabbed her finger. "Shake that thing in my face again and I'll—"

Her eyes widened until she saw the twinkle in his eyes. "Or you'll do what?" she challenged.

"Or I'll do this." He cupped her face and covered her lips with his, giving her a long, breathless kiss.

"Hmmm. I think I'll shake my finger at you more often," she whispered against his mouth before kissing him this time.

With his lips still against hers, he replied, "I think I'll let you."

Chapter Fifteen

Over the past five days, Barrett had been by to see Audra every day, bringing her meals, cards - some humorous some serious, various stuffed animals, candies and chocolates from all around the world, and roses. Lots and lots of roses. Her living room, kitchen table, and bedroom were now overrun with pink roses, and her whole house smelled like a rose garden.

Standing in front of the vanity mirror, she leaned down and buried her nose into one of the two dozen roses that were arranged in a vase on her vanity and breathed deeply. "Ummm. They smell so-o-o good," she told Louey who was lying on her bed paying no attention whatsoever to her.

Audra slid her paisley cotton dress on and tightened the belt around her waist. Today, she and Barrett were going to Erik and Olivia's. Camara and Chase Lamar would be there.

She sat down and painted her nails and toenails lemon yellow to match one of colors in the paisley design on her dress. She added a coat of tiny fluorescent glitter strips on top and let them air dry.

With a sudden bark, Louey darted off her bed and bolted out the door, yapping happily all the way to the front door.

In the next instant, the doorbell rang.

Audra glanced at the clock and groaned. Late again. Still in her bare feet, she hurried to the top of the stairs. Leaning over the banister, she hollered down at the front door, "Come in, Barrett."

He stepped inside, and before even looking up at her, he handed Louey a treat, and when Louey took off running, he glanced up at her. "Let me guess. You're running late."

"You guessed right. Have a seat. I'll be down in a few minutes."

"More like fifteen or twenty."

"I heard that. Ha. Ha. Very funny. Remind me to laugh."

His smile brightened her day.

She whirled and rushed to her room, grateful her leg was doing better and that she could finally move around much easier. She slid her feet into her sandals, applied her mascara, lipstick and perfume on, snatched up her Coach bag, and headed downstairs. "I'm getting better. Only twelve minutes late instead of fifteen."

"Only?" He hiked a brow.

"You complaining? 'Cause if ya are, I can just call this whole thing off, and you can go to Erik's by yourself." Even though she had absolutely no plans to do that, she teased him just the same by turning around and acting as if she were going to head right back up the stairs.

"Oh no you don't." In less than a second, he was in front of her, threading her arm through his, and guiding her rather quickly toward the front door.

Audra laughed the whole way and playfully resisted his tug.

When he stopped at the door, she eyed him up and down. "You look nice." *And you smell really nice too. Like pinewood and rain all rolled into one.*

"So do you. Beautiful as always." He leaned over and planted a kiss on her cheek. "Don't want to mess up your lipstick."

"Who needs lipstick? Besides, I can always apply more."

"In that case…" He gathered her into his arms, his firm but soft lips captured hers, and his spearmint breath mingled with hers.

Warmth spread through her and she locked her knees into place.

Seconds ticked by on the Grandfather clock. Those tick, tick, ticks were drowned out by the fast beating of her heart as his kiss soared throughout her veins, landing in her heart.

Not wanting to, but knowing she had to or they would really be late getting to Livvy's, Audra pulled back. "We'd better go, or we're gonna be late." Her voice sounded breathy even to her own ears, she could only imagine what Barrett thought about that. She didn't have to wonder for very long.

"Who cares about being late?" His throaty voice matched hers.

Audra couldn't help herself, she giggled.

Barrett raised his head and the dreamy look in his eyes vanished, replaced with a frown. "Care to tell me what's so funny?"

She smiled. "Did you just hear what you said?"

Dawning lit his face. "Oh man." He groaned, laying his head back. "Your bad habit is rubbing off on me. Lord, have mercy on me."

She slapped his upper arm. "Smart Aleck. Let's go." She pinched his shirt sleeve and tugged him out the door.

"What about your lipstick?"

"Forget it. I just may need another kiss before we get to Livvy's."

"Sounds good to me."

It sounded good to her too. *Lord, I am a goner for this man, have mercy on me.*

They climbed into his roadster, and as they headed to the Coles', Barrett grasped Audra's hand. At the house, they headed around back to their patio. Laughter and voices drifted out to them when they rounded the corner. "Is this a private party or can anyone join?" Audra asked as she and Barrett neared the small group of people.

"Audra!" A beautiful petite blonde woman wearing a yellow summer dress and flip flops with tiny yellow daisies on them hurried over to Audra and hugged her. "So good to see you again." She stepped back and lifted Audra's hand up and inspected them. "Love your nails."

"Only because they're yellow." Audra chuckled.

"Guilty. Yellow's my favorite color." The woman smiled at Audra, then looked up at him. "And, who is this handsome gentleman?"

Audra looped her arm through his and gazed up at him. "This is my boyfriend, Barrett Camden. Barrett, I'd like you to meet Camara Lamar. She's Erik's sister."

"Figured she might be," he said while shaking her hand. He couldn't help but notice the rough calluses and the grease under her nails when he did. Definitely not soft and manicured like Audra's. "Hear you like to race and build engines."

"Ya heard right." Camara smiled, her brown eyes and white straight teeth sparkled. "My equal half does too. Come on and meet him." She clutched him by the wrist and tugged him forward. Barrett had no choice but to follow the little spitfire. She reminded him of someone else he knew. He glanced over his shoulder at Audra. "You coming?"

"Yup."

They stopped in front of a man with dark spiked hair and green eyes who was several inches shorter than himself, but what the man lacked in height, he made up for in muscle mass. "Chase, this is Barrett Camden. The one Erik told us about."

Erik told them about him? Why would Erik tell his sister and brother-in-law about him?

"Nice to meet you, Barrett." Chase held his hand out.

Barrett accepted his hand. Chase's grip was firm and solid. He liked that.

"Erik says you're helping him get the motocross races set up."

"Trying to."

220 | Debra Ullrick

"That's great. I hear you've done a lot of that yourself. I'm familiar with quite a few of the motocross teams. Who'd you race for?"

Barrett told him.

"I know Jim. He's a great guy."

"He sure is." Barrett often wondered how Jim was doing. He'd love to call him, but that was one of the many bridges he had to burn along his way to standing here.

"So," Chase said. "You ever do any mud bog racing?"

"No. You?"

"Yeah. My wife and I live for it."

"That's the truth." Erik walked up alongside them with Olivia on his arm. "You should see all the trophies these two have won. You could fill a shop with them.

"Well, you could fill a shop with all of them monster truck trophies you've won too, bro." Camara's southern drawl was as strong as Audra's.

Erik shrugged. "Don't I wish. I haven't won that many, but I love it and keep doing it anyway."

"And you're good at it." Pride for her brother was evident in Camara's voice.

"Before the end of the race season, you should try mud bogging, Barrett. How about this evening?" Chase took a drink of his Coke.

"I don't think so."

Chase lowered his drink. "Why not? You'll love it."

"After what happened in my first, and only," he emphasized the words *and only*, "demolition derby, I think I'll pass."

"Why? What happened?" Chase turned confused green eyes on him.

The pause was long. So long in fact that Audra ended up filling them in on what had happened.

"Wow. Man, that's too bad. I understand your hesitation, but if you do change your mind, let me know. We brought four trucks with us, and you're welcome to run one of them if you'd like. You too, Audra."

"Me?" Audra squeaked. "No way." She waved her hand and her head in opposite directions as she said it.

"That's what you said about the demolition derby, Audie, and you ended up loving it," Olivia goaded Audra.

"True, but at least I was able to see out the windshield in the derby car. Can't say the same thing for mud bog racing. I don't know how y'all do it." Audra shook her head in short choppy waves. "How do you?"

Barrett listened with great interest as they explained what they did. Temptation to run a mud bog race just once ran over him, but his soul still stung from knowing he'd hit Audra and the little girl the last time he'd tried something that sounded fun. He'd have to pass on the mud bog racing.

"Barrett, are ya listening?"

At the sound of Audra's voice, he gave himself a mental shake. "Sorry. What?"

"I said, 'I'll do it if you will.'"

"Do what?" He'd missed something somewhere.

"Do the mud bog race."

His eyes widened at that. "You? Get muddy? Oh, this I've got to see."

Audra wrinkled her nose up at him. "Get ready to eat dirt then, Hotrod."

He hiked his eyebrows upward. "You mean mud, don't you?"

"Moot point." She casually studied her nails.

"A lot of difference between mud and dirt," he countered.

"Only one difference. Water."

"Then game on," he challenged.

Her eyes shot up to him. "Game on, Hotrod."

"Are they always like this?" Camara asked.

"Most of the time," Erik answered. "Reminds me of another couple I know." Erik glanced at Camara and Chase.

"I smell a story here." Barrett rubbed his chin, loving how at ease he felt around these people even though they'd just met.

"You would be right about that." Erik chuckled.

"I'd love to hear it."

"These two used to be bitter rivals and even worse enemies." Erik gave a quick nod toward his sister and brother-in-law.

"You're kidding? How did you two ever end up getting married?"

"Well, it all started with a wager." Camara glanced over at her husband and smiled at him. "If I lost the race, I had to go out with Chase, something I did not want to do, and if he did, he had to wear a cap and a jacket with a yellow Chevy emblem on them." She giggled. "To this day, he's still a Ford man. To make a long story short, we ended up going on a date. But only because someone sabotaged my bogger," she quickly added.

"Sure, Honey," Chase said. "You believe that if you want to. We all know the truth about who's the better mud bog racer." Chase pointed his thumb toward his chest and winked at his wife.

"In your dreams," Camara shot back with a wink and a smile.

These two were something. Barrett could almost picture himself and Audra like that in a few years, not talking about mud bog racing, but the same easy bantering back and forth. Something they already did now.

"We can tell you more about it over dinner. Here comes Mickey and Virgil with the food." Camara nodded toward the patio doors.

Mickey and Virgil headed toward them, carrying platters and trays on their arms and in their hands just like waiters and waitresses would do in a restaurant.

At the same time, everyone stepped forward and took a plate or something from the couple and set them on the table, filling the center of it rather quickly.

"You're joining us," Erik informed them.

"Can't. We've got a hot date." Mickey winked. "Dinner and a movie, then a late night swim." Mickey smiled and gazed up at her husband Virgil, who was smiling down at her with admiration shining through his eyes.

Their love for each other was evident. Same with Erik and Olivia, and Chase and Camara.

Barrett hoped that someday he'd get to share that same devotion and love with Audra. For the umpteenth time, he prayed his past wouldn't ruin his future.

They all sat down at the table, and after Erik said the blessing, they dove into the banquet spread out in front of them.

Halfway through lunch, Camara tapped her glass with her knife. The chatter around the table stopped and all eyes went to her. "I have an announcement to make." She reached for Chase's hand. She smiled up at him then looked over at Erik. "We're going to have a baby."

Erik's chair scraped across the patio floor. Within seconds, he was hugging his sister and lifting her off the ground, swinging her around.

"Put me down. I'm pregnant." Camara laughed.

Erik set her down very carefully. He shook his brother-in-law's hand then pulled him into a bear hug. "That is so awesome. Congratulations."

Olivia joined him, then Audra, and finally Barrett.

"When is the big day?" Olivia asked.

Camara's face glowed. "February 3rd."

There was something so beautiful about a pregnant woman. A vision of his wife's glowing face the day she informed him she was pregnant drifted through his mind. He quickly squelched it. The pain of knowing he'd lost his unborn child sent daggers through his chest. With all the force of a wrecking ball, he slammed that thought from his mind.

"So happy for you, sis."

"Me too," Livvy added.

"Congratulations." Barrett stepped up and shook their hands, but his smile never quite reached his weeping heart.

With the congratulations over, everyone sat back down and finished their meal. Well, most everyone did. Barrett just mainly pushed his food around his plate since his appetite had vanished.

Audra stood, and clasped Barrett's hand. "Would y'all excuse us a moment?"

Confused and concerned, Barrett let Audra lead him toward the pool area.

"What's up?" Barrett asked her as soon as they reached the privacy of the pool.

She turned and put both hands on her hips. "That's what I wanna know."

He frowned. "What do you mean?"

"You barely spoke three sentences all through lunch. What gives?"

"Nothing."

"No." She waved her forefinger in protest. "No nothing this time. What's wrong, Barrett? And don't even think about not telling me." She stared up at him. After a second, she lifted her eyebrows as if challenging him.

Barrett ran his hand over the back of his head. "Okay. The truth is, watching Camara and Chase got me to thinking about us."

"Huh?" She cocked her head to the side. "Us? Why?"

"They remind me of us."

"How so?"

"You didn't much care for me when you met me, and now you love me."

"Guilty." She smiled. "But I still don't know what that has to do with you being so quiet."

Barrett's cell rang in his pocket. "Hang on." He grabbed up his cell and checked the Caller ID. "I have to take this. Excuse me a minute." He strode toward the other side of the pool, away and out of earshot of her.

Audra watched him, walking away, bent in conversation with whoever was on that call, and it took everything in her not to turn and run. Minutes later, as she watched, Barrett ended the call and put his cell back in his pocket. But rather than come back to her, he just stood there. His head bent as if the weight of the world rested on his shoulders. Audra didn't know whether to go talk to him and ask him what was wrong or to give him a few minutes. She decided to wait until he was ready to come to her.

When he finally did, with every step he took, she debated about whether or not to ask him again what was wrong. One look and she decided that now was not the time to ask him why he was so quiet. The look of sadness and disillusionment on his face told her he needed her support more than her questions. So, instead she placed her arms around his waist, settled her head onto his chest, and held him. Instantly, his arms wrapped around her, holding her tightly in their embrace.

They stood there for several minutes just holding each other. Finally Audra whispered, "It's okay, Barrett. You don't have to tell me what was bothering you earlier, or what's bothering you now."

His chest heaved against her ear. "Thank you," he whispered softly.

Audra leaned back in his arms and gazed up at him. Stormy, weighty eyes stared down at her. Her heart went out to him. Whatever was the matter it was not a passing thing. It was deep and held a myriad of pain.

"Thank you for understanding and for being so patient with me. I love you, Audra."

"I love you too."

Barrett's lips touched hers lightly at first. Then he closed his eyes and yanked her to him. "I don't want to lose you too." His breath brushed against her ear.

Wait. What did he just say? That he didn't want to lose her *too*? What did he mean by *too*?

The second Audra stiffened, Barrett realized his mistake. All this time he'd been so careful. He'd guarded his words so diligently. Until now. *Lord, please don't let her ask me what I meant by that. I can't tell her about my wife. Too much is at stake.*

Audra stepped out of his arms and gazed up at him. "What did you mean by you didn't wanna lose me *too*?"

Barrett pressed his lips together. *Please, help me out here, Lord.* "I just meant that I've lost so many loved ones already. I can't bear to lose another one."

A second of decision and Audra's frown disappeared. She nodded. "Oh, okay."

Barrett breathed a sigh of relief. *Thank you, Jesus.*

"Hey, you two, I hate to interrupt but…" Olivia stepped through the gate. "We need to get to the speedway and get ready for this evening's events. Y'all are coming, right?"

Barrett looked down at Audra and sent her a mischievous grin. "Not only are we coming, but we've got a mud bog race to enter."

"But, but," Audra sputtered, as the three of them made their way back to the others.

"But nothing. I'll take you home to change. You can't race in that." He pointed to her paisley dress.

"Wait. I can't race tonight. I forgot all about my cut."

Oh man, so had he. How could he have forgotten so quickly?

"I don't get my stitches out until Wednesday. How about next Saturday? We can do it then if y'all are still here that is." She looked over at Camara and Chase.

"We'll be here for a couple more weeks. So, whenever you're ready to race, you just let us know." Camara wove her gaze between Audra and him.

"We certainly will." Barrett sent another challenging look Audra's way. By then her leg should be healed enough to race. If it wasn't though, there was no way he would let her. He'd call the whole thing off first.

Audra laid her head back and closed her eyes. "Why me, Lord? What did I ever do to You to warrant You sending me this… this—?"

"Wonderful, loving, caring man," Barrett finished for her with a grin, knowing she meant that the Lord had sent her another challenge to overcome.

She shot him a look that said don't mess with me boy-o. He just grinned again.

The past seven days had flown by in rush of meetings, visits with Audra and running errands. Today was the day Barrett and Audra would compete in their first mud bog race. Barrett made sure Audra's leg was better before he agreed to go ahead with this whole crazy idea. Audra had assured him it was. In fact, she'd told him that the day her doctor had removed her stitches, that her doctor had informed her she could resume her normal activities.

Even so, it took a lot of talking, but Barrett finally convinced her into wearing extra padding and using extra protection on her wound. Audra reluctantly complied, and for that Barrett was grateful.

He just wished he felt better about this whole thing, but truth was, he still struggled with what had happened the day he had competed in his first derby race. Because he still was a bit apprehensive to do this thing, he knew he needed to take his cue from Audra's life and face his fear by doing it.

That's why he was now standing in the contestant pits at Cole Speedway with Audra at his side, listening to Camara and Chase explain to them over the loud rumbling and crackling engines of the other mud bog racers the ins and outs of mud bog racing. Of what to do and what not to do and what to watch out for and so on.

"Audra, you can drive The Black Beast." Camara nodded toward a black '74 Chevy with the white Chevy emblem and words - The Black Beast - on the doors only yards away from them. She looked so femininely masculine and cute dressed in those yellow coveralls and yellow Chevy cap.

"And, Barrett, you can drive the Mud Boss here." Chase yanked his thumb toward a yellow Ford Coupe with bogger tires and a lift kit.

"Sweet." Barrett nodded his head, admiring the '34 Ford Coupe with the words Mud Boss on the doors.

"Better than that black Chevy, right?" Chase winked at Camara, who sent him what even Barrett knew to be a fake frown of disapproval.

"That Chevy can still out race your Ford any ole day."

"Care to make a wager on that, shrimp?" Chase gave his wife a smirk of a grin and waggled his eyebrows.

"Call me shrimp again and you'll find your spark plug wires cut and water in your fuel tank." She grinned, but Barrett didn't get the joke.

As if Audra sensed his silent confusion, she said, "Someone had actually put water in Camara's fuel tank, and she hates being teased about being short."

"Oh." Barrett nodded as he remembered them saying something earlier about how someone had sabotaged her bog truck.

"I'll take ya up on that wager, mister." Camara turned her Chevy cap around until the bill of her cap was on the back of her head.

"Oh, oh." Chase placed his hand over his heart and wobbled. "I've gone and done it now."

"Done what?" Barrett still didn't get the joke.

"She only does that," Chase pointed to Camara's cap, "when she's angry or teasing me that she's angry."

Camara wrinkled her nose up at him. "You got that right."

Chase looked over at Barrett and Audra. "She's teasing."

That looked didn't exactly say teasing to him. "How do you know she's teasing?"

"Because, in the past when she did that, there was no smile," Chase said with a shrug. "She'd close her eyes and count to ten. Most of the time she'd only get to one or two before she'd blast someone."

Camara gave a shrug and a smile and nodded in agreement.

"Okay. Now, back to our bet, Ca-mare-o." Chase waggled his eyebrows again.

"Watch it, buddy." Camara narrowed her eyes at Chase.

"She doesn't like being called Ca-mare-o." Chase said in a fun manner. "Let's shake on it."

Instead of shaking her husband's hand, the feisty blonde shook and wiggled her body.

"Oh, are you gonna get it." Chase grabbed his wife and tickled her.

Barrett watched their playfulness and smiled. When they finished flirting with each other, they shook hands on their friendly wager.

"There's one tiny detail I forgot to mention about our wager, Cam. It's based on which of these two," he nodded at Audra and Barrett. "wins the competition."

"What?" Audra sputtered, and Barrett swung his attention to her. "That's not fair to Camara. I've never driven a bog truck before."

"Neither have I."

Audra narrowed her eyes at Barrett. "But you've raced motorcycles before."

"And you drive one," he tossed back.

"Driving and racing are two different things."

"Okay, you two. You sound like me and Cammy."

They both looked at Chase. "We'll call off the wager. That'll solve your argument."

"I don't think so." Audra planted her hand on her hip.

"But you just said…" Chase looked to Barrett for help.

Barrett shrugged and sent him a look that said you're-on-your-own-with-this-one.

With a smirk and a quirk of her eyebrow at him, Audra tipped her head. "Forget what I just said and let the race begin. Catch me if you can, Hotrod."

Barrett laughed at the shocked look on Chase's face and the smug grin on Camara's.

This ought to be interesting.

Chapter Sixteen

"Me and my big mouth," Audra mumbled. Sitting behind the wheel of Camara's mud bog truck, getting ready to drop into the long mud pit, suddenly she didn't feel quite as smug as she had earlier when Barrett had challenged her.

"I know I already asked this before, but are you sure it's okay for you to do this in your condition?" Audra glanced over at Camara who was harnessed in on the passenger side of The Black Beast.

"I'm sure. The day I found out I was pregnant, I asked my doctor. He said it's fine, especially since I'm healthy as a horse and because my body is used to it, and because I'm only a few weeks along. Besides, you're not getting out of this that easy." Camara grinned at her.

Audra wasn't voicing her concern so she could get out of it. She was genuinely concerned for the welfare of Camara and her unborn child. Okay, if she were being completely honest, perhaps a small part of her saw it as a way to get out of this race, but it definitely wasn't her main motive. Nowhere even close. With a sigh of uncertainty, she said, "As long as you're sure."

"I'm positive."

Audra nodded.

"How about you?" Camara asked. "Olivia said you have quite a nasty cut on your leg."

"It'll be all right. The doctor removed the stitches and said it was pretty well healed. I've got it padded pretty good. Barrett's idea." She grinned, patting the bulging spot as if to prove her point.

The announcer's voice mentioning her and Barrett's names and the names of the boggers they were driving snagged her attention back to the bog truck.

Her hands shook as she gripped the steering wheel and gazed out into the three-foot deep mud pit. Three feet? Add another two feet, three inches and the thing would be as deep as she was tall.

Even though Camara had Audra drive The Black Beast around the back lot of Cole Speedway for over an hour while she instructed Audra what to do, Audra still wasn't sure she could do this. A picture of those fake clacking teeth flitted through her brain. That's what hers was doing now.

"You can do this, Audra. You have to, or I'll never hear the end of it."

No pressure there. "Neither will I." They both laughed.

Audra glanced over at the other pit that looked every bit as deep and treacherous as the one in front of her. Her attention shifted to the Ford Coupe in front of it.

Barrett and Chase were sitting inside it with Barrett behind the wheel.

Audra wondered if Barrett was as nervous as she was. Knowing him, probably not. He mostly oozed confidence. They looked her way, but she couldn't see their faces through their dark helmet visors.

Barrett leaned forward. With his finger and thumb shaped like a gun, he flipped it forward. Game on.

"Don't let him intimidate you. Have fun with it, Audra. This is a timed event, and my truck has the power to hold its own."

Audra nodded at Camara.

The flagger standing between the two mud pits raised the flag.

Her heart revved up like a racing motor. She pulled the visor down on her helmet.

The flag dropped.

Doing just what Camara had instructed her to, they dropped into the pit, her stomach dropping with them all the way to her toes.

She struggled to keep the truck from going up and over the sides. Mud spun up from the pit and covered the windshield. Audra couldn't see a thing and found herself wanting to panic. But being in the middle of a mud pit was not the time to freak out. So instead, shouting above the noise of the truck, she asked Camara, "What do I do now?"

"Keep looking out the window. Make sure you stay away from the wall."

Audra felt the pull of the mud, dragging her to the side and down. On instinct, she moved the steering wheel in the opposite direction of the rear end of the truck.

"You got it, Audie. Keep it up!" Camara cheered her on from the other side of the cab.

Mud soaked Audra's left arm and leg. Ech. Whoever thought mud baths were great had to be crazy. *No more crazier than you for doing this, girl.*

She cut a glance to the other pit. From what she could tell, she and Barrett were running side-by-side.

"Hold on."

Audra glanced at Camara who extended her arm toward the dashboard control panel. She flipped a switch and The Black Beast lurched forward, power surging through its engine. Audra's adrenaline kicked in right along with it.

She shot a quick glance toward Camara, wondering what she had just done.

"NOS." Camara stated with a smile.

Whatever NOS was, the truck was suddenly moving twice as fast through the pit. It took all of her strength to hold the power.

The mud yanked the wheels back and forth as Audra strained to keep it from hitting the outside edges. Her arms ached with the strain. How much longer they would hold up, she had no idea. Though she lifted weights, she wasn't a muscle bound girl. Then again, neither was Camara and yet she managed to do this all the time. How? Audra had no clue.

Suddenly The Black Beast lunged up and out of the pit and Audra's heart and stomach bounced out with it.

At the same time she let up on the gas, Camara reached over and flipped the NOS switch off.

It was over. She could breathe again and hopefully stop shaking like a bobble head doll.

"Lean your head out the window and head back to the pit. Go slow."

Camara didn't have to tell her to go slow more than once. Slow sounded pretty good after what she'd just been through. Mud bog racing definitely wasn't for her.

They pulled up alongside the mud-encased Coupe. Barrett hopped out, removed his mud soaked helmet, and handed it to Chase.

Audra sat there, willing her legs and stomach to stop trembling. "Did we win?" she asked Camara.

"Don't know yet. But we're fixin' to find out." Camara opened her door and slid out.

Audra's side of the door flung open, and Barrett stood there, staring up at her. Mud smattered his handsome face, covering most of his lips. At some point he must have raised the visor on his helmet, Audra thought, or his lips and face wouldn't have been as muddy as they were now.

"So what did you think?" He held his arms up for her.

Looking down at him and all the mud dripping from his clothes, she started to shake her head until she glanced down at her own mud-soaked clothes. She didn't look any better than he did. Hiking a shoulder, she willing slid down into his arms. When her feet touched the ground, Barrett put his muddy lips on top of hers. "Eww." She turned her face sideways.

"Ah, come on. Where's your sense of adventure?" He tugged her closer to him.

"Not there." She squirmed, trying to get away, but he was too strong for her. He kept trying to kiss her.

Despite the mud, she found his antics funny. Giggling, she turned her head left and right, dodging his muddy lips. All of a sudden, his lips found hers. He'd outsmarted her and had anticipated her next move. Why fight it? She gave into his kiss and was so glad she did. That man sure knew how to kiss.

Audra was disappointed that neither she nor Barrett had won. Erik pulled a fast one on them and didn't time them. He figured it was best that way, and he was probably right. Whichever one of the two of them that won would probably rib the other one with no mercy, and not just her and Barrett either, but Chase and Camara too. Erik was a smart man.

They headed to the private showers Erik provided for them to clean up and to change their clothes. Unbelievably, Audra made it out first and had to wait outside the building for Barrett. This was a first for her. Usually it was Barrett waiting for her. She made mental notes of all the things she would rib him about it. This was definitely one for the history books, and it would probably never happen again.

She laughed at her own dramatic flare.

Minutes later, when he stepped around the corner, Audra whistled. "Boy, don't you like nice. But," she placed her fingertip to her chin. "I think I like you better the other way." She smiled.

"I can go back and change into my muddy clothes if you'd like." He turned and headed toward the men's shower room.

Audra rushed up to him and grabbed him by the arm. "I don't think so, Hotrod."

"What? Don't you like mud?" He waggled his eyes.

"Uh, no." She shook her head and laughed as she put her hands up and over the back of his neck.

"To be honest, I don't much care for it either." He hugged her to him long and hard.

"Didn't you like mud bog racing?" she asked when he released her and took her hand.

"Loved it."

"But you just said…"

"I said I didn't care for the mud. The racing, oh yeah."

"Think you'll do it again?"

"Definitely." He eyed her up and down. "You?"

"Uh. No."

"Chicken."

"Bawk, bawk." She tucked her hands under her arms and flapped them like a bird.

"You're a nut, you know that, don't you?" He drew her back into his arms.

"No more than you are."

Barrett laughed and then kissed her.

Hugging her to him, Barrett raised his head and rested his chin on top of Audra's head. Movement around the corner of the building caught his eye. Earlier, he'd noticed two men watching him. Those same two men were watching him now, and a ping of ice slithered across his heart. As soon as they noticed that he saw them, they darted around the side of the building.

"Hold that thought." Barrett released Audra and took off after them. He wove his way through the crowd of people, searching for the two men, but in mere seconds, he realized they were long gone. Anger and a finger of fear needled into him.

Deep in his gut, he felt something was wrong about those two. That was not random although he sincerely hoped he was wrong. Wrong like that time in Fort Worth when he was sure there were guys following him, and they were just trying to find the coffeeshop. No, Barrett knew that his nerves sometimes led him in directions logic would never go.

Feeling like an idiot and wondering how he would explain, he hurried back to Audra.

She didn't exactly look calm or carefree. "Is everything okay?"

"Fine." Barrett knew to make it stick, he should look at her. So why did that feel so impossible?

"Do you always take off running when something's fine?"

"Point taken." He glanced over his shoulder. "Listen, I need to make a quick call. Stay put, okay?"

Her gaze drilled into the side of his face. "You're being all mysterious again."

There was no way he was going to tell her that he thought he saw someone watching them. But he did need to tell Andy. "Most women love a man of mystery." He tried to make light of things so she wouldn't ask any more questions.

"Not this woman. What's going on, Barrett?"

Then he did look into her eyes, and even he didn't like the distrust swimming there. "Audra, can you please just trust me when I say it's something I can't share?"

Her eyes searched his face. "I'll try."

He smiled as a small semblance of relief trickled through him.

"But," she held up her hand.

His relief was short lived.

"I'm not saying that I'll be successful. I only said I'll try."

"That's all I ask, Baby." He kissed her cheek. "I'll be right over there. Promise you'll stay put."

She frowned but nodded.

Barrett walked several yards away from her, making sure he could keep her in his line of sight while he punched in Andy's number.

On the third ring, Andy answered. "Hey, buddy, what's up?"

"Hey, Andy. Listen, I have to make this quick. I hope I'm not overreacting here, but there are two men following me around. I noticed them earlier today, and I didn't think much about it, but just now when I saw them again, as soon as they noticed me watching them, they took off. I tried to find them, but it's like they vanished. I don't like it, Andy. You don't think it's those two men who killed my wife and parents, do you?"

"How would they know where you are? Besides you don't look the same, remember?"

"I still have some of my old features."

"You think enough of them for these men to recognize you?"

"They knew everything about my family. Where we went, what we did, who we were with. So, I wouldn't put it past them to have memorized every line on my face." He knew he was probably overreacting, but nonetheless he had to use caution.

"You still haven't answered my question. How would they know where you're at?"

"Because that incident at the derby was plastered all over the news, remember?"

"Yeah." And now Andy didn't sound so sure. "How'd that happen anyway?"

"I have no clue." Putting his hand up to the top of his head, Barrett tried to think that moment through. It wasn't working any better than it ever had. "I don't remember seeing any cameras that day." With great effort because he hated the memory, Barrett turned his thoughts back to the day his derby slammed into Audra. He remembered looking up, but he'd been so concerned about Audra and the little girl, he didn't see much. A shadow passed through his mind.

A shadow of a man.

Taking pictures of the races.

Of the cars.

Of the event.

Of Audra.

Of him. "Oh man," There it was lodged into his memory. "Why didn't I cover my face?"

"Don't overreact, Barrett. It could be your imagination working overtime too. Hearing about the two men, then finding out your face was on the news, and now seeing two men. It could all be a coincidence."

"Or not," Barrett interjected, certain that it wasn't his imagination working overtime.

"Or not," Andy agreed. "Listen, hang tight. I'll call the agency and have them send a couple of men to keep an eye on you and Audra."

"I'd sure feel better, if you did."

"I'll do it now. Talk to you later. And, Barrett?"

"Yes?"

"If you see those men again, don't do anything stupid. Call me or tell the agents, and they can trail them. Promise me you'll do that."

"I promise I won't do anything stupid." That was all he could promise though.

"That's not the promise I was looking for."

"It's all I can give you for now."

Andy's heavy sigh came over the phone loud and clear.

He wanted to ease his friend's mind. "Don't worry, Andy. I'll be careful. You've trained me well, remember?"

"I remember. But I also don't want something to happen to you too."

Barrett's gaze bounced over to Audra. It wasn't his safety he was concerned about.

"Keep me informed. I'll call Winslet and Dowers now."

"Thanks."

"Any time. Luv ya, bro."

"Love you, too."

Barrett hung up and before heading back to Audra, he panned the area again. No sign of those two men. He had the feeling he'd be doing that a lot from now on.

His perusal started with Audra and ended with her. She was talking to a woman wearing a black leather mini skirt, a black leather vest with a yellow T shirt underneath it. The young woman had bright pink hair and tattoos all up and down her arms. Arms that were wildly moving as fast as her lips were.

Barrett immediately wondered who this woman was and how Audra knew her. With a determined purpose to find out, he strode up to Audra.

Pinky looked up at him and did a double take. "Whoa. So this is the new man, huh? No wonder you've been keeping him all to yourself. Hi, I'm Angela. You must be Barrett." She held up her fingerless gloved hand as if she expected him to kiss it.

He looked over at Audra.

She shrugged a shoulder as her lips twitched and her eyes twinkled.

Audra was no help. Fine. He raised the woman's hand to his lips and he went to kiss it, but discreetly put his thumb where his lips pressed, then he released Angie's hand. "It's a pleasure to meet you, Miss Angela." From his peripheral vision, he noticed Audra's mouth drop open and her eyebrows rise. He hid his grin.

He stepped over to Audra's side.

"Please, call me, Angie. All my friends do." She batted her heavily mascaraed eyelashes at him.

Barrett resisted the urge to roll his eyes, instead he smiled. "Angie it is."

He gazed down at Audra, and without moving his head, his eyes darted toward Angie. Barrett hoped Audra latched on to his silent question.

"Angie works for me." So, Audra had caught on, but her answer pert near shocked the boots right off of his feet.

His face must have registered his shock because Audra added, "Angela is on her way to a masquerade ball with her boyfriend. After the mud bog races, that is."

"Oh." Was all Barrett could come up with for a response. He was still processing through the initial shock of thinking the woman worked for Audra - looking like that - when Audra's salon was obviously a very upscale establishment.

A tall, lanky man sporting a black leather vest, black leather chaps with fringe, around his skinny goiter neck a spiked choker that resembled a dog collar Barrett had once seen at a major pet store chain, and square-toed boots with metal buckles across the tops of them, stepped up alongside Angie. "Are you ready, my darling? We must be on our way or we shall be late for Mother's party. And you know how angry Mother gets when we are late. You did promise me, Angela Darling, that you would come if I attended your little race event thing." His comment was accompanied with a brush off wave of his hand taking in the circumference of the place.

Barrett mentally shook his head. He didn't expect such formality out of the man who looked like someone on the front cover of a bad-boy, biker gang magazine, minus the stocky build. Barrett couldn't help himself. He had to ask. "Who did your tattoos?"

The man looked at him and eyed him up and down with very little appreciation for what he saw. "And who, sir, are you, may I inquire?"

"Yes, you may. Name's Barrett. Barrett Camden." He extended his hand toward the man.

"I am Bradford Farlington the sixth." He looked at Barrett as if Barrett should know who he was, but the name didn't ring any bells.

"Nice to meet you." When they shook hands, Barrett felt as if he'd just shaken hands with a frail woman instead of a man in his mid-twenties.

"In response to your question, sir, these are henna tattoos. Mother would kill me if they were real. My lovely Angela here, hers are henna as well. And now, if you will excuse us, we must take our leave. Come along, Darling."

Bradford looped his arm through Angie's and turned to leave. Angie looked over her shoulder and said, "It was nice meeting you, Barrett." With a wave, they were gone.

"Now that's the weirdest couple I've ever met," he uttered under his breath.

"I heard that."

Not that he cared that she had, but... "How could you with all the trucks firing up around here?"

Squinting up at him, Audra raised her eyebrows. "I have great hearing. And they say your ears are tuned to the things you love." Her lips shifted into a smile.

The ramification of her words went all the way through his soul, landing firmly and tenderly into his heart where he would later bring them up and hug them to himself. He returned her smile, then asked, "So, who was that man?"

"The Farlingtons are one of the wealthiest families in West Virginia. Angie says Mr. Farlington started out by purchasing a small mom and pop grocery store. They built it up and sold it for a nice profit. They kept buying up companies that were going under and turned them all around until they made a huge profit. And now he's a multi-billionaire."

"That explains the formality."

"I've only been around him a few times, but for someone so young, he sure is a stuffed shirt. He needs to loosen up a little. Angie's trying to get him to, but as you can see, it isn't working very well. *Mother* would not approve." She mimicked Bradford's regal tone.

They laughed.

"Shame on me. That wasn't very nice. To be honest though, I don't know how Angie does it. I could never be with someone like that. Someone so stuffy and pompous. I like a man who knows how to have fun."

He reached around her and took her by the waist. "I like to have fun."

"I know. And that's one of the things I love about you." She wrapped her arms around his neck and raised her chin.

Barrett was more than happy to comply with her silent request. He kissed her, enjoying the soft feel of her lips under his. Hopefully, he'd get to do this the rest of his life. Only time would tell.

Chapter Seventeen

A udra's four o'clock alarm went off way too early. With it still dark outside, she wanted to ignore the blaring thing and go back to sleep, but after not working most of the week before, she had a backed up schedule this week.

She shut the alarm off and stretched her legs against the crisp cotton sheets, almost knocking Louey to the floor when she did. "Sorry, Louey." She picked up her dog, kissed him on top of the head before placing her feet on her fuzzy pink rug and heading to the shower. Even though she was tired, she couldn't wait to get to work. Today she'd go in early to try and catch up on some paperwork before her first clients showed up. Audra smiled. Ingrid and Elsa were her first appointments of the day. In the short time she'd known them, she'd grown to love those two caring, eccentric women.

She slipped her soft pink dress on. The one that had a single stem with a bunch of fuchsia and lavender bell shaped flowers hanging from it down the left front side. She strapped her feet into her sandals and headed downstairs where she fed and watered Louey, grabbed a quick bite to eat, and headed out to her car.

On the way to work, she sang along with an upbeat contemporary worship song. By the time she walked up to the door, her spirit was soaring. Beautiful day. Going to work. Being in love.

It was still dark out when she pulled the key from her purse. As she extended her arm to insert the key in the lock, the hair on the back of her neck stood. She felt as though she were being watched, which was silly because no one else was even around this early.

Still, she turned slowly and panned the area. A man dressed in all black wearing a baseball cap way down over his eyes ran and hopped into a black car parked up the block a ways. Within seconds, the car slowly came up the street with its headlights off.

Audra quickly unlocked her door and hurried into her shop, bolting the door behind her. She discreetly peered through the slat in the small side window blind.

The window in the car went down. An arm covered in black tossed something at her shop.

Glass shattered.

Alarms blared.

Audra screamed.

Tires squealed.

Audra watched as the car tore down the street, its lights not coming on until it was almost out of sight.

Her hands were quaking as she yanked her cell phone out of her purse and tapped out 911. Still shaking like a leaf in the wind, she told the operator what had just happened. The operator told her to stay on the line. She said she would and fought with her heart to stop hammering as her gaze went over to the thing now lying in the middle of the floor.

A police car drove up in front of her salon, and a tall, broad shouldered officer in a blue uniform with a badge came to her door. Quickly she told the operator the police were here and hung up the phone. Within seconds she had the door unlocked. "I'm so glad you're here." Audra glanced at his nametag, "Officer Tallis." She quickly explained what happened, stepping outside to point out where she had seen everything.

"Did you get a plate number?" His blue eyes were penetrating and intimidating but comforting at the same time.

"No. It was too dark." She described the car and told them what direction it had headed.

Officer Tallis called it in.

They stepped inside and Audra pointed out the thing on the floor, and that's when she noticed it had a note wrapped around it, held on by a rubber band. She leaned over to pick it up.

"Don't touch that." Officer Tallis's authoritative voice stopped her. "It's evidence."

He pulled a pair of plastic gloves out of his pocket and put them on his large hands before he picked up the rock. He removed the rubber band from around it and carefully unfolded the note.

"What does it say?" Audra asked, her eyes never leaving the note.

He held the piece of paper in front of her so she could read it.

Audra read the words out loud, "I'm watching you." She turned her eyes up at the policeman.

"Do you know who might have done this, Ma'am?"

Audra shook her head as her eyes went wide with fear. Her brain spun with possibilities, but she x'd them off as soon as they came up. "No."

"Do you have any enemies?"

"No. None that I'm aware of."

He continued asking her questions. When he finished his report, he asked, "Is there someone you can call to stay with you or to help you board up this window?"

"Yes. I'll call them now." Audra grabbed her cell. She thought about calling Barrett, but he lived too far away. Erik was closer. So she called Erik instead.

"Audra, is everything okay?" Erik asked, his voice sounded rather groggy.

She knew why he asked because it was only 5:15, and she never called them early. The only reason she did this time was because right now she needed the security that a man offered. She wanted the man to be Barrett, but she also had to be practical. "No, I'm not okay." It was crazy how long a body could keep shaking when it was rattled like that. "Someone threw a rock through my salon's window."

"What?" The grogginess from seconds ago was nowhere in his voice now.

"I'll explain later," she said as the shakiness returned with a vengeance, "but right now I was wondering if you could come down here to my salon and bring something to board my window up with."

"I'll be right there. You're not alone are you?"

"No, the police officer's with me."

"Let me talk to him."

"He wants to talk to you." Audra handed her cellphone to Officer Tallis.

"This is Officer Tallis. Yes, I'll stay until you get here. Yes, she's fine. Will do." He handed the phone back to her.

"I'm on my way out the door." The words rushed out of Erik.

"Thank you." Those two words didn't do her gratitude any justice whatsoever. Audra hung up, and her mind immediately zipped to Barrett and how she wished he was here with her right now. Nibbling on her lip, she debated about whether or not she should call him. She really wanted to, but with a heavy sigh, she finally decided against it. It was just too early to call him. And honestly, she didn't want him to worry about her, which, of course, he would.

Twenty-five minutes later, Erik pulled his Chevy truck up in front of her salon.

Before he even had the engine even shut off, Olivia hopped out of the truck and ran toward Audra. Fear and worry cascaded over her face. "Are you okay?" Olivia pulled her into a quick hug before scanning Audra from head to toe.

"I'm fine. Can't say the same for my window though." Audra smiled, hoping to ease some of the worry from Livvy. Now that her friends were here, it was much easier to be brave.

"This isn't funny." Olivia frowned with worry.

The sigh slid out of her. "I know it's not, Liv. I was just trying to not make you more upset."

"Well, it didn't work. Who would do such a thing?" Olivia looked at the shattered glass all over the floor.

"I don't know." Audra shook her head, her attention drifting to Erik and Officer Tallis.

The two men were outside on the sidewalk in deep conversation. Minutes later, they both strode toward her and Olivia.

Officer Tallis pulled a card out of his pocket and handed it to Audra. "If you remember anything else or need me for anything, here's my information. Don't hesitate to call." In his hand was the clear bag with the rock and note in it. Officer Tallis glanced around the shop one more time before his attention came back to Audra. Noted concern flitted across his face, but he immediately masked it.

Still, Audra saw it nonetheless. "Thank you, Officer Tallis." She took his card and slipped it into the pocket of her dress.

The instant the police car drove away, Olivia asked, "What did the note say?"

"It said 'I'm watching you'."

Olivia frowned and shook her head. "Who would do something like this?" That was the second time she'd been asked that question.

Audra shrugged and answered the question again. "I have no idea, and I have no time to figure it out now. I've got to get this mess cleaned up before my clients arrive."

"You're still going to work after all of this?" Olivia blinked, pointing to the broken window and to the mess.

"Yup. I don't run from fear, remember?"

"I hardly call using caution in this case running from fear," Olivia shot back, clearly perturbed with Audra.

"What am I supposed to do, Liv? Go into hiding somewhere? I have a business to run."

"And you have a life to protect."

Audra stepped over to her friend and put her arm around Olivia's shoulder. "I'll be careful, Liv. But I can't stop living because someone tells me they're watching me."

Olivia studied her for a moment. "I'm scared for you, Audra."

"Well, the truth is, I'm scared for me too, Liv. But I can't let that ruin my life or my business."

While Erik boarded up the window, Audra quickly made coffee, then grabbed a broom, a dustpan, and a trash can from the storage closet, and immediately got to work, picking up and sweeping up the shattered glass.

Olivia jumped right in and helped her.

As the sun peeked into the world, Audra dumped the last of the mess in the trashcan and hauled it out back. When she returned to the front, Ingrid and Elsa were chatting away with Erik and Olivia, waving their hands and arms frantically.

The instant they spotted her, they hurried toward her as fast as Ingrid's arthritic knees would allow her.

"Oh my, dear, are you okay?" Ingrid's brows crinkled, her concern evident.

"What happened?" Elsa inquired in that no nonsense tone of hers.

Audra didn't want to distress the ladies any further so rather then tell them that someone had thrown the rock through her window, she simply said that a rock flew through her window. They seemed to accept that.

"Why didn't you call us? We would have rescheduled our appointments." Elsa didn't give Audra a chance to answer. Instead she took charge. "Come on. You need to sit down." Elsa pointed to a chair.

"What she needs is chocolate," Ingrid informed them.

"Ingrid, you think the solution to the world's problem is food. Especially chocolate."

"Isn't it?" Ingrid looked surprised, but her lips and eyes twinkled.

Audra smiled, biting back the giggle that rose at those two caring women's antics. "I'm fine. Really I am."

"That is not fine." Elsa pointed her wrinkled finger toward the boarded up window.

"No, but it will be. I'll call the glass man and have it repaired as soon as possible."

"I'll take care of it," Elsa stated.

"And I'll take care of the lettering," Ingrid added.

Before Audra had a chance to protest, Elsa and Ingrid had their cellphones out, and within seconds they were both deep into conversation.

Their words faded when the front door swung open and Angie rushed inside. "What happened?"

Audra looked at Olivia. "Liv, would you mind taking Ingrid and Elsa to the waiting room and get them a cup of coffee or tea?" Audra looked at Ingrid and Elsa who were now heading toward her. As soon as they reached her, she said to them, "I have a couple of things to take care of here before I cut and style your hair. Would y'all mind following my friend Olivia? She'll get you a cup of coffee or tea."

Elsa looked at Audra.

Both Elsa and Ingrid seemed uncertain as to what to do, so Audra sent them a reassuring nod.

"Ladies, if you will follow me." Olivia motioned toward the waiting area. Surprisingly they both started walking that direction.

"By the way, I'm Olivia. Olivia Cole."

Knowing they would be well taken care of, Audra turned to Angie and took her aside. Angie looked normal again, her hair was no longer pink and all the henna tattoos were gone. A simple light teal summer dress replaced the black leather costume. Keeping her voice down so that Elsa and Ingrid didn't by some strange chance overhear her, Audra told Angie, "Someone threw a rock through the window. I don't want our clients to know that. So please, just tell them that a rock hit the window."

"I wonder if it was those two men who were watching you last night. That one was sure glaring at you."

Audra frowned. "What two men?"

"The two men at the mud bog race. Both Bradley and I noticed them. I'm surprised you didn't."

Audra remembered Barrett suddenly taking off.

Had he seen those men and that's why he did?

She had to know.

Had to call him.

And now.

~♥*~*

"Hi, Sunshine, what's up?" Barrett loved seeing Audra's number pop up on his caller ID, and he couldn't wait to hear that sweet Southern drawl of hers.

"Morning. Listen, I need you to be honest with me. This is extremely important."

At the worried tone in her voice, Barrett set his coffee cup down on his breakfast nook counter. "What's up?"

"I need to know something. Last night when you took off all of a sudden, was it because you noticed two men watching me?"

Watching *her*? They weren't watching her, they were watching him. How did she know about them? "Why do you ask?"

"Just answer the question, Barrett, please?" Something about the nervous quiver in her voice dropped even more concern into him.

"Yes. I noticed two men watching *me*." He emphasized the word me, hoping she would catch that.

"Could you describe them?"

He already had, at least as much as he could anyway, to Andy. "Why?"

"Barrett!" Audra's frustration came through loud and clear.

"I think so."

"Good, well then would you please meet me at the police station around noon?"

Police station? He shoved his mahogany kitchen chair back and shot to his feet. "Audra, what's going on?"

"I'll explain everything when you get here. I've gotta go now. Ingrid and Elsa are here and they're waiting for me. See ya at noon." With those words, she hung up.

Barrett stared at his ended call. What was going on? Why were Elsa and Ingrid at Audra's shop so early in the morning? And why did Audra want him to meet her at the police station?

Barrett had no answers to any of those questions, but one thing was for certain, he wasn't going to wait around until noon to find out. Before he headed to Audra's shop though, he called Andy hoping he had some answers.

After his talk with Andy, the whole long drive to Audra's salon, Barrett prayed like he'd never prayed before.

Chapter Eighteen

Answering the same question over and over the past two hours was beginning to drain Audra. Every client that came to the salon wanted to know what had happened. She had instructed all of her hairdressers to tell them a rock had merely hit the window.

Ingrid and Elsa strolled out of her salon arm-in-arm with their heads held high, smiling. Their new haircuts and styled hairdo's looked great, which surprised Audra considering her mind was mostly on the rock and the note and wondering who was behind it.

The women said their goodbyes with the promise of seeing her again and the promise of following up on the men they had contracted to take care of her window.

Exhausted, Audra dropped into her office chair, her arms hanging limp at her sides. How she wished the day were already over. One thing she was grateful for was at least she didn't have the arduous chore of finding someone to fix her window. Later on in the afternoon, someone was coming to put the window in and to replace the lettering on the glass. Normally it took a couple of days to get someone out to do those things, but with one phone call from Ingrid and one from Elsa, the whole thing would be taken care of in less than eight hours.

"Thank You, Lord, for Elsa and Ingrid. They are two of the sweetest people I have ever met. Thank You for placing them in my life. And please, bless both of them in a special way. Amen." Audra laid her head back and closed her eyes.

"Audra."

Her eyes darted open, and she bolted up straight in her chair.

Blinking, she looked toward her office door.

There stood Barrett, watching her, and looking as if he'd aged overnight.

She glanced at the neon scissor clock next to him on the wall. "Barrett? You're early."

"I couldn't wait." He walked around her desk and stood next to her, piercing her with his eyes. "What's going on? Why is your window boarded up? And why didn't you call me?"

"Close the door and I'll tell ya."

Shaken by the fear lacing her eyes, Barrett went over and closed the door. Coming back, he settled one hip on the corner of Audra's desk, leaving his leg dangling.

He listened as Audra explained about the car, the rock through the window, and the note.

His heart sank lower and lower with each detail she related to him. All of it was because of him. He owed it to her to tell her everything. After all, she had trusted him when he'd asked her to, and now he needed to trust her. It was only right. But it wouldn't be easy. Still it needed to be done. "Look, Audra. I have to tell you something. But before I do, I'm going to ask you to promise me something."

She looked skeptical but nodded anyway.

He glanced out her office window into the salon and waiting area. The place was filled with customers, and while they weren't within hearing distance of Audra's office, Barrett didn't feel comfortable talking to her here just in case for some reason or another someone overheard him. "Let's go someplace where we can be alone."

"We're alone here."

"I don't want anyone overhearing what I'm about to tell you. It's important." It was a risk trusting her. But after what she'd just told him, what other choice did he have? Because of him, her life was in danger.

"Okay."

Barrett stepped to the side so she could go first, but he shadowed her every movement from her office out to his car.

While he opened Audra's door and waited for her to be seated, he caught sight of the agents following both him and Audra. Having them around helped ease his mind. A little bit at least.

As he walked around to his side of the car, he prayed for God to help him tell her what happened and for her to be understanding.

Making sure the agents followed, he drove to a nearby park and parked in a secluded place. The agents weren't far away, but the world felt a million miles from the spot.

He shut the engine off and shifted in his seat toward her. His gut churned, but he had to do it.

He had to protect her even at the risk of his identity being exposed.

Audra watched the struggle skitter across Barrett's face. She reached over and took his hand. "Barrett, you can trust me. Whatever you tell me will stay between us. You have my word on that."

His chest expanded, and he nodded. "I know. You trusted me, and now I need to trust you. You are the only person besides Andy and a few of Andy's secret agent friends that know what I'm about to tell you. I need you to promise me, that even if you hate me afterwards, you won't tell anyone what I'm about to tell you. It's extremely important. Can you do that?"

"I told you, you have my word." Breathing was scarce at the moment. Was this what she'd been waiting for? For him to reveal his past secrets to her? If so, no matter what he revealed, she wouldn't betray his confidence. She even made up her mind that no matter what he revealed, she would love him. She hoped.

Barrett stared out the window with a faraway look on his face. "I'm not even sure where to begin."

"At the beginning," Audra spoke softly.

~♥*~*

Though his gaze was out the window, Barrett saw nothing but the shadows of his past. He struggled to dredge up the words he needed to say in some order that made sense. It had been years since he had talked fully about or even let himself think fully about that night.

That night seven years ago that had changed everything.

God, help me here. And help Audra to understand why I've done the things I've done. Father, help her to understand why I have to say goodbye. Give me the strength and the grace to do it. For her sake. He pulled in a long breath and slowly blew it out. "I wasn't born Barrett Camden." There, he'd said it.

"Huh? What does that mean?"

He looked over at her.

A confused frown stretched across her forehead.

"I was born Kelly Hudson."

"You had your name changed?" Her frown deepened.

"Yes. I had to," he paused and willed a massive dose of courage to himself before continuing. "Do you know who Gage Lincoln is?"

Her answer was immediate. "I sure do. He's that smoking hot actor who starred in several motorcycle and comedy romance movies."

He smiled at her description.

"Why?" Audra frowned, weaving her head back and forth. "What's he got to do with any of this?"

"Everything." He released a weighty breath. "Audra, I'm Gage Lincoln."

Shaking her head, she closed her eyes for a split second before looking over at him. "Ha ha. Very funny.

Quit joking around and tell me what was so important that you made me promise not to tell anyone about."

"I just did."

Audra eyed him skeptically.

Barrett clamped his lips together and stared hard at her, not blinking even once, making sure she understood just how serious he was.

Her mouth fell open.

She blinked once.

Twice.

Three times before she finally spoke. "You're—?"

"I'm Gage Lincoln." He finished her sentence for her.

The skepticism returned. "No-o-o." She dragged out. "You can't be him. You don't look anything like him. Gage's eyes were sky blue, and he had beautiful blue-black hair, like Rhett Butler's in *Gone With The Wind*. Your eyes are hazel, and your hair is sandy blond."

"I was born with blond hair and hazel eyes, Audra."

She pressed her eyelids together and shook her head. "Okay. Wait, I'm confused."

"I can see that."

Audra opened her eyes, lines creased her forehead as she stared at him as if searching for the truth in his eyes.

"Before I started acting, my agent thought I'd get further if I dyed my hair black and wore blue contacts. So, I did. Before I knew it, I had more offers than I knew what to do with, and I was on my way to stardom."

Audra shook her head, confusion dancing across her beautiful face. "But, but you don't look like him."

"You said that. And you're right, I don't. It's a long story, Audra."

She crossed her arms over her chest. "Well, I've got the rest of the day."

Considering what he'd just told her, Barrett was surprised that was all she'd done and at how calm she really was. He expected her to fly off the handle, to yell or something. Anything but this.

Was this the calm before the storm?

Or had the truth not quite hit her or sunk in yet?

It would, of that he was certain. Then what would she do?

"You're stalling." She removed her seatbelt, twisted sideways in her seat, and crossed her arms over her chest again. "Now spill."

He removed his seatbelt and shifted in his seat to face her. "Do you ever watch the news or read magazines?"

"No, can't stand the stuff personally."

"Well, did you ever hear about Gage Lincoln's wife, *my* wife—"

"Your... your wi—wife?" She uncrossed her arms and eyed him as if he were some sort of evil monster or something. "You're—you're married?" Horrified was the only way to describe the look on her face.

"No, Audra, I'm not married." He swallowed the lump of emotion clogging his throat. "My wife was murdered seven years ago and I never remarried." He closed his eyes against the gruesome memory that was certain to come. It always did. When he opened his eyes, Audra was staring at him. But instead of horror, he saw only confusion and compassion. He was right in trusting her with his deepest secrets.

"Murdered? Your wife was murdered?" Sympathy brushed through her words.

Barrett closed his eyes and nodded. "Along with my parents and unborn child."

"Oh, Barrett, no. I'm so sorry." She moved closer to him and took his hand in hers.

"It was my fault, Audra." The pain of admission clogged his throat again.

"How could their deaths be your fault?"

He cleared his throat, forcing out the words. "The day they were murdered, I had just gotten back from being on location. The crew wanted to celebrate by going and having a few drinks. When I called Felicia to tell her I'd be late, she was disappointed. Said she missed me and that she had made reservations for the four of us to celebrate the completion of my newest film.

"I asked if she could change the reservation to eight. She said she'd try. I knew she was disappointed that I wasn't coming home right away, but I had already promised the crew I'd go. I figured I'd just go and have a drink with them and then go home. Just one drink." He rubbed the back of his head. "One drink led to two, then three and before I knew it, it was seven-thirty, and I still had to call a cab to take me home which was about twenty minutes away.

"I called my wife to tell her the cab was on its way, but she never answered. I figured she was upset with me.

I didn't blame her. I kept calling. I left several messages telling her how sorry I was and that I loved her and to please forgive me for being late and for upsetting her. I hated that. Especially after the autopsy showed that she was six weeks pregnant."

Audra gasped, and squeezed his hand, saying nothing more, for which he was grateful.

The pain of losing his child rolled over him like a tidal wave. His dream of becoming a father was there one moment, and gone in the next.

Dwelling on that fact now was just too painful for him, so he forced himself to blot it out and continue. He cleared his throat again. "When I got home, Felicia and my parents' vehicles were there. Inside the house, I searched for them and hollered for them. When they didn't answer I went around back and…" He closed his eyes, as the images of seeing his loved ones blindfolded, with their mouths, legs and hands duct taped, shot execution style slammed into his consciousness. Tears burned the back of his eyes. He struggled to keep them back because he knew once he let them go, he wouldn't be able to stop them.

He leaned back in the seat, putting his head back and fighting not to let the memories completely take his sanity. It took several minutes for him to swallow the bile that rose to the surface and to keep his insides from releasing their contents.

Audra gave his arm a gentle squeeze. "It's okay. You don't have to tell me."

Barrett looked over at her, thankful for her understanding way, and nodded. When his gut finally quit churning, he continued, "If I would have just taken them out like Felicia had wanted, all four of them would be alive today."

"You don't know that, Barrett." Audra's gentle voice washed over him. He wanted to reach out too, to let it soothe his soul like a healing balm. But he couldn't. The guilt of their deaths was too heavy. "You could have been killed right along with them."

Hadn't he thought that very same thing a million times over? And each time he did, it always came back to the same thing. He'd never know, and that truth haunted him still to this day. "That's something I'll never know. What I do know is how merciless the press and the paparazzi were. They hounded me and followed me everywhere I went. They were driving me crazy, literally.

Anger over how detestable they were crashed in on him. He pulled himself together, he had to finish what he'd started. "I craved peace and quiet. It had gotten so bad that at one point I wanted to die. And almost did. In a car accident."

"Were you trying to end your life?" Audra asked barely above a whisper, sadness wrapped around her voice.

"No." Barrett shook his head. "I'll be honest, I thought about it a time or two, but somehow I kept putting one foot in front of the other and kept going through the motions of living."

"You mentioned a car accident. What happened?" Audra asked.

270 | Debra Ullrick

"After months of them hounding me, the day I wrecked my car, I was trying to get away from the cameras. I was driving way too fast when I rounded a corner. I lost control and my car slammed into a concrete wall. I was trapped in the car and was in pretty bad shape. In fact, they told me later that I would have died if I hadn't been wearing my seatbelt.

"Andy was the first person on the scene. He talked with me through the mangled metal, assured me I wasn't alone, asked me if I knew Jesus." Barrett smiled at that particular memory, the only good one in the whole batch of evil ones. "I was in such bad shape, Andy was afraid I was going to die, so before anyone else arrived, he asked me if I knew the Lord.

"My parents and Felicia were Christians. They were always trying to convert me, but I wanted nothing to do with God. I was afraid he'd ask me to give up partying or my fame and fortune if I did.

"This time though, when I heard about Christ and his sacrifice on the cross for my sins—and by that time I was very aware of all the things I'd done wrong—those very words that used to drive me nuts now filled me with hope and peace. Which was something I desperately needed. Right there, in that mangled up car, I accepted Christ as my Lord and Savior.

"That's the last thing I remember before waking up in the hospital. When I did, Andy was there. He used his influence and contacts to secretly have me transported to a hospital where no one could find me.

"Because of the broken bones in my face, I underwent several reconstructive surgeries. The first time I saw myself in the mirror, I was shocked. It was me, yet it didn't look anything like me. My hair had grown out. The black hair was gone. My contacts weren't in, so my eyes were there normal hazel color. Right then, I decided this was my chance for a new start in life.

"This was the one time I was actually glad for the press. They believed I had died in that crash and had been secretly buried. Since the only family I had was gone, I let them believe that so they'd finally leave me alone, and so that I'd finally have some peace. I saw the whole thing as my chance to leave Hollywood. To get away from the fame I'd worked so hard to gain." He gave a disgusted snort. "Ironic how I had gotten exactly what I'd always wanted, always dreamed of, and when I did, it wasn't anything like I had made it out to be. Oh sure, I enjoyed the fame and the fortune, all the glitz and glamour of Hollywood. Until that fame cost me my loved ones and very nearly myself.

"After that, none of it mattered anymore. That old saying about be careful what you wish for is so true. Sometimes what you wish for isn't always all it's cracked up to be. And it sure isn't always what's best for you.

"So that's why as hard as this is for me, for your sake, Audra, I have to say goodbye to you." Even though his heart was shattering into a million pieces, he had no choice but to let her go. He loved her too much to try to keep her, knowing the danger she would be in forever if he did.

"What do you mean you have to say goodbye?" She frowned. "Are you saying *I'm* not what's best for you?" The confusion and fear were back on her face.

This wasn't coming out right. "No, I'm saying *I'm* not what's best for you."

"I don't understand."

He could see that, and he wasn't quite sure how to make her understand, but he'd do the best he could. "Look what happened to your salon. The men responsible for my loved ones deaths have obviously found me."

"How could they have found you?"

"My face was plastered all over the national news last week."

"You know what, Barrett? I seriously doubt that whoever did this to my salon had anything to do with your family. I was a huge fan of yours, and I didn't recognize you at all. You really think the killers will figure out you're still alive and come looking for you because of one television news report?"

When she said it like that, it sounded ridiculous. But still… "I don't know. But what I do know is you didn't have anything happen like this before we met, right?"

Even she couldn't deny that even though she clearly wanted to.

"True. But that doesn't prove a thing. Listen, Barrett, I can't imagine how much you've struggled, even I'm having a hard time wrapping my mind around what's happened to you and who you really are. I don't think my mind has quite caught up to any of those facts yet. But none of those things, while shocking, has changed how I feel about you. I love you, Barrett. And nothing will change that. Not you leaving or anything else."

She gazed up at him. "Barrett, please trust me when I say, I know what fear can do. I've seen it paralyze people. Myself included. Especially when it came to trusting a man again. But, I also know that if you don't get past this, then there really can't be a future for us. Not because of me backing away but because of you throwing away what we have together."

She took a slow and calming breath. "Having said that, I'm also not willing to let you go or throw it away. As you very well know, I'm not someone who backs down from a challenge or runs when the going gets tough. And just to clarify, I am not in this relationship for the challenge. I'm in it because I love you. So just know, I'm not giving up on you, and I'm not giving up on us. We're gonna figure out a way to get you through this fear. It tears me up seeing the fear and pain in your eyes. But I know together we can get through this if you'll trust me."

Though her words touched him deeply, he knew she didn't completely understand the risk involved. He had to make her see, make her understand. Somehow, even though it killed him to do so. "Don't you get it, Audra? I can't allow you to take that risk." With his eyes, Barrett begged her to understand.

But her eyes were placid and filled with love. "Love is always a risk no matter what the circumstances are. I know this is hard for you. All I'm asking is that you think about what I've said. And in the meantime, I'll figure out a way to talk you into it." The sound of an alarm cut through her words, and she jumped. Audra grabbed her phone and pushed a button.

Barrett's heart hammered like he'd been shot. "What was that?"

"With all that's gone on this morning, I didn't want to forget my appointment with the police, so I set my phone alarm so I'd get there on time."

"You on time?" He tried bantering, though not feeling it, but giving it just the same.

"Ha Ha. Very funny. Remind me to laugh. Hang on a sec, I need to call the police station and reschedule. This is more important right now."

"Wait, don't do that. You're right, this is important, but we need to keep that appointment so that we can try and catch those men."

She eyed him for several seconds as if debating what to do before she finally nodded. "We will continue this, Barrett," she said firmly.

"You're right, we will continue this." His voice sounded bland and emotionless even to his own ears, but his emotions were raging inside him like a tsunami out to destroy everything in its path.

Numbly, he started the car and drove toward the police station. Her knowing about his past had done little to remove the weight he'd been carrying like he had thought it would. The only thing that helped a little was that she hadn't bolted. Then again, perhaps it would have been better if she had. It would have made saying goodbye easier, right? He had no answer to that question. Regardless of everything wonderful she'd said about staying with him and trying to figure out a way to talk him into staying together, he knew what had to be done.

"I want you to remember one thing, Barrett." Her small voice filled the silence in the deafening cab.

"What's that?"

"You promised to go parasailing with me."

What? Parasailing? Was she joking? Parasailing was the last thing on his mind at the moment. Saying goodbye was first. "Audra…"

"No. Don't 'Audra' me, Barrett. You promised."

He couldn't argue, so he didn't even though if she kept demanding, he would have to sooner or later.

At the police station, while they waited for Andy to arrive, Barrett gave the sketch artist all the details he could remember about the men from the mud bogging incident. When the woman finished, she turned one of the pictures around and showed him.

"Does this look like him?" the brunette with the questioning brown eyes asked.

"It looks almost identical to the man I saw." Barrett was amazed at just how much the drawing did resemble the man he'd noticed watching him. It gave him the creeps and angered him at the same time, seeing that face and knowing that the man in the drawing might very well be one of his family's killers.

Working hard to remember every detail he could, he described the second man.

"How about this one?" The artist turned the sketch toward him.

Audra's gasp jolted him and yanked his attention from the drawing and onto her.

"What's wrong?" he asked, standing to his feet as concern fisted into him.

"That... that's Neil!" Audra pointed to the artist's sketch.

"Neil?" Barrett shook his head not quite understanding. "The married man you dated?"

She nodded, her eyes wide with shock as she swallowed. "That's him. That's Neil."

"Do you know that man, Audra?" Andy asked, stepping in behind her.

Audra stopped staring at the sketch and shifted her focus to Andy. "Uh-huh. I used to date him."

"Okay. Do you know why he would be following you?" Andy asked.

She looked positively stunned speechless as she kept staring at the drawing. "I don't know. We haven't seen each other in a long time."

"Barrett said 'the married man you dated'. You dated a married man?" There was no condemnation in Andy's voice, only a serious question looking for information.

"I didn't know he was married." Audra shook her head.

Andy gave a quick nod, and the look on his face said he believed her, which Barrett was glad for. "We'll bring him in for questioning." Andy turned to one of his police detectives, and the two of them discussed having Audra's ex-boyfriend brought in.

Suddenly the reality of the situation hit Barrett with all the force of a runaway train, and all strength fled his body. He searched for the closest chair and slinked onto it.

"Barrett, are you okay?" Audra laid her hand on his arm.

Though he felt numb, he masked the turmoil going on inside him. "Just need a minute by myself, all right?"

She stared down at him, finally nodded, and walked over to the vending machine. Not that she got anything or even looked like she saw the thing.

Barrett's mind processed what he'd just heard. The men he'd seen following him had nothing to do with him. They'd been following Audra. There was no relief in that fact, knowing that those two men were out to hurt her. There was also no relief in that fact that those two men weren't his family's killers. Killers that were still out there somewhere. And until they were caught, he couldn't rest, knowing they could hurt the woman he loved.

Even though it would kill him, for Audra's sake and despite her protests, he had to say goodbye. After he took her parasailing that was. After all, a promise was a promise, and he'd given her his word that he would. He would also take that time to memorize every inch of her face because it would be the last time he'd see it. It had to be. He had to leave knowing she was in danger. And yet, how could he leave her knowing that she was in danger? Either way he looked at the whole thing, it was a no-win situation. One he had no idea how to fix.

~♥*~*

Audra bounced her focus between Barrett and the vending machine. She knew a part of him was relieved that it wasn't his family's killers, and yet he probably wished they had been. Her heart ached for him. She still couldn't believe he was Gage Lincoln, the actor who she had crushed on for years. Only thing was, she didn't see him as Gage Lincoln, but as Barrett Camden, the man she'd fallen completely and hopeless in love with. She only hoped and prayed that Barrett would change his mind about them.

"Audra, we're ready." Andy's hand settled on her shoulder. "I'll get Barrett. Meet me over there." Andy pointed to what Audra assumed was an interrogation room.

The lines around Barrett's eyes were still there. She wanted to take the burden from him and then cast it on the Lord, but only Barrett himself could that. No one could do it for him.

Audra and Barrett stood outside the two-way mirror, listening while Andy and one of Charity's police detectives interrogated Neil.

The other thug, who the detectives identified as Eugene Santos, was in another room going through the same interrogation as Neil.

Andy strategically hounded Neil until finally Neil broke down and buried his face in his hands. "All right already. It was me who hired Santos." Neil looked up at Andy with pleading eyes. Eyes Audra had once loved gazing into, but that now turned her stomach. "I only wanted him to scare her. To torment her the same way I'm being tormented now."

"Why?" Andy's voice rang with authority.

Neil's face hardened. "Because of her, I lost my wife and children." Venomous anger spewed through his words. "If she would have denied having ever known me, let alone ever dating me, my wife and I would still be together."

Audra gazed up at Barrett. "Can you believe him? Blaming me for his cheating ways. I've heard enough." Audra spun on her heel and strode away from the interrogation room.

Barrett fell in step alongside her.

"I can't believe he blames me for his wife leaving him. I had no clue he was married. None whatsoever. But he sure did. That poor, poor woman." Audra shook her head. "My heart still goes out to her. And to Neil's children." Anger replaced her compassion, but it wasn't directed at Neil's wife and children, but at Neil himself. "What a sleaze ball. And to think, at one time, I really cared for the man. I must've been crazy, right?"

"No. You weren't. You're just too trusting."

Audra frowned. She had a feeling that Barrett's words had a double meaning behind them. She only hoped and prayed he wasn't still planning on saying goodbye. If he did, though, he'd have a fight on his hands. Of that, she was certain.

Chapter Nineteen

Audra tossed and turned all night. After Barrett had left for home the night before, she'd fretted about whether or not she'd see him again. He promised her he'd take her parasailing. She just hoped he kept that promise.

No longer able to stand not knowing, she decided to call him. She glanced at the clock. 6:03. It was too early to call him. Unable to sleep, she crawled out of bed and climbed into the shower. She shampooed her hair. When she finished rinsing it off, she stared at the suds swirling down the drain, wishing that the gigantic problem between Barrett and herself could be annihilated as easily as those suds were just now.

Several minutes later, dressed and ready, chores all finished, she once again looked at the clock. 6:45 Still too early to call Barrett. "That's it," she muttered to Louey who was lying on the sofa with his head resting on his paws.

He raised his head, looked up at her as if to say *yeah, what do you want,* then laid his head back on his paws and closed his eyes. Dogs had it made. They ate, laid around, barked once in a while, and slept. They didn't have to deal with all the complications of a love relationship between males and females.

Unlike humans.

This human in particular right now. "Ech," she groaned. "C'mon now, Audra. Get busy and do something. You've gotta get your mind off of Barrett." She rolled her eyes at the ludicrousness of that idea. "Good luck with that, Audra." Her words floated across the room on dead air as she stomped into the kitchen.

Audra cleaned her kitchen that was already spotless, dusted everything in her living room that had no dust, and organized a stack of hairstyle magazines that didn't need organizing. When she finished, she glanced at the clock and moaned. It was only 7:15. Even though her first client wasn't until eleven, she decided hanging around here would drive her crazy. So rather than call, she was going to drive over to Barrett's. By the time she got there, it would be close to eight. Surely he'd be dressed and up and around by then.

She grabbed her keys, locked her door, and made the drive to Barrett's that seemed to take three times longer today. All the way there, her insides jangled with nerves as one question after another flew through her brain.

What if he was gone?

How would she find him?

Did he still love her?

Did he ever love her?

Was he doing okay?

Did he regret telling her everything the day before?

Forty five minutes later, she pulled up to the gate. But, without a remote, it wouldn't open. So, she parked her car and walked until she found a tree she knew she could climb. Having climbed trees with her brother, she trekked her way up it, and dropped down inside Barrett's property.

As soon as her feet touched the ground, she took off toward the lane and followed it until she reached the clearing and his place came into view.

She let out a long breath of relief the instant she spotted his roadster in the drive. Barrett was still here. He hadn't left yet.

Everything was so quiet. No noises. Except for the birds singing their happy songs.

Audra wondered if Barrett was inside or if he was even awake yet. Maybe this hadn't been such a good idea after all. Should she turn around and leave?

Should she ring the doorbell?

Or what should she do?

Then she remembered Barrett telling her that sometimes he had breakfast in his butterfly garden. Would she find him there now?

Only one way to find out. She hurried around to the butterfly garden. There, she spotted him, sitting on a bench, with his face buried in his hands.

He looked so dejected, her heart broke. Slowly and quietly, she made her way toward him and sat down beside him on the marble bench, careful not to touch him or to startle him.

As if he sensed her presence, he slowly raised his head and looked at her. "Audra? What are you doing here?"

"I came to see you."

"What for?"

"You promised to take me parasailing, remember?" That sounded lame even to her, but she didn't know what else to say.

His gaze lowered to his hands and then drifted back up to hers. "I haven't forgotten."

She weaved her head back and forth like a slow pendulum. "I didn't come here about parasailing. I came because I was afraid you'd leave, and I'd never see you again. Barrett," she wrapped her hand around his and gazed up at him. "I don't wanna lose you." Tears snuck down her cheeks.

He reached up and brushed at the tears with his thumb. "I don't want to lose you either, Audra. I just don't see any way out of this though." He rose off the bench and stood with his back to her, his shoulders stooped forward, and his head hung.

In one fluid motion, Audra was behind him, placing her hand on his back.

His muscles tightened underneath her touch.

He took a step forward.

Her hand slid away and dropped to her side. She honored his silent wish by not touching him again. For now anyway.

Barrett looked around, then turned and faced her again, his gaze landing on her. "Do you know why I built this butterfly garden?"

Huh? What did that have to do with anything? "No. Can't say that I do."

A shield dropped over Barrett's face. He was here and yet he wasn't. That same faraway look he had the day he'd told her about his family was back. That's where he was now. Back in time with them.

Minute after minute passed in silence, broken only by the soft sound of Barrett's throaty voice. "Felicia loved butterflies. After we had visited one of those butterfly pavilion places, she wanted one. For her twenty-fifth birthday, I had one built for her. She was so happy with it." A smile so small that Audra almost didn't see it tampered with Barrett's lips.

"She loved spending time in it, taking care of it. She wouldn't even let me hire anyone to help her with the garden. She wanted to do it all. It took a lot of talking, but eventually she finally allowed me to help her. I enjoyed working alongside her.

"When I wasn't on location filming, we would go there and just sit and talk for long periods of time. It was so peaceful. It was the one place I could go to get away from the world. Away from the crazy pace of Hollywood, the paparazzi, the news media, the fans. Just life in general. When I first built this one, I used to come out here and talk with Felicia. Sometimes I thought I could even see her face, smell her perfume, hear her voice. Sounds crazy, I know."

"Doesn't sound crazy at all," Audra said quietly. In fact, it sounded beautiful, poetic even. Anyone who spent time in this tranquil garden would understand.

"Now, I come here to meet with God. He seems closest to me here."

"I can see why."

Barrett slowly turned and gazed down at her. A blink and he was back from the indelible black hole of his past. "Audra, I'm so torn. I don't know what to do. I love you so much it hurts. How can I leave you? And yet how can I stay?" He closed his eyes as pain etched itself over every inch of his face.

A step and Audra closed the gap, pressing her head into his chest and wrapping her arms around him. His strong arms immediately went around her.

He held her tight.

Drops of moisture landed on top of her head.

She leaned her head back but only far enough until she could see his face. Her heart wept at what she saw there.

Tears streaked down Barrett's face, and he didn't even try to hide them.

God, help this man. Heal him. He needs You, Lord.

In the next instant, his lips came down hard on hers, not hard in a painful way, but fast and as if he might never kiss her again.

She kissed him back, willing her love for him to flow into him, praying it would be enough, yet knowing it wasn't.

All of a sudden, he set her away from him and took two steps back. "Audra, please go. I need time to pray and to think, and I can't do it with you here. I'm sorry."

"I don't wanna leave you." How could she, knowing he was hurting?

"I know. I don't want you to either, but please understand I need some time alone."

She studied his face, memorizing every line, every crease, every inch of his handsome face, firmly embedding every feature of it into her heart where it would remain forever regardless of his decision. When she finished, she asked one final favor of him, "Promise me you won't leave."

"I promise I won't leave without saying goodbye."

"No!" That wasn't good enough. She needed more. She had to have more. "Promise me you won't leave. Period."

With sad eyes, he shook his head. "I can't do that."

Indignation replaced her worry. The man had walked into her life and swept her off her feet, knowing that he might never be able to stay. He owed her. Big time. And she wasn't letting him get away without a fight. She crossed her arms over her chest. "Then I'm not leaving."

She stared up at him hard, daring him to say no to her.

He twisted his mouth in annoyance. "You're incorrigible."

"That I am."

"Well, at least we agree on one thing." His lips curled into a small smile.

"Two things." She tilted her head and sent him a smirk. "We love each other."

His smile fell. "That's what makes this whole thing impossible. I won't leave until I've prayed this whole thing through. That much I can promise you. Anything after that…"

Seeing his mind was made up, she had no choice at the moment but to leave. She hated to, but she also knew it was what he wanted. This whole thing wasn't just about her. It was about Barrett too. She needed to be considerate of his feelings and his desires as well. So, without pretense, she reached up and kissed his cheek. "Okay, then. I'll be here, waiting. And praying. I love you, Barrett." With those words she turned and left, not once looking back.

~♥*~*

"Wait!" Barrett darted after her.

She turned and faced him.

Seeing the hope on her face and knowing why it was there, he hated having to dash it. "How did you get here?"

It was just as he suspected. The hope slipped away with his question.

"I walked."

"All this way?"

"No silly, I drove my car to the end of your drive until I found a tree I could climb to get over your fence."

"You climbed a tree?" He eyed her up and down.

"Yup."

That made him nervous. After all, if she was able to climb a tree and get onto his property then anyone could as well. He made a mental note to check into that and rectify the problem.

"I used to climb them all the time with my brother Josh. We used to have races to see who could go the highest and the fastest."

"Let me guess." He rubbed his chin. "You won, right?"

She smiled.

"You're one of a kind, Audra Darron." He couldn't help but smile at her.

"Yup, I sure am. And don't you forget it."

He knew what she was saying. As if he could ever forget her. Even if he left, he'd never forget her. Stifling his sigh of hopelessness, and knowing there was no way he'd let her walk back to her car alone, he said, "I'll take you to your car."

"Normally, I'd say no, that I'd walk. But I do have several clients coming in, so I'll take you up on that offer."

They hopped in his roadster, and he drove her to her car still parked at the gate.

As he watched her pull away with a wave of her hand out the window, his heart grieved, knowing he very well might have to say goodbye to her forever.

He turned his vehicle around and drove back up the lane.

Close to the house, a raccoon darted out in front of him. He slammed on his brake, and something hard hit the back of his boot.

He twisted and peered down at the floorboard. His stomach took a hard hit the second he saw the rock with a note wrapped around it.

One thing he'd learned from Andy was never to touch evidence with your bare hands.

Knowing he had gloves in his butterfly garden, he parked there, jogged to it and grabbed a pair. When he opened the note, the sucker punch to his gut hit even harder. The note had the same cutout, glued on magazine letters, just like the ones he received several months prior to his family's murders.

He dropped to a nearby bench and shook his head. If only he'd taken those notes more seriously back then. Sure, he'd told the police, but they said it was just some kids pulling pranks. How they came up with that conclusion, he had no idea other than they said several others in the neighborhood had gotten them too.

Barrett yanked out his cell phone and dialed Andy.

"What's up, buddy?"

"I need to see you. Can you come out here right away?"

"What's going on?" The concern flooded into Andy's voice.

"I'll tell you everything when you get here. How soon can you come?"

"I can be there within the hour. Is the gate code the same?"

Barrett changed it often and Andy knew that. He gave him the new code.

Knowing he'd go crazy while waiting for Andy to arrive, he got busy pruning the plants, praying the whole time.

"I knew I'd find you out here." Andy strode over to him. "What is it? What has you so riled?"

Barrett set down his pruning shears and handed the note to Andy.

"So that's what it said?" Andy scrubbed his chin with his fingers.

"What do you mean?" Barrett was completely baffled by Andy's comment and by his lack of concern.

"That nut Neil hired said he dropped a note in your car too."

"I'm confused."

"That Neil guy said he told Eugene to give you a note too. He wanted to throw you two off track, so hers was handwritten and yours was this." Andy held the note up.

Barrett wasn't convinced that this was the same note. "Don't you find it strange that it's identical to ones back in California?"

"Normally, yeah, I would. But not with that Neil character's confession." Andy frowned, then his eyebrows rose. "Wait. You thought this note was from your family's killers? Oh man, Barrett, no wonder you're so upset. I should have told you, but I had no clue how long you'd stayed outside that window listening. I thought you heard everything."

"Why didn't you ask me for the note after he mentioned it?"

"Because we didn't need it. He signed a confession admitting his guilt."

Barrett ran his hand over the back of his head. "Is this ever going to end?"

"I just told you, he confessed."

"Not that."

The radio on the front shoulder of Andy's uniform squawked. He reached over and turned the volume nob down. "You were saying."

"This thing with my family. I figured since no one recognized me after all those years that maybe I was free to live and love again. Then I met Audra. I love her, Andy."

"Like that's news." Andy smiled. "Anyone who's been around you two can see that."

"For all the good it does me." Barrett all but snorted.

"What's that supposed to mean?"

"It means, I have to say goodbye to yet another loved one." And it was tearing his insides up just thinking about it.

"Why?"

What did he mean why? Of all people, Andy should understand why and yet he looked genuinely confused. "As long as my family's killers are running loose, and I now know they are, I'll never feel like I can lead a normal life. Get married. Settle down. Have children." A butterfly landed on his arm, and he gently set it to flight.

"Why, Barrett?"

How could he make him understand? "Because, I'll always be looking over my shoulder wondering if they've found me and if they're going to hurt more of my loved ones."

"*They*, along with everyone else, believe you're dead," he said nonchalantly. "Your fear is unwarranted, buddy." Andy picked up a flower Barrett had cut off and pressed it under his nose.

Barrett wanted to grab onto that hope, but doubt crept in like it always did. "Is it? Remember Lonnie, the guy I raced motocross with. His wife said I reminded her of Gage Lincoln."

"What did you say to her?"

"I laughed it off and said, 'Isn't he that actor that died in a car crash or something?' She said no one really knew if he did or not. That scared me. That's when I quit motocross racing. I knew it was only a matter of time before someone recognized me."

"Does Audra know who you are?"

"She does now. I told her." He was still amazed at her response. He'd expected her to throw a fit or toss him out or something other than the understanding and the acceptance she offered.

"Did she know who Gage Lincoln was?"

Barrett smiled at the memory of when she found out. "Yes. She said she was one of my biggest fans."

"Hmmm. Interesting. She was one of your 'biggest fans'," Andy made quote marks with his fingers when he said the words *biggest fans*. "She's spent all this time with you and yet she never recognized you. That says something, buddy."

Barrett thought about it. He wanted to believe in the hope that he was a free man, but that niggling doubt that was always there residing in the back of his mind, spewed like a geyser. "I don't know what to think anymore, Andy." He raked his hand through his short hair and collapsed onto the edge of the large concrete planter. "I told Audra I was leaving."

"What?" All creases left Andy's forehead. "Why would you do that? She's the best thing that's happened to you since Felicia and your parents died. She's brought life back into you."

"I know. But I can't risk them finding me and hurting her too."

"Barrett," Andy hooked his large hand over Barrett's collarbone and gave it a firm squeeze. "You've got to let the past go."

"It's not that easy," Barrett snapped. Andy didn't understand. He couldn't. He'd never had his loved ones snatched away from him so mercilessly and so brutally.

"I know. I never said it was easy." Andy's voice was filled with compassion and understanding. "Life isn't easy. But you're giving those two men way too much power over you. You're letting them rule your life with fear."

Barrett hated hearing what Andy had just said, only because he knew it was the truth. A truth that drove a spike through his chest. "I don't know how to stop it. I've lived with fear and guilt for seven years now. I don't know how to not feel them."

"Don't you think it's time you said goodbye to them, instead of to Audra?"

"How, Andy? Tell me how?"

"Barrett, I don't know how, but I know the One Who does. I suggest you pray about this. Ask God what He would have you to do. Ask him to heal you. To set you free. And I wouldn't do anything rash or stupid like giving up Audra either. Let me tell you, love doesn't come around every day, and sometimes we've got to decide to love despite the risk. In fact, love is a risk— you risk getting hurt, you risk losing the other person, you risk loving them and them not loving you back..."

"Andy, this is not helping," Barrett said, barely getting levity he didn't feel into his voice.

Andy smiled. "Yeah, well, sometimes the truth isn't as easy as the fantasy. But in all of that, what I also know is that love is worth all the risks. It's worth putting your heart out there and being loved and loving because otherwise, you're not living, you're just existing and waiting to die."

"Boy, you are a bucketful of depressing today."

This time Andy laughed. "I'm really not trying to be. Look, Barrett, I know this isn't easy, and me telling you that it is isn't going to help anything. I can't say, 'Just move on' because you can't do that."

"But it's been seven years."

At that, Andy sat down on the planter beside his friend. "Yeah, and next year it will be eight, and the year after that, it will be nine. And if you don't find a way to let this go and live again, you're going to still be right here, with your butterflies. I mean, don't get me wrong, they're beautiful and all, but this isn't living. You know that as well as I do."

Knowing he had to somehow make the leap but not knowing how, Barrett looked over at Andy. "Will you pray with me?"

"Sure thing, brother."

They lowered their heads.

"Father," Andy said softly. "You know the weight my dear friend's been carrying here. A weight You never intended for him to carry. A weight that's burdening him, tormenting him, and causing him to live in fear. This fear is not from You, Lord. It's from the evil one, the devil. So, Father, I'm asking You today, right here and now to set my friend free as only You can. As we come boldly to Your throne of grace, we pray for mercy and grace to help Barrett in his time of need. And help him not to do something he'll regret by saying goodbye to Audra and turning his back on love. Amen."

Andy looked over at him with compassion in his eyes. "It's up to you now. You can either choose to continue to live in fear and guilt, to let those thugs control you the rest of your life, or you can step out in faith and trust that God's got your back."

Barrett recognized that term. Cops used it often. They trusted their partners to have their back when they went into danger. Barrett knew in that moment he had a choice to make. Trust that God did indeed have his back or not trust God and live in fear forever. As much as he knew what should be the right answer, at that moment, the right answer seemed as dangerous as the wrong one. After all, the danger didn't involve just him, it would Audra as well. That's what made this whole decision thing so difficult.

Chapter Twenty

Audra's fingers trembled as she buttoned the blouse she put on over her one-piece bathing suit. Neon green shorts covered the bottom half of her swimwear. This was one time she refused to be late. She had no idea what today would hold or if this would be the last day she'd get to spend with Barrett or what. He'd been rather vague on the phone, and life had taught her she could have trouble reading him on a good day.

At least he was keeping his promise to her by taking her parasailing. Even that she had mixed emotions about. After all, what would she say afterward to keep him around if he was determined to say goodbye?

Audra snatched up her beach bag, the one with the picture of a sandy beach, a clear blue sky, and a white picket fence with several pairs of multi-colored flip flops leaned up against it. She'd packed it the night before so something wouldn't happen to make her late. With Louey already fed and taken care of, all she had left to do was to put on her sandals and head downstairs to wait.

At the bottom of the steps, she glanced at the time. Twenty minutes early. Barrett would definitely be shocked. She knew she was.

She decided to wait for him out on the front porch swing. The rocking motion would hopefully help to calm her nerves.

Ten minutes later, she heard the familiar rumble of Barrett's roadster coming up the street, and every part of her suddenly tensed.

By the time he came into view and pulled into her driveway, she was already standing there waiting for him, holding her beach bag.

Just seeing him made her insides leap like a nest of rabbits on caffeine.

God, please don't let him leave me.

Barrett hopped over the side. He held his hand over his heart and held onto his car door, bending his knee. "Whoa. I can't believe my eyes. Miracles really do happen."

"Ha ha. Very funny. Remind me to laugh."

He chuckled, and in two steps was in front of her, leaning over and kissing her on the cheek.

On the cheek, and not on her lips. Did that mean something? Or was she reading way more into it than what was really there?

"Ready?" Barrett stood at the passenger side, holding the door open for her. That short sleeve peach colored Polo shirt he was wearing did nothing to hide his rock solid biceps or his broad chest. His white shorts showed off tan muscled calves.

He grabbed her beach bag from her and set it on the back seat.

She sat down and clicked her seatbelt on. Within a minute they were on their way toward Lake Bouey to go parasailing.

Audra shifted as much as her seatbelt would allow. "Everything is arranged then?"

"I called ahead." He glanced at her then shifted his attention back onto the road. "Did a weather check. Made sure the men are licensed, experienced and have a good record. I had them investigated."

"Another background check, huh?" She sent him the same smirk she always did even though he couldn't see it because he was looking directly ahead watching the road.

"To quote you… yup."

They both chuckled.

"Thank you for taking care of everything."

"Glad to do it. Are you nervous?"

"Scared silly is more like it."

"You sure you want to do this?" He did another quick glance her way.

"I'm sure. I'm not one to back down from a challenge or to let fear control me." She hoped he got the double meaning of her words.

"Good." He reached over and squeezed her hand.

Audra was trying her hardest to act normal, but normal was highly overrated. Especially since she had no idea what was going through Barrett's mind, and what the end of the day would bring concerning their relationship.

Barrett parked near the dock, and while he talked to the man he'd made the arrangements with, Audra looked around the lake.

Boats dotted the blue-green water. Trees surrounded the entire lake. Cabins lined one side of the lake and were spread out far enough to give the people next to them privacy. Audra thought about how nice it would be to come back here sometime and rent one of those cabins, if they were even for rent that was. Parking a camp trailer at the spacious campground close to the lake sounded just as enjoyable as renting one of the cabins did.

Children and parents lined the beach. Parents fished while children played in the sand.

Audra laughed at a tall, gangly teenage boy chasing a petite teenage girl with a fish. The girl screamed while he laughed.

She remembered her brother doing that to her. Until the day she turned tail on him and had chased him with a crawdad, something Josh was petrified of. She later learned it was because when he was four, he'd stuck his hand in a bucket of them and several of them had latched onto him with their pinchers. No wonder he was so scared.

"Ready."

Audra turned at the sound of Barrett's voice and looked up at him. "Ready as I'll ever be I guess."

He opened her door, and she stepped out. Barrett grabbed her beach bag and another black bag from the back seat. Holding onto both of them, he took her hand and led her toward the dock that had several boats tied to it.

Water lapped up against the dock, leaving a hollowing echo sound in its wake. White foam rode atop each wave.

They stopped at a boat with a big flat deck in back. A long pole stuck out of it with a cable attached to a parachute.

"This is it. What do you think?"

Audra took one look at the thing. What little courage she'd arrived with, which wasn't much, sank to the bottom of the lake like an anchor. "I think I wanna leave and forget this whole thing. That's what I think."

Barrett smiled down at her. "Can't chicken out now."

"Yeah? Well, neither can you." She arched her brows.

"Touché," he answered with that and nothing more.

He handed their bags to a young man onboard, then held her hand and stabilized her while she boarded the boat. Barrett climbed onboard right behind her.

A handsome African American man in a white shirt, white shorts, and a white cap strode up to her and extended his hand. "Hi, I'm Captain Trevon Williams, and that's my helper Roy Dubbs." He jerked his thumb toward the young man who took their bags. A short, stocky built boy with bleached blond hair, spikes in his ears, and covered in tattoos.

"Hey." Roy gave her and Barrett a short nod before turning back to whatever it was he was doing with the cable machine looking thing before he'd taken their bags.

"Hi, I'm Audra Darron."

"It's nice to meet you, Ma'am." Captain Williams extended his hand, and Audra shook it. "I hear tell you're scared of parasailing."

Audra glanced up at Barrett. *Big mouth.*

He hiked a shoulder, looking all innocent like. Innocent? Uh, not hardly.

"Don't you worry none, Ma'am. I've been doing this for eight years, and I ain't never had no accident."

"Well, let's hope I'm not your first." Her teasing, nervous laughter did nothing to ease the tension in her stomach. She was shaking like a ribbon streaming from a cooling fan set on high speed.

"You're perfectly safe with me, Ma'am. I promise you that."

"Please, call me Audra."

"Yes, Ma'am, Mrs. Audra."

Mrs?

Oh, she loved the sound of that. Only thing that would make it sound even better was if Camden was at the end. As in Mrs. Barrett Camden.

"I'm just teasing ya, Audra." When he smiled a row of bright white teeth and big brown eyes sparkled back at her. "Gotta get you to loosen up a might cuz you're gonna love it."

"I'll take your word for it."

"Well, let's get you two harnessed up then."

Captain Williams had them put a life jacket on first. Then they stepped into their harnesses and pulled them up to their waists.

"Set that seat under your thighs," Captain Williams instructed them.

That seat, as he called it, was nothing more than a thicker piece of strap. Sweat beads sprouted out across the top of Audra's nose.

"No need to be nervous." Barrett unbuttoned his shirt pocket and removed a monogrammed handkerchief from it and held it up in front of her. "I came prepared." He grinned.

Audra shook her head and laughed, a very nervous laugh.

Barrett dabbed the beads of sweat off of her nose with the thing. "Everything will be fine. You'll see."

If only he meant that about the two of them, and not just parasailing. Parasailing she could handle, losing him, now that she couldn't.

They did as they were instructed, the seat was now under their thighs.

Captain Williams hooked each of them up.

He headed to the back of the boat, gave his helper Roy some instructions, and then the captain fired up the boat.

This was it. She was really doing this.

As they slowly headed away from the dock, Audra watched as the flat parachute ballooned out.

"Follow me," Roy said.

On shaky legs, Audra rose and with Barrett at her side, holding her hand, she made her way to the platform at the back.

"Sit down with your legs straight out in front of you."

They did.

Barrett blotted the top of her nose again.

Roy hooked their harnesses up to the parachute hardware. "You ready?"

Was she? She looked behind her at the parachute, then upward, then over at Barrett. "No." She shook her head vehemently. "I can't. I can't do this."

"Why not?" Roy looked at her as if she were crazy.

Maybe she was. Her mind was going too fast to tell, and her heart was in a race to keep up with it.

"Give us a minute," Barrett told the young man.

Roy glanced at the captain who gave him a quick nod yes.

"K. When you're ready, holler." Roy strode over to the captain.

Again Barrett blotted her nose. "Audra, what are you so afraid of?"

Of you leaving, she wanted to say but blinked that back. Panic began to take over her senses. "I've always thought this looked like so much fun, but the idea of being pulled up into the air, way above the water, and then falling to my death? That scares me."

"What makes you think you'll fall to your death? Where does that fear come from?"

"I don't know, it's just something I heard about years ago, and ever since then, I've been afraid of it."

"So why do it now?" He touched his handkerchief with the initials B C on it to her nose again.

"I told you. I face my fears. It might take me a while to face them, but I do." Once again, she hoped he got the message she was sending… overcoming fears takes time. And it was no different for him.

"I won't let anything happen to you."

"Oh, yeah? How ya gonna stop it?"

He looked at the rigging above them. "Good point. Tell you what, let's pray and ask God to keep us safe. Do you believe He will?"

"Do you?" She sent him a look that could not be mistaken.

He put his lips together and never let her gaze go "I know what you're getting at. We'll discuss that later. Right now, we're going to do this together. Now, I'm here to help you overcome this fear, and so is God." He bowed his head and she did too. "Father, we ask You to watch over and to protect us and keep us safe as we take this parachute ride. Help Audra to enjoy it. And ease her fear. I'm running out of dry spots on my handkerchief."

Audra swatted him on the arm, and he laughed.

"What? I am."

She shook her head at him and rolled her eyes.

"Well, you ready to this thing?"

She drew in a calming breath. "No, but let's get it over with."

Barrett motioned for Roy and let him know they were ready.

Roy slowly let the cable out.

Audra's legs slid against the deck as she was being pulled backward. She slammed her eyes shut and clutched the straps. *Jesus, Jesus, Jesus,* she recited his name over and over in her mind.

She could feel herself being raised higher and higher.

Her feet tingled.

Her nose beads popped up. *If he wipes them off again, I'm gonna slug him.* That was her fear talking.

You're gonna crash.

You're gonna crash.

You're gonna crash.

She pinched her eyes shut tighter and squeezed the harness handles so hard her fingers tingled.

"Audra, it's okay." Barrett's hand rested right above her knee.

"No it's not."

"Yes it is. Open your eyes. The view is spectacular."

"No," she whimpered.

"Yes. Do it, Audra."

"Bossy."

"Sure am."

One second ticked by. Then two. Then three, four, five...

Was Barrett still there? Why wasn't he talking anymore?

"Barrett!" Her eyes shot open and she looked to make sure he hadn't fallen out of his harness.

"I'm still here."

He was too. Right beside her. In the air. Hundreds of feet above the water. Where no one should be. And yet he was here. With her.

"Look at the view, Audra."

"I am." Only she wasn't looking at the view he was referring to. She was looking at him. The best view around. "I'm looking at the most handsomest guy ever."

"I'm flattered." A grin tugged at his lips. "But..." He suddenly looked down. "Well, will you look at that?"

"What?" Audra looked down and all around. All she saw were trees, sparkling water, a few boats and... "Wow, this is amazing. I feel like I'm flying."

"In a way you are."

Audra glanced at Barrett. "In a way you're right." She smiled and continued to enjoy the breathtaking view. Seeing the tree tops from up high, the shiny silver streaks in the water, the people on the beach, everything from up in sky was truly breathtaking. Her fear vanished, and she spent the rest of the time, holding Barrett's hand and enjoying one of the most thrilling, fascinating rides of her life.

When the ride was nearly over, as they were being lowered slowly to the boat, Barrett asked if she wanted to get wet.

"What do you mean get wet?" She wasn't sure she wanted anything to do with that. It sounded dangerous dangling in the air from a parachute.

"They can control the parachute. We can let them dip us in the water."

"No, no." She shook her head. "I'm not ready for that."

"Chicken."

"Bawk, bawk."

Barrett gave a nod to Roy. Within seconds cool water splashed over her legs and part of her upper body before she was lifted up again and pulled onto the deck of the boat, where they landed safely on their feet.

"I did it! I did it!" Her insides beamed with delight and joy, and she wondered if it showed on her face. "I conquered another fear."

"No, we did it. Together." He kissed her hand, never taking his eyes that were filled with pride off of her when he did.

Her heart soared as high as the parasailing chute of moments before. "We sure did." She turned serious eyes on him. "Okay, Hotrod. Your fear is next."

The rest of the day passed by parasailing and enjoying the yacht Barrett had rented when they were finished parasailing. Something Audra was now hooked on.

She couldn't have asked for a better day. Parasailing, boating, lunch on the deck of a beautiful yacht on the middle of the lake, dinner on the beach, roasting hotdogs and coconut marshmallows, all of which Barrett had arranged beforehand, and now watching the sunset on the water snuggled against Barrett's chest and with his arms wrapped around her.

Pinks, purples, and streak of white in the center, along with a ribbon of blue surrounding the sky, it was a made-for-romance sky. Only one thing was missing, the feel of Barrett's lips on hers. Not once had he kissed her all day, except for the kiss on her cheek, but that didn't count. She wanted to kiss him, but for the first time, she didn't have the courage to do something first. No, he needed to be the one to initiate the kiss. After all, he was the one who said he needed to end their relationship, not her, and she wasn't going to go chasing someone who didn't want to be caught. A change of mind from earlier.

Minutes later, the pink and blue colors reflected in the water disappeared with the sun.

"God sure knows how to paint a spectacular, live picture, doesn't He?" Barrett's voice drifted with awe on the soft evening breeze.

"He sure does." He made you, she wanted to add, but didn't.

"Well, we'd better get this thing ashore."

Audra stood, but made no effort to move away. Barrett stood too and gazed down at her. Audra held her breath. Was he finally going to kiss her?

Suddenly Audra shook a chill. When her back was nestled against Barrett's chest on the bench seat on the vessel, she never noticed the chill in the night air. But now that he was behind the wheel of the yacht, a place where he looked completely at home, she rubbed her arms and shuddered again.

"Cold?" Barrett asked.

"Little. If ya don't mind, I'm gonna go below and change into something warmer."

"Don't mind at all. I'll just get this thing turned around and head to shore. Unless you want me to wait so you can see the view on the way in."

"No, that's fine. Go ahead."

He gave a short nod.

Audra grabbed her beach bag, headed down below and changed into her royal blue hip-huggers, white button down long sleeved blouse, white slip on sneakers, and her royal blue cardigan sweater. By the time she finished, Barrett was pulling into the dock.

Barrett docked the boat, and Audra waited while he went below and changed into a pair of black jeans and a light gray slipover hoodie. While he returned the keys to the boat rental place, Audra waited on the long wooden dock.

Fishy water, wood smoke from campfires, and mosquito repellant smells filled the air. Soft gentle waves lapping onto the shore and under the dock, along with buzzing mosquitoes, and the distant voices of happy campers, drifted through the darkness.

"It's really beautiful out here," Barrett said from behind her as he rested his hands on her shoulders.

"Sure is."

"I hate to leave, but we'd better get going."

All the joy and peace of the day vanished from her like campfire smoke on a windy day. Neither of which were good.

She didn't want to go. Mostly because she didn't know if this was the last time she'd get to spend time with Barrett or not.

They loaded their stuff into the back of his roadster and headed back to Charity, only Barrett didn't get off on the main exit road heading back to Charity. He took a different road instead.

"Where are we going?"

"To my place." He glanced over at her. "You got a problem with that?" He laid his arm across the back of her seat and his hand cupped the top of her arm.

"Nope." Knowing she was getting more time with him, as the breeze lifted her hair, she laid her head back against his rock solid arm and gazed up at the sky. "Not at all," she said with a dreamy sigh of contentment.

They pulled around back and parked near his butterfly garden. He came around, opened her door for her, and with his hand on the small of her back, he led her into his garden.

When she neared the fountain in the center of the garden, her eyes widened and her mouth dropped open.

Various colored vases, flooded over with pink roses, lined the base of the fountain wall. Tall, flickering, battery operated candles that looked amazingly real, ringed the fountain ledge and were scattered throughout the back wall where the water didn't reach.

Audra shook her head. She whirled around to tell Barrett how beautiful it was, but her words died in her throat.

There in front of the bench across from the fountain, surrounded by pink roses and candles was Barrett, kneeling on one knee, holding a velvet box out with one hand and a single pink rose in the other.

"Audra Darron, today I held your hand while we overcame your fear of parasailing together. Now, I'm asking you to hold mine as I overcome my fears. Together, I believe we can do this. Alone, I cannot. I love you, Audra. I don't just want you in my life to help me overcome my fears, but to love me, to be with me and to let me love you. I want you to spend the rest of your life with me. Will you do that, Audra? Will you become my other half and make me whole?"

Audra stared at him. She couldn't believe her ears. Tears streaked down her face. "You're, you're not leaving?" Was all she could say.

Barrett stood then and was in front of her in an instant. "Is that a yes?"

She shook her head. "No."

He frowned. "It's not?"

Her smile flooded her face and heart. "It's a yup. A great big, ginormous yup!"

A huge smile replaced his worried frown as he took her in his arms and his lips found hers. Joy spread through her. He wasn't leaving. She wasn't going to lose him. She deepened the kiss, and when they finally pulled apart, he whispered, "Your ring fell in the fountain."

"What?" Audra whirled. Losing her balance, she fell into the water. Pink roses and candles fell right in along with her.

Barrett stepped over the ledge and offered her a hand up. "Well, that was graceful."

"Ha. Ha. Funny man." She settled her hand in his, and he helped her to her feet.

Then they both leaned over running their hand along the bottom of the fountain, searching for the ring box. Audra was the first to find it. When she stood and opened her mouth to tell Barrett she'd found it, seeing him stooped over, her lips slowly curled upward. One push was all it took.

He went down with a splash, and she flopped down beside him right in the middle of the fountain.

For a second he sputtered and choked. Then he looked at her, soaked just like he was.

They sat in the fountain, laughing. "We've got to stop meeting like this," she said, laughing.

"I don't know what your problem is, but I have no problem with it." He took the box from her hand and placed a gorgeous pink rose-cut diamond on her ring finger. "I saw this and thought of you. I'll get you a different one for our wedding day."

She held it up and admired it. "I don't want a different one. This one is perfect." Her eyes turned to his, and she cupped his face. "Just like you. I love ya, Barrett Camden."

"I love you, Audra Darron, soon to be Audra Camden."

Audra smiled, and her heart joined the joy spreading across her upturned lips.

Barrett pulled her into his arms, and their wet lips met, ending in one of the sweetest kisses ever. It was the perfect ending to the most perfect day ever.

Epilogue

It had been the longest winter of Audra's life, and yet it was the shortest. Today she was marrying Barrett Camden, aka Gage Lincoln, the famous movie actor, who would've surely been even more famous if anyone on the planet knew he was alive. Besides Andy and a few agents, only she and Barrett knew who he was. Even without him even asking her to, she would have promised Barrett that she would never reveal his true identity to anyone, including Olivia and Erik and her family. No one else needed to know. The past would stay right where it was, in the past. The future started today. And she could hardly wait.

Standing in front of the dressing room mirror at the church, Audra put her back to the mirror, pulled her hair off to the side, and turned enough so that she could see the back of her dress.

Shoulder straps made of the finest rose and leaf pattern lace flowed down the inside of the backless dress that hugged her waist. That same lace covered the top of her silk bodice and tulle skirt.

"You look lovely, Audra."

Audra gazed into the mirror at the reflection of her mother standing behind her.

She and her mother shared the same facial features, the same hazel blue eyes, auburn brown hair, and the same short stature. "The dress Ingrid and Elsa bought you is exquisite."

"I'm so glad their gift didn't offend you, Mom. They just wanted to be a part of things since they've kind of adopted me as part of their family."

"Just like you did me, Mom," Olivia said, sweeping into the room, holding Audra's enormous bouquet of pink roses. Olivia hugged Audra's mom.

Keera, Andy's wife, walked in behind her.

"You look so beautiful, Audra."

"So do you, Keera. In fact, you all do. Y'all will outshine me."

"Nonsense," Elsa swept into the room, followed by Ingrid. Both of the women's hairdos had turned out great. They refused to let Audra fix it on the day of her wedding, but they trusted her judgment that Angie would do a great job. And she had too. Ingrid's petal curls looked great, and Elsa's bouffant hair was styled to perfection. "A bride always outshines everyone in the room. We all know that."

Not if sparkles counted. Elsa's dress was peach, Ingrid's was blue. Both were sequenced knee-length dresses that sparkled like prism glass in the sun. Audra had made them her honorary bridesmaids. She wanted them to stand up there with her, but they said they were too old to stand that long. Audra smiled at that. Those two might be old as far as years went, but they were as young as they felt.

"We wanted to give you this before you walked down the aisle." Elsa extended a long black velvet box toward her.

"We asked your mother if it was okay first, and she assured us it was," Ingrid added.

"But you've already given me so much."

"Nonsense, Child. Here." Elsa set the box in Audra's hand.

Audra opened it and gasped. "Oh, Elsa. Ingrid. They're beautiful." In the box was a necklace of pink rose cut diamonds and a strand of three teardrop matching diamonds that started out small and ended up larger.

"We thought you'd like them." Ingrid smiled at her.

"I love them. Thank you." She hugged both of the women and kissed them on their cheeks.

Her mother clasped the necklace for her while she put her earrings on.

"We bought something for you ladies too." Elsa and Ingrid handed each one of them a velvet box.

"You shouldn't have," Audra's mom said, and Keera and Olivia agreed.

"We most certainly should have." Elsa said with that no nonsense tone of hers.

All three held up a strand of elegant diamonds with a swirly teardrop design dangling from the center and a set of matching earrings. Olivia's had a purple stone in the center of the swirl, her mother, who loved blue, had sapphires, and Keera's had rubies, her favorite gem.

Those two women didn't miss a thing. Audra loved them almost as much as her own mother. Almost. No one could ever take her mother's place.

"I hate to break this up ladies, but it's time to go." Her father's voice broke up the round of hugs going on inside the room. "Hope you don't mind that I didn't knock first, but you left the door open." Her father stepped inside the room. He looked so handsome in his black tux. The gray at his temples gave his black hair a regal look.

"I'm ready, Daddy."

Barrett stood at the front of the church. Andy stood next to him. And Erik stood beside Andy.

He was glad that his side of the church was full with friends and family of Audra's. He would have hated looking out and seeing his side empty. Seeing Audra's brother and his family, her sister who he had flown in from Thailand, along with Camara and Chase and whole slew of people he had yet to meet, his heart swelled with contentment.

Barrett watched as the usher walked Audra's mother up the aisle. It saddened him that his own mother wasn't here to see him get married. Or his dad. They were the only family he had, and he would miss them forever and always. Starting today, however, he would have a whole new family to love forever and always as well. Somehow he'd never realized that part all those years he'd let the fear keep him from life. No more. Now, with Audra by his side, he would face his fears even while he held her hand as she faced hers.

The ring bearer and flower girl, cousins of Audra's, made their way up front.

Next Elsa and Ingrid walked up the aisle arm-in-arm, beaming. They took a seat on the chairs set up front for them close to where the bridesmaids would stand.

Keera stepped into view.

She had on a soft red dress. The skirt was an inch or two above her knees in the front and hung clear to her ankles in the back. It looked like she had on a mini skirt with a sheer silk gown over it.

Next Olivia stepped into view. She had on an identical dress as Keera, only hers was lavender.

Audra loved all colors. Neon colors included. So he wasn't surprised that everyone was dressed in a different color.

The orchestra started playing *Canon in D*.

Barrett's eyes stayed glued to the back of the church.

Audra appeared on her dad's arm. Her face glowed with a smile he knew he would remember forever.

Her beauty took his breath away.

Their eyes connected.

He smiled.

She smiled.

Within seconds, she was standing only two feet from him, but even that was too far.

"Who gives this woman to this man?" the pastor asked.

"Her mother and I do," Audra's dad answered proudly. "Take good care of my girl," he said before placing Audra's hand in to Barrett's.

"You bet I will. I'll guard her with my life." And he meant it. Even though his family's murders hadn't been found, he knew God was with he and Audra, watching over them, and protecting them. Ecclesiastes 4:12 popped into his mind. "Though one may be overpowered by another, two can withstand him. And a threefold cord is not quickly broken." The three of them together would be a mighty force to be reckoned with.

They repeated their vows.

"You may now kiss your bride."

Barrett pulled her into his arms and kissed her. He raised his head and whispered, "Looks like I finally caught the woman who didn't want to be caught." He smiled right before he kissed her again.

When he raised his head, the words he longed to hear flowed from the pastor's lips. "I now introduce to you, Mr. and Mrs. Barrett Camden."

After the reception, they hopped into his roadster and drove toward the airport where they would board his private plane and head out to London, England. Audra's choice.

Instead of the sound of tin cans tinkling against the pavement, they heard the clunking and banging of the auto parts and die cast demolition derby cars that streamed from the bumper of his car. Gratis of Erik, Olivia, Camara and Chase who had also put a large sign on the trunk that read…

Catch me if you can
Challenge accepted
JUST MARRIED

About the Author

Debra Ullrick is a hot rod, figure-eight races, classic cars, mud-boggin', monster trucks fanatic, who loves Jesus. Her hobbies include, going to classic car auto shows, collecting muscle car and monster truck models, reading, writing, drawing western art, feeding wild birds, playing with her Manx cat Tickles, visiting with family and friends, surfing the Internet, watching movies, especially every available version of Jane Austen's stories, Monster Jam World Finals DVD's, Ma and Pa Kettle, Little People, Big World, CASTLE, COPS, and the PBS documentaries, Frontier House, 1900's house, and Manor House.

Debra and her real-life hero of forty years, along with their now married daughter lived and worked on cattle ranches in the Colorado Rocky Mountains until a few years ago. Now they live down in the flatlands where they're still experiencing cultural whiplash from big city living.

Her debut novel, *The Bride Wore Coveralls,* the first book in the Racing series is available through all major retail book sites.

Debra loves to hear from her readers.

To contact her visit her website at **www.debraullrick.com** or write her at **christianromancewriter@gmail.com.** You can also find Debra on **Twitter @DebraUllrick** and at **www.facebook.com/debra.ullrick.**

Other Books by Debra Ullrick

The Bride Wore Coveralls
Racing Series, Book 1
(Barbour Publishing)

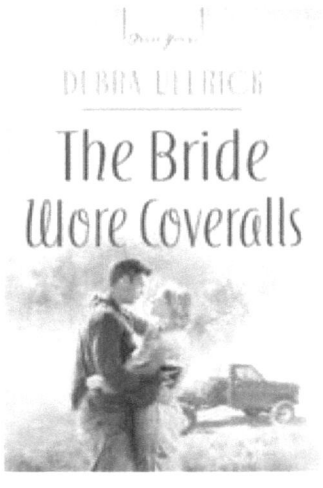

Can bitter rivals come to love each other? Fighting deep prejudice against her femininity, her choice of vehicle, and even her heritage, Camara Cole is determined to win the mud-bog racing championship this year. Her biggest competition seems also to be her worst enemy. Chase Lamar has been racing mud-boggers as long as Camara, and he grudgingly admits she's the best driver-mechanic he knows. Their rivalry has been long and bitter. But Chase is a new Christian. As he begins to change, he finds his relationship with Camara changing, too. When Camara's vehicle is sabatoged, she naturally blames Chase, despite a growing attraction. Chase must prove his innocence, but evidence points his way. When the smoke clears and the truth is known, will each be able to extend forgiveness, maybe even love?

Déjà vu Bride
Racing Series, Book 2

Furious with God, Olivia Roseman vows to never trust Him again. Why should she? Once again her prayers have gone unanswered, and once again another loved one has been ripped from her. With no job and only a few dollars, Olivia makes a choice to start over again. Without God and without love. However, her handsome new boss isn't going to make forgetting God or keeping her vow to never love again very easy. Erik Cole questions the sanity of his moving from Swamper City, Alabama to Charity, West Virginia. That is, until he hires airbrush designer Olivia Roseman to paint his monster truck. When he senses that she's a gal who is down on her luck, he vows to do whatever he can to help her. Only problem is, the little beauty creates more challenges than one. As his feelings toward her deepen, all Erik can do is hope and pray that one day Olivia will open up her heart to Christ—and to him.

Forewarned
A Contemporary Christian Suspense Romance Novel

He loves her... but can he save her from her own mistakes?

After a near fatal accident in the Colorado wilderness, the pain Jasmine Moore lives with has made her a recluse.

To fill the void the harsh Steamboat Springs winter brings, she goes online seeking companionship. Her loneliness overrides all caution, bringing with it a deadly peril.

Jackson Warren has loved Jasmine for years. When he discovers she's talking to strangers on the Internet, his internal alarms blare. Especially after strange and suspicious incidents occur close to home. Can he convince her to heed his concerns before it's too late?

A Log Cabin Christmas
A New York Times & CBA Bestseller

Experience Christmas through the eyes of adventuresome settlers who relied on log cabins built from trees on their own land to see them through the cruel forces of winter. Discover how rough-hewed shelters become a home in which faith, hope, and love can flourish. Marvel in the blessings of Christmas celebrations without the trappings of modern commercialism where the true meaning of the day shines through. And treasure this exclusive collection of nine Christmas romances penned by some of Christian fiction's best-selling authors.

The Unlikely Wife
Love Inspired Historical

The arrival of Michael Bowen's bride, married sight unseen by proxy, sends the rancher reeling. With her trousers, cowboy hat and rifle, she looks like a female outlaw—not the genteel lady he corresponded with for months. He's been hood-winked into marriage with the wrong woman!

Selina Farleigh Bowen loved Michael's letters, even if she couldn't read them herself. A friend read them to her, and wrote her replies—but apparently that "friend" left things out, like Michael's dream of a wife who was nothing like her. Selina won't change who she is, not even for the man she loves. Yet time might show Michael the true value of his unlikely wife.

The Unexpected Bride
Love Inspired Historical

After the disaster of his first marriage, Haydon Bowen has no intention of marrying again. Unfortunately, his brother has some intentions of his own, and plans to see to it that Haydon finds happiness once more.

So he answers a "groom wanted" advertisement—in Haydon's name—and sends Haydon to meet his new bride at the stagecoach stop!

For beautiful, cultured Rainelle Devonwood, any dangers she may face in the Idaho Territories are preferable to staying with her abusive brother. So even when Rainee learns she's a mistakenly ordered bride, she won't let Haydon drive her away. She's up to the challenge of life on the difficult, demanding frontier...and the great challenge of opening Haydon's heart again.

Find a complete list of Debra Ullrick's books on her website: www.DebraUllrick.com

www.ingramcontent.com/pod-product-compliance
Lightning Source LLC
Chambersburg PA
CBHW020228180626
46810CB00006B/2093